Drug Clouds ⌐   )

By Rick Blaine

To Son + Jane,

My best wishes

R.B.

(Rick Blaine)

07971820659

Foreword

I was staying in Tangier, Morocco the third time I watched the film Casablanca. It was my sixth visit to this enigmatic country spread over more than thirty years. Maybe it was because I was watching it in Morocco, I wanted more than anything else to follow in the hero's footsteps – to go to that iconic location and do something heroic. This book tells the story of how I found a way to do that.

For the film's most famous character, the story did not have the perfect ending: he sacrificed the love of his life for a greater good. However, if my story has the same influence on the world as the film had, the ultimate ending will be a happy one. Millions of lives will be saved, there will be less crime, and families torn apart will be reunited.

Although I have changed their names, much of the content is fact. You will not have to look to closely to know what fiction is; those are the circumstances leading up to the horrendous event that has not happened yet. Hopefully writing this book means it never will.

For reasons that will become obvious, I write using a pseudonym. As the story unfolds, readers will realise the one I chose could not be more synonymous with the outcome.

Rick Blaine Jr.
Casablanca, Amsterdam, New York and London
May 2021

Preface

Morocco's links to drugs, terrorism and organised crime are responsible for some of the worst drug related problems in the world. While living there, I discovered this terrible truth. From my experience as a recovered drug addict, careers as a business development adviser to the pharmaceutical industry and police officer, I came to realise that by changing some of their drug policies there was a much better way forward.

The first time I saw the street children of Casablanca I was confused. Later, I realised how they lived; when I discovered the consequences, I was horrified. On this occasion there were three boys. One was begging at the window of cars stopped at red traffic lights. His accomplices were lying in a doorway holding filthy plastic bags that contained the solvent they sniffed every few minutes. The boy, who was begging had his bag in a pocket. When he needed a fix, they rotated their roles. It was midday and each was already stoned out of their eight-and nine-year-old minds. They were the youngest drug addicts I had ever seen.

Because of the Islamic tradition of giving charitably, the boys knew that begging would pay for their drugs. Either they had run away from home after much domestic abuse, or their parents had thrown them out; now drugs were their only priority. They were unwashed and dressed in rags. At the end of the day, they would spend the night sleeping rough with others just like them. There are an estimated 70,000 street children in Morocco, at least 10,000 are drug addicts. For them, the next step on the ladder of life is to descend onto harder drugs and be exploited by seasoned criminals. They have no other option.

Their journey into addiction and its consequences would have been vastly different to mine or drug addicts in almost any other country. As Morocco is the world's biggest grower of cannabis (source UN), their next step would be to move onto that drug, meaning they automatically become criminals. After that they would abuse alcohol, heroin, cocaine and synthetic drugs, as well as Morocco's exclusive drug cocktail, karkoubi, known as 'the drug of mass destruction'.

All this time they would almost exclusively be living with other criminals, in trouble with the police, society and poverty. Each of these facts making it easy to radicalise some into terrorism. There would not be a time in their lives where they would be free of drugs and tortured by the hell of living in addiction and all its manifestations.

As a former drug addict and alcoholic, some of this scenario had been the same for me. But because the drugs I, and millions like me got hooked on were alcohol, tranquillisers and sleeping pills, we were not branded criminals. So, what a difference being a drug addict with money living in a different country makes to being one in Morocco! The questions are, who and what are to blame?

Just before I witnessed the scene with the street children, I had a meeting at the Addictology Unit in Casablanca's Ibn Rushd University Hospital. I had been there in my capacity as a member of Narcotics Anonymous and Alcoholics Anonymous advising the hospitals psychiatrists on how these 12-Step Fellowship programmes could help treat Morocco's million plus drug addicts. The irony of seeing addicted street children begging less than three hundred metres from the hospital, only minutes after my meeting with people at an institution remitted to solve Morocco's drug problems, left me frustrated.

Had I seen this pathetic sight and realised the juxtaposition of Morocco's drug situation before the meeting, my approach would have been more direct.

My knowledge of Morocco's links to drugs, European mafias and terrorism compelled me to write this book. By exposing the truth, I hope it will save the lives of many people and stifle the seeds of another jihadist attack like this century's previous Moroccan influenced bloody outrages in Barcelona, Paris, Brussels and Casablanca. It is well documented that some of the perpetrators of these were under the influence of drugs and their crimes were financed by drug trafficking.

Although the story is fictionalised, it depicts the reality behind this plague of organised crime and puts forward an approach that would stop it.

Part 1

Drug Clouds Over Morocco

Chapter 1

Arthur Cyriax made a lot of money out of one pharmaceutical drug. In 1995, when he bought a magnificent home in Sotogrande, on Spain's Mediterranean coast, he was worth £16,000,000; by the time he bought a superb 35-metre yacht four years later he was worth £43,000,000; three years after that he bought a private jet, which hardly dented his first £100,000,000. He also bought apartments in Monte Carlo, Tel Aviv and Florida during this time, as well as continuing to live in his Hampstead, London home.

Having inherited a successful paints business from his father, Mortimer, a stockbroker friend, suggested that Arthur's company, Cyriax Paints, buy a single-product shell company with tax losses listed on the London Aim stock market. That product was an opiate painkiller. Through clever marketing, Cyriax Paints plc's opiate drug became a blockbuster, then, after hyped-up presentations to City institutions, Arthur's firm's share price doubled, trebled and quadrupled in just eight years. He also changed its name to Cyriax Pharma plc.

Although it was no secret that Arthur made his money from drugs, at the golf clubs, ski resorts and in Monte Carlo where he now spent most of his time, he was endlessly teased that it was not just this prescription drug that enabled him to amass a fortune. But as Arthur was generous and knew all the 'right' people, no enquiries were made to establish if there was anything untoward in his business affairs. In fact, there were not. His business practices were ethical; his tax dodges, though, were highly dubious.

Arthur had a son, Randolph. After school at Eton, where he was introduced to cannabis and homosexuality, he went to Oxford University to study chemistry. There he was nicknamed Randy, but dropped out in his second year having discovered a new way of life. He had become a daily cocaine user, and the hedonistic lifestyle that went with this was far more attractive.

From the moment Randolph's parents divorced during his third year at Eton College, his father showered him with money, but not love. The result was that Randolph became insecure, and to compensate for this he gave notoriously wild parties to boost his low self-esteem. His wild habits led to his being arrested twice for possession of drugs, once for being drunk and disorderly, and once for assaulting a police officer. The trouble was, the more drugs he took, the more his problems increased, both socially and mentally. As a result, he began to hate his parents for bringing him into a world which got bleaker and bleaker.

When Arthur became aware of Randolph's drug problem, he decided work would be the answer, so he put him on his firm's payroll by making him its representative in Spain. As Randolph's original ambition had been to become a pharmacist, to his father this seemed a perfect solution in every way.

But Randolph had other ideas; he only agreed to it to appease his father, who threatened to disinherit him if he did not quit drugs.

By the age of sixty, being on his own, Arthur had virtually stopped using his Spanish villa and yacht. He spent most of his time working or in his other homes in America, Monte Carlo and Florida. Over lunch one day with Randolph, he told him he had decided to sell the boat and Sotogrande home as he no longer used them; he also told him he was hoping to reunite with his mother, whom he had been seeing again recently.

After a stay in an Arizona treatment centre, and clean from drugs for two months, Randolph returned home. A few days later, he told his delighted father that he thought the best way to continue his recovery was to return to Spain and stay well away from his drug connections and partying playground in London. For maximum effect he added that this would help him kick his drug habit for good.

When his father responded positively, he suggested he investigate the possibility of a convenient tax dodge and give him the property and boat if he hadn't sold them yet. He hadn't, so Randolph, already born with a silver spoon in his mouth, now had two more. In the back of his mind was the knowledge that Sotogrande was not far from the Strait of Gibraltar, and he would have a boat to cross back and forth to Morocco and the famed 'cannabis coasts' as often as he desired.

Having developed a cannabis habit in his teens, Randolph had visited Tangier several times. On these trips he discovered that Bob Marley and the Rolling Stones went there to smoke hashish, and Barbara Hutton gave lavish jet-set parties, which meant it became one of the 'in' places to go, and Randy made sure he did so as often as possible. Indeed, he had frequently made the short crossing by boat between Sotogrande and Morocco, each time returning with enough hashish for personal use and to sell to friends visiting from the UK.

So, in a small way, Randy had become an international drug dealer, which he saw as a slap in the face for his father, whose business was legal despite dealing in much stronger and potentially lethal drugs.

After several more recent visits to Tangier, Randy had developed a relationship with a cannabis grower, so to cut out the middleman, he started buying directly from him.

This man operated from a factory near the 'blue city' of Chefchaouen, on the edge of the Rif mountains, the cannabis growing and production region, where smoking hashish in cafés is as common as drinking alcohol in bars in the West.

The more time Randy spent in Morocco, the more he got to know its cannabis business and his supplier. On one of his visits, the supplier, who spoke good English, asked him if he knew of the drug cocktail, karkoubi and its powerful effects. Randy's answer was no, and he asked what it was. The information he was given was that it is a mixture of a commercially available benzodiazapine, solvent, cannabis and alcohol. The supplier added that it was used mostly in Morocco, which triggered an idea in his chemistry-trained mind.

If Randy could deceive his father into sponsoring him, he could put in play his own real-life version of *Breaking Bad*. In that hit TV series, a seemingly legitimate chemistry teacher manufactured and trafficked a lethal mood-altering drug – crystal meth. Randy's time had come, and he was ready.

****

Although they are in close proximity to each other, the difference between Sotogrande and Gibraltar is like chalk and cheese. 'Soto' is well known for its golfing millionaires who play at the Severiano Ballesteros-designed Valderrama, and other golf clubs, and for having multi-million-pound yachts in its harbour, while 'Gib' is famous for harbouring tax-dodging scoundrels, and as a British Overseas Territory that is unpopular with the Spanish government. What is also well known about Gib is that it lies between Cadiz and

11

Malaga, a short boat ride from Morocco, adjacent to the main cannabis and other drug trafficking routes to Europe and beyond.

Most of the 30,000 people who live on the Rock of Gibraltar are British. However, 8000 of the people who work there are Spanish and cross the border every morning from La Linea, returning home in the evening. It means this crossing is relatively easy. Knowing there are one thousand Moroccans living in Gibraltar, when Randy first heard about karkoubi, a possible new development in his life and livelihood began to take shape in his mind.

After talking with drug-using friends, he realised the potential for Europe's untapped karkoubi market, and knowing the quality of Morocco's already established and varied drug trafficking routes, he took the view that if he could tap into that potential, a whole new drug business could open up. Then, what he discovered by going into the history of opiates gave him an idea of the advantages of establishing a laboratory in Spain to manufacture karkoubi's main benzodiazapine ingredient. The other ingredients of the cocktail, solvent, cannabis and alcohol, would be easy to obtain anywhere.

It started when he read about one of Tangier's famous literary sons, William Burroughs, who wrote about his experiences after moving there in 1954. '... I had every drug I wanted. Very soon I found a connection for junk, an opiate called Eukodol, which they sold over the counter.'

Then he read Norman Ohler's book *Blitzed,* published in 2016, and discovered further and even more interesting details about karkoubi. It revealed the amazing story of the Third Reich's relationship with drugs, including heroin, morphine and speed, and that Hitler was an opiate-injecting junkie.

Towards the end of the Second World War, due to increased Allied success, Germany grew desperate. So, in 1944, Admiral Hellmuth Heye of the German navy ordered their pharmaceutical industry to develop a drug that would provide users with superhuman strength and boost self-esteem. The drug they came up with was the opiate, Eukodol, a clonazepam which is a tranquilliser of the benzodiazepine class, which, mixed with other drugs, could have a similar effect to karkoubi.

This fact Randy now added to his knowledge that Eukodol was much loved in Tangier during its literary heyday in the 1950s, just as karkoubi is today. He assumed it had been established there partly due to Tangier's incredible past. In the preceding thirty years alone, it had been beset by conflicting European interests. This was because of its geographical location just nine miles across the Mediterranean Sea from Spain, which meant that it was viewed by Europe's leading naval forces as occupying a commanding strategic position. In 1923 the governorship of Tangier was given to France, Spain, Britain, Portugal, Sweden, Holland, Belgium and Italy. This had some extremely negative consequences. Not much had changed since, except that now karkoubi had spread all over Morocco.

The next thing Randy undertook was an internet search for privately owned Spanish pharmaceutical companies that made their own drugs. He found five, but only one was in Andalucia – Ibyx Pharma SA, near Algeciras. This company manufactured a small range of generic products, including the opiate codeine. Further research showed that since Spain had gone into recession in 2009, Ibyx had suffered badly.

Arranging a meeting with the man who owned and ran Ibyx, Raphael Cortez, was easy. All he had to do was tell him that he was the son of the chairman of Cyriax Pharma, and they were looking for a partner in Spain. Their meeting went well, and after lunch they visited Ibyx's manufacturing site together. Raphael explained that he was eighty-four years old, and for health reasons wanted to step down, adding that he had no successor.

Randy's primary reason for wanting to visit the factory was to see if there was sufficient manufacturing space and compatible machinery available to test and produce the benzodiazepine he needed for karkoubi. If there was, all he had to do was isolate it in such a way that only he and a select group working on it would know what was happening in the cordoned-off area. He would do this by explaining to Ibyx staff that a new drug was being tested and only personnel who had signed a non-disclosure agreement could enter. To begin with that would be just him and one other pharmacist.

For Randy's eighteenth birthday, his father had given him one million shares in Cyriax Pharmaceutical plc. At the time their value was £4,500,000; today they are worth £11,000,000.

Ever since Randy could remember, his father's win at all costs, greed-driven attitude drove him to rebel; the more he told him what to do, the more Randy disobeyed. Over the years this had turned into a deep loathing on his part, which his drug-using exacerbated, eventually causing a huge rift between them. Now, however, he needed his father's support for what he was proposing to do.

A few days after meeting the owner of Ibyx, Randy phoned his father and suggested he come to the family home the following Sunday for lunch. He explained he had a business idea he wanted to discuss that needed his blessing. Delighted at this sudden change of heart from his wayward son, Arthur readily agreed.

When lunch that day was finished, Arthur took Randy into the library to discuss his idea. After a chat about the recent failures of England's rugby and soccer teams, Arthur broached the subject.

'You said you had a business idea you want to discuss. As you know, I have always said I would do anything I can to help you get on your feet. So, fire away. What is it?'

This was just the opening Randy had hoped for, so he began confidently. 'Thanks, Dad, I knew I could count on you. I discovered through a friend in Gibraltar that there is a small pharmaceutical company called Ibyx, near Algeciras, which is possibly for sale. After doing some research, I met the owner to discuss it.'

'It must be small because I have never heard of it. A few years ago, we were looking at buying one near Barcelona, but nothing came of it. I suspect it won't be big enough for us.' Arthur, always sceptical of any of his son's ideas, automatically showed no enthusiasm for this one.

'We discussed their products, sales and distribution, and the chairman showed me their offices and took me around the factory. I liked what I saw and what he told me, gave me an idea,' Randy responded.

'Do they make their own products or are they distributors for other companies?' Arthur asked, still sceptical.

'Both. But before I go into detail about the company, I want to tell you my idea. I like living in that part of Spain, and it has helped me to quit cannabis and cocaine. In the past nine months I have hardly used any drugs, and since

15

rehab, none. My aim is to do all I can to keep it that way. The problem is, I get bored as I don't have enough to do all the time.'

'I'm not surprised. I always told you a man needs to work. I would go insane if I didn't have my company to run. That has always been your problem – too much time on your hands, and laziness. So, what's your idea now?' Arthur asked, evidently expecting it to be some sort of insane fantasy.

Randy, prepared for this, did not rise to his father's negative attitude towards him. Instead, he said, 'Firstly, to persuade the owner, Raphael Cortez, to meet me again. I told him I was your son and that I have a background in chemistry. We met on Wednesday, as I already mentioned. As our discussion progressed, he told me he is eighty-four years old and made it clear he would be more interested in finding someone to run Ibyx for him than selling it. At the same time, he kept saying how good it would be to work in partnership with a company like Cyriax Pharma.'

'My boy, I'm impressed.' That was a first, Randy thought. When had his father last said something positive about him? 'This is the sort of thing I hoped you would do. My time will be up as chairman in a few years and if you are able to take over the reins, it would make another old man very happy. Does he have a successor?'

'Thanks, Dad, but I hope that is a long time off. I'm a long way from being ready for that. The good news is, he does not have a successor. Both his children are lawyers, and neither is interested in the company.'

His father smiled. "I was jumping the gun, but it is still good news. Tell me more.'

Randy braced himself; what he would say next was the tricky bit. 'Currently Ibyx are strapped for cash and their running costs exceed their income. Borrowing from banks is no longer possible, so they need around 2,000,000 euros to survive this year. That is partly because they have a new product that the market does not know about, and if it takes off, as seems likely, it will return them to profit in its first year on the market.'

At the mention of money problems, Arthur was all ears and his naturally sceptical disposition returned.

'So, they want Cyriax Pharma to bail them out, is that right?' he said, his tone not concealing his view.

'Not exactly. I was sceptical, too, until they showed me the product and told me their plans for it.'

'What is their idea then?' Arthur asked, even less enthusiastically.

'I wish I could tell you more, but I can't as I had to sign a confidentiality agreement before he would show me the factory and the new product's test results for human applications. But everything I heard and saw was extremely positive.'

'I understand, but I still don't know what your idea is. Explain it.'

Put on the spot, Randy said as positively as he could, 'You always told me I need to stand on my own two feet. Well, I believe this gives me a way to do that and make money at the same time. First, I sell my shares in Cyriax and go to work at Ibyx, to begin with as Raphael Cortez's understudy. For the money I put in I get 51% of the company, and six months later he will make me chief executive. If the figures they produce are half as good as those he showed me, Ibyx will be profitable again well before the first year is up. Best of all, he agreed that Cyriax would get first option when he sells it. As I would be CEO and controlling shareholder, if you like the results, there would be nothing to stand in your way.'

Arthur was surprised to hear Randy's idea, but most of all he was taken aback by the air of confidence with which he presented it. He had never heard him speak so enthusiastically about a business opportunity before. But like all such things in life, he needed time to mull it over, so he replied, 'Well, Randy, this time you have surprised me. I need time to think it over and will ask one of our analysts to check it out. I suppose the reason you came to me is to get permission to sell the shares. Is that right?'

'Yes, and to get your approval of my idea.'

This new approach from his son pleased Arthur. As far as he could remember, he had never asked his advice before. 'Give me a few days to get back to you. I'm sure I can find out all I need to know from our contacts in the Spanish market.'

'The problem is, you won't find out anything about their new drug, and that is where their future success will come from.'

'Leave it with me. Finding out about the history of the company and its chairman should tell me a lot.'

'Thanks, Dad. I have never felt so good about something to do with work in my life. If I do this, and make it succeed, other than quitting drugs, it will be the best thing I'll ever do.'

The sincerity with which Randy said this and the reminder of his reason for doing it caused Arthur not to make any of the usual negative responses that came to mind whenever his son dreamed up an idea. He had always put him down, believing he was lazy and useless, and telling him so. He had constantly reminded him that considering all the money he had spent on his education, not to mention bailing him out of drug-related problems and paying for his treatment, he should be more grateful and show it in his attitude to himself and his mother. So, on this occasion he said, 'I have never known you to be as enthusiastic as this about work. If my research confirms you are right, I will give you all the backing I can to make it a success. I always knew you had the skills, and now it seems you may be about to put them into practice and follow my example.'

While his father was saying this, Randy's mother, Alison, quietly entered the room. Picking up on the last thing her husband said, she could hardly believe what she was hearing. It seemed too good to be true. In order not to disturb them she sat near the door and waited, hoping for an opportunity to be alone with her son when they finished. A few minutes later Arthur left the room, so she went and sat next to Randy on the two-seater sofa.

What she said moments later was the icing on the cake of his visit, and due to its profoundness and the sincerity with which she said it, it almost brought tears to his eyes, but for historical reasons, not quite! 'God forbid you are a chip off the old block, Randy. But as this is the first time I've heard your father praise you, whatever you told him you will do, I will move heaven and earth to make sure he gives you the support you need to do it.'

'Thanks, Mum, I appreciate that,' he replied, surprised. But he was even more astonished when she continued, 'It saddens me to say it, but unfortunately all through your adolescent years, I let you and your sister down by not supporting you. Many times, I let your father's know-all, pompous, arrogant attitude rule our household, when all the time I knew it was wrong and should have stood up to him. I am deeply sorry and hope in time you will forgive me. The reason I agreed to live with him again was not because I wanted to. It was because I believed it would be the best way I could be here to support you for the rest of our lives.'

In one way this extraordinary statement from Randy's usually passive mother was music to his ears. In all other ways it was too late. Too many wedges and too much drug-taking had been driven into the barrier between him and his family to put that right in a few heartfelt sentences. However, he was pleased and wanted her support, so he replied, 'I appreciate your saying this, and doing so can't have been easy. Dad is not an easy man for anyone to get on with. I hope it works out for you and that it is a turning point in our relationships, for all our sakes.'

All his life Randy had wanted parental love, but until now had never been given it. At the age of seven he had been sent to a well-known preparatory boarding school where he was sexually abused by a male teacher. Aged thirteen, he went to Eton where he was only slightly happier.

From his third year at Eton onwards, after his parents separated, Randy got the highs he needed in life from a daily cocktail of mood-altering substances. This meant that except for receiving from his father the monetary gifts he needed to feed his habit, he wanted less and less to do with his parents and increasingly turned his back on them.

Such monetary gifts had always been forthcoming from a father who in the past had boasted on many occasions to anyone who would listen, 'Don't talk to me about families. I have given my children everything they could possibly need for their education and much more. I work day and night for them and their mother, but what thanks do I get? None. She left me and my kids have become nothing but blood-sucking leeches.'

The previous night, when Arthur and his wife had discussed the lunch they were to have with Randy the following day, he repeated most of this, adding, 'What more could I have done? You tell me.'

Her reply was one he did not want to hear. For the first time in Alison's life, she stood up to him and told him the truth in no uncertain terms. 'You could have shown them unconditional love,' she said, anger flooding through her veins. 'That is what both our parents should have shown us and that was what our children needed, but what they got was the opposite. Money, money, money and what it would buy, including people, was all you and I ever thought about. And your tax dodges during the last ten years of our marriage meant we never had a proper home.'

Almost lost for words, but not quite, Arthur retorted, 'You think you're some kind of saint, but you're not. You're as much to blame as I am. When did you say no to visits to Champneys, shopping sprees at Harrods or a fortnight at Sandy Lane?'

'That's not what I am saying. What I now know is what I should have done. I should have threatened to leave you years ago and taken the children with me. But I did not have the courage to do that, and when I did, it was too late, they had already left home.'

Arthur snarled back, 'Well you can pack your bags again as soon as you like. After tomorrow, I don't want anything to do with you if that's how you see me.'

This was not going the way Alison had wanted. Her aim was to bring the family closer together, not tear them apart even more. 'You don't understand. I'm not blaming you for the way you are. I feel sorry for both of us. What you did was the result of the lack of love your parents showed you. All you were ever given were extremes of discipline by an army officer father who never once told you he loved you and a mother who was the least maternal woman I have ever known. What I did came from never answering my father back, and a weak mother. And I became just like her. Those are the reasons we grew up to despise our parents and now we have done the same to our children. What I want is that from now on we try to be the best parents we can be and stop fighting. Do we really want to go to our graves with our children hating us? I know I don't, and I am sure you don't either.'

For the first time ever Arthur's response was not to say anything. His wife had touched a raw nerve by saying things he had always known but never faced up to; also, she had never before challenged his authority.

While Alison was speaking, Arthur's head gradually lowered to the point where he was looking down at the floor. After a few minutes he got up and walked to the door. He was thinking about something he had read earlier that day in Benjamin Franklin's autobiography: 'There are no gains without pains.' As he went to his bedroom, he knew he was going to have a long night reflecting on what she had said.

The following week Arthur received the results of his enquiries into Ibyx. The reports were that it was a good, well-managed company that had been badly affected by the slump in the Spanish economy. His sources added that the founder and owner was well respected, but that it was time for him to step down.

As a result, he called Cyriax's chief executive, the finance director and one of its non-executive directors and said, 'For personal reasons, I am authorising our stockbrokers to sell a block of my family's shares to a spread of existing institutional shareholders.'

****

As soon as the £11,000,000 he received from the sale of his Cyriax Pharma shares was in his bank account, Randy made another appointment to meet Raphael Cortez. A few days later he was back in Spain at the meeting. The following week meetings with lawyers were arranged, and six weeks later after some basic due diligence the deal was concluded.

For the next three months, Randy made every effort to learn from Raphael Cortez's experience. He was determined that when the handover occurred he would be in the best possible position to run the company efficiently. To help him do this he took what he thought was a balanced daily cocktail of drugs – cocaine first thing in the morning, three joints of cannabis during the course of the day, several glasses of wine in the evening and one or two sleeping pills at night. Everything worked more or less as planned, because after six months Randy took over as chief executive of Ibyx Pharma, no longer needing Raphael Cortez's guidance.

In the case of takeovers redundancies are common. But in this instance the only change Randy needed to make was to employ a pharmacist he could trust to study karkoubi's benzodiazapine' s constituents. Together they would work out its formula, then manufacture a pill identical to the one which Algeria exported to Morocco. The right machinery would do the rest.

Getting access to karkoubi's psychotropic component was relatively easy through doctors' prescriptions in Spain and elsewhere. Within another month Randy had made the perfect copycat drug. Now he was ready to start business.

The first thing he did was send 1,000 tabs of his benzodiazepine – each tab containing ten pills – on an empty boat returning to Morocco that had originally shipped cannabis to Spain. There he sold them for 5,000 euros to a drug dealer he was liaising with in Tangier. Although this price was less than half their street value in Morocco, his plan was to use this ready-made market to test them and get started. If that went well, his aim was to do something much bigger and far more profitable in Europe.

Within a month he made two more shipments with no hitches, as boats going in that direction were not apprehended by the police. From every angle it seemed a winner.

Algeciras is the main port for car and people ferries between Spain and Morocco. In addition, there are similar ferries from Algeciras to Ceuta, the Spanish enclave in the north of Morocco. As Ceuta is near the Rif Mountains, the trafficking of drugs by small fast boats and ferry passengers was well established. These links are some of the most successful of all drug supply chains in the world. In his third month of making his karkoubi ingredient, Randy exploited these as well.

After cannabis reaches Spain, the networks transporting it to all corners of Europe are well established. Knowing this, Randy started to plan how he could use them to transport his benzodiazapine and, stimulated by cocaine, his thinking went from small to grandiose as he contemplated distributing it to the whole of Europe, and if that worked, from China to the USA and everywhere in between and beyond.

Once he had pondered on this, he decided the best place to start was Amsterdam in the Netherlands.

Chapter 2

The same week Randolph Cyriax took control of Ibyx Pharma SA in Spain, six Moroccan terrorists met in Amsterdam to discuss its implications for them. They were not interested in the legal drugs Ibyx would make; their interest was in another drug they had heard this otherwise legitimate company was going to make clandestinely. That drug was a copy of the benzodiazepine used in the lethal drug cocktail, karkoubi.

The single agenda of these four men and two women was martyrdom. Their aim was to get the maximum amount of publicity to benefit their Islamist fundamentalist ideals. Ibyx making the karkoubi ingredient and their trafficking it would provide the funds they needed, its 'Rambo' effect helping to stimulate the feeling of invincibility they needed to carry out their plans, especially taking Western capitalist and non-Muslim infidel lives.

Karkoubi had not been christened 'the drug of mass destruction' and 'drug of the poor' in Morocco for nothing, where it also generated huge funds on the black market. For the Moroccan brothers, Yashine and Hamid Abu Zoubeir, their girlfriends Nadia and Mariam, and their childhood friends, Mahi and Nabil, poverty, resentment and disillusionment with the authority and the rich was in their genes. Karkoubi had been the vehicle to turn them into cold-blooded killers. Their meeting today was to decide what European city would be the next target and when.

Eighteen months ago, the men had come to the end of incarceration in Casablanca's Oukacha prison in Morocco. Each had taken drugs since they were eight years old and, while in prison were introduced to karkoubi. Originally from London of Moroccan parents, Nadia Benazzi and Mariam Idrissi had been cannabis drug mules between Morocco and Europe. When Yashine and Hamid introduced them to karkoubi it helped radicalise them, in the same way it had many poor, angry young Moroccans.

The men had grown up in Al Hoceima, one of the largest cities in Morocco. It is on the Mediterranean coast in the Rif Mountain cannabis-growing region, renowned for being all that reflects badly on the king's aim to create an attractive image for his country. Extremes of poverty, drugs and crime provided the background for national protests in 2016, 2017 and 2019. Corruption, unemployment and the brutal death of a destitute fisherman, badly treated by local police, helped create the region's bad reputation.

The two brothers were serving prison sentences for being involved in the protests. At the same time, Moroccan Mounir el-Motassadeq was returned to Morocco from imprisonment in Germany for his role in America's 9/11 terrorist attacks. As news of his arrival and deed spread, he became a hero for many. This meant the radicalisation of young people to be jihadist martyrs became easier than ever before, especially among the homeless and those in prisons on karkoubi.

It was a combination of these factors that led Hamid, Yashine, Mahi, Nabil, Nadia and Mariam to embark on their personal mission to achieve martyrdom. Their aim that day was to put in place an especially bloody terrorist attack that would send them on a magic carpet ride to salvation.

A year after being freed from prison in Morocco, Yashine and Hamid moved to Amsterdam, taking with them Nadia and Mariam. Mahi and Nabil were already there, and they had arranged to meet them on the evening of the day they arrived. After getting high on local cannabis and wine,

Yashine produced what they had all been waiting for, strips of cellulose-wrapped karkoubi cocktail pills the girls had smuggled in from Casablanca in their underwear. Within minutes of taking one their moods changed, reflecting the potency of this highly dangerous drug mixed with alcohol.

Nadia Benazzi and Mariam Idrissi were from North Kensington in London, where they lived in a Moroccan community. On a visit to Casablanca in 2018 they had met Hamid and Yashine soon after they had come out of prison. A few days later the pair introduced Nadia and Mariam to karkoubi; immediately they were singing from the same jihadists' hymn sheet as the brothers.

As Nadia and Mariam had British passports, and did not have police records, it meant they could come and go to Morocco and Europe as they pleased. Whereas Hamid, Yashine, Mahi and Nabil were restricted to Morocco and the Netherlands because of their police records and family connections.

Although they made regular visits from then on to Amsterdam to be with their boyfriends, it was not until a year later that all six were reunited in the Netherlands. In that time Hamid and Yashine had joined an offshoot of an ISIS cell in their community.

Yashine's deeply imbedded hatred of all non-Muslims, belief that armed combat was the only way to prevent further American imperialism, and his high level of intelligence meant he quickly became a leader, forging contacts in ISIS in other countries, including the United Kingdom.

The Netherlands is home to a large number of former Moroccan citizens, spanning nearly three generations. In the 1960's many went to live there to find work. Today there are nearly 400,000 spread across the country, with 70,000 living in Amsterdam.

Dam Square is in the heart of Amsterdam. As it is next to the famous red-light district, this popular square for tourists in a city that has 18,000,000 visitors a year is always crowded, day and night.

With Amsterdam being the recreational cannabis capital of Europe, and Morocco the world's biggest producer of cannabis resin, it was natural it would become a hub for drug trafficking in Europe. As this has been happening for more than fifty years, there are well established drop-off points in between its source in northern Morocco and every country in Europe.

The business this produced gave birth to the 'Mocro-Maffia', the nickname for the Netherlands Moroccan mafia which has become the largest drug trafficking operator in the Netherlands, Belgium and Spain. Renowned mafia writer Roberto Saviano, whose *Gomorrah* is based on the organised crime world of the Camorra network, believes the mafia influence in Amsterdam is worse than in Naples. He wrote in the *Volkskrant* newspaper, 'There are clans from all over the world, because the Netherlands is one of the most important transit ports. They know whoever controls the Netherlands has one of the arteries of the global drug market.'

Billions of euros are earned on the Dutch black market. Synthetic drugs with a street value of €18.9bn were produced in the Netherlands in 2017. Illegal drugs have been imported from Colombia and North Africa for 30 years. Today a significant portion of synthetic drugs – MDMA, LSD, amphetamines, GHB and crystal meth – are produced in the Netherlands.

To drug traffickers themselves, what they do they see is no worse than the police officers, politicians, lawyers, pharmacists, bankers or doctors who criticise them; they want to make money. And for poor Moroccans, if you aren't a great footballer or don't have the brains to wrestle yourself honestly out of a life of poverty, dealing in drugs is the obvious means. This was Yashine's raison d'être and through karkoubi he wanted a slice of the action.

Being aware of the same facts, Randy Cyriax chose the Netherlands as the best place to begin selling karkoubi in Europe. Although he originally thought using existing traffickers to ship his benzodiazepine would be good, it would involve people he would not trust. He needed a safer, economical way to get it from the south of Spain to the Netherlands and avoid the Mocro-Maffia.

The port of Algeciras is the gateway for much of Morocco's fruit and vegetables that are exported to Europe. Through a friend in Gibraltar, Randy was put in contact with a family-owned freight company that made daily shipments of Moroccan fruit and vegetables to France, Belgium and the Netherlands.

To instigate his perceived need, Randy bought a disused shop near Algeciras port; as Ibyx Pharma's manufacturing site was only eight kilometres away, the location was perfect. All he had to do then was a deal with the freight company's owner, who, after being offered enough money, was happy not to question what 'vegetables' he was transporting once a week from Algeciras to Amsterdam. Randy also knew any drug checks would be *before* his karkoubi ingredient pills were put in the vehicles.

To make sure he got every detail right, he went to Amsterdam every few weeks to establish dealer contacts, always driving there in a rented vehicle and going alone. By the time he had completed five visits, he had been to forty of Amsterdam's 170 coffee shops at least once, and the ones where he made the best connections, several times. This led to him meeting three well-established dealers, two Dutch and one Moroccan, and by the end of his fifth visit, he believed he had the one connection that would be perfect: the Moroccan.

Mohamed El Abbas was a second generation thirty-four-year-old whose family came from Ketama, a town in the main cannabis-growing region of Morocco. For more than thirty years his family had been involved in trafficking cannabis from Morocco to the whole of the Netherlands. Best of all, in all that time they had never had problems with the police in either country; generous bribes in both worked wonders.

Mohamed knew all about karkoubi and for years had worked on an idea to introduce it to the Netherlands, but getting enough of the right benzodiazepine to create a market had never been possible; the timing for Randy to meet Mohamed could not have been better.

After a successful trial run of Moroccan-labelled citrus fruit boxes, Randy sent his first shipment of benzodiazepines in identical boxes to Amsterdam. Within six months, the Netherlands had received enough to establish the karkoubi cocktail as the drug of choice for more than 400 drug users. As he had expected, Moroccans living there loved it and word quickly spread to other Dutch cities. After all, it is human nature to experiment with drugs, especially when they are illegal and make people who normally feel inadequate believe they are all-powerful. Each innocent-looking pink benzodiazepine helped users have exactly that effect.

Packed in foil and plastic strips identical to the codeine medication Ibyx made, all it needed were weights to be added to the boxes to make them the same as those for citrus fruit. The difference between the effects of the contents, though, could not have been more different: one boosted human beings' immune systems, the other destabilised their brains.

As addiction took hold of some people the casual user network expanded. So, for the next few months, Randy held back on providing all the karkoubi pills his dealer requested, his aim being to double the demand and therefore increase the price.

In that time the price more than doubled, while the amount of karkoubi pills being delivered to the Netherlands every week stayed the same. This result was beyond Randy's wildest dreams, while the consequences for the Netherlands citizens were horrendous nightmares.

The first consequence was an increase in street violence, especially knife crime and theft, plus mafia assassinations. To begin with the police had no idea as to the cause, but as more and more people were arrested, the single common denominator was a pink pill none of them had seen before. It was only when two teenagers were arrested after stabbing to death three people living in an old people's home that the link between the 'pink pill' and violence was recognised. Each was carrying a half-used strip of the drug.

The enquiries the Dutch police made meant they found out for the first time what karkoubi was capable of and why it was called 'Morocco's drug of mass destruction'. As they looked back over the recent wave of violent crime, they saw the connection and realised the havoc it had created on Dutch soil in this very short time.

The murder of the pensioners caused a public outcry and the media's exposure of the effects of karkoubi sent shivers down the spines of the Dutch police; but it was a different fear that infiltrated the minds of Dutch businessmen and politicians. Amsterdam's tourist industry attracts millions of people because of its cool attitude to cannabis, sex shops, prostitution and associated hedonistic lifestyle. As these are interlinked, curbing any of them, or exposure by the international media to the greater prospects of crime, could have a huge impact on the Dutch economy, shops, hotels and restaurants. So as much as possible was done by authorities to prevent this happening, and after a brief spell of extra police activity, life in Amsterdam returned to more or less normal.

It did not take long for Yashine to understand the Dutch government's motives. He had lived there long enough to know the importance of money in their society, especially as the district in Haarlem where he lived was a more affluent part of the Netherlands. The effect such negative influences would have on tourism would be devastating, so when he discussed it with Hamid and their friends, he described it as reminding him of the American greed in the film Jaws and the reasons why visitors to Amity were not warned of its killer shark. Yashine realised the current scenario played into his hands. It convinced him now was the perfect time to make a terrorist assault because the knock-on effect would rock Amsterdam's hedonistic – to him Satan-driven – lifestyle to the core.

And there was another reason Yashine thought the timing was good. Of the countries in Europe that had a significant number of Moroccans living there, the Netherlands was the only one that had not had a major terrorist attack. Many people thought this was because of the Dutch government's liberal attitude to cannabis, resulting in millions of euros being made by the people who lived there, especially the Mocro-Maffia, as well as those with political and business influence back in Morocco; a view he had held for a long time.

Before he was radicalised, Yashine had been an aimless, bitter young man, aware of the financial injustice inflicted on his family and most of the other residents of North Morocco. Their harvests of cannabis were taken from them by the police, who then hiked the price, whereas he and his friends received a pittance and were classified as criminals. So, like other young men in Al Hoceima, to subsidise his income he had sexual relations with western tourists who visited his town in search of cannabis.

Because of his intelligence, he was a quick learner. He became attuned to these men's preferences and was invariably spot on at knowing who liked gay sex just by looking them. But as he walked through the alleyways thronging with people, donkeys and motor scooters, local men would make lewd comments to him, hurtful and humiliating, because everyone knew his business.

Being sensitive, Yashine had to learn insensitivity so he could carry on doing what was financially good for him; no one was going to help him get by, so it was on the streets of Al Hoceima that he learned to help himself. This rural region had no other sources of income, so as he saw it, he had little or no choice if he wanted to survive.

For years, the resentment this caused festered inside him and grew, eventually making him want revenge. Now he believed that opportunity had come.

****

For over a month Yashine had kept strips of karkoubi pills in his home for when he thought it would be the right moment for him and his friends to use them. After a tagine lunch and smoking cannabis, the six friends' mood had become lighthearted. This was the moment. He gave each of them another bottle of beer and a crushed karkoubi pill to swallow.

Sitting in a lotus position on the floor, he put one on his tongue and downed his beer. Then he raised his left arm and said, '*Almawt lilkifaar*' – 'Death to infidels'. With that the others did the same.

After discussing the pros and cons of where to hit that would have the greatest effect, it was decided the four men would stay in Amsterdam targeting two well-known tourist attractions and the women go to London, targeting one. As their minds had already been filled with hate while taking karkoubi cocktails in Morocco, they no longer needed drugs to maintain an attitude of disillusionment with authority and an abhorrence of the rich; just an occasional top-up of karkoubi was all that was necessary to do that.

Today, the effect of what they had taken, and the prospect of what they were going to do gave them highs the like of which they had never reached before. The crowd-pulling importance of their targets, Dam Square in Amsterdam and Trafalgar Square in London, were enough to do that.

Chapter 3

Letter to the King

In the film Casablanca, my namesake said his reason for going to live in Morocco was for its life-giving waters. Mine was the opposite. When I did the same, it was because of its infamous life-taking drugs: one of which I had not heard of before, karkoubi, probably the world's most dangerous drug cocktail.

My intention when I moved there was to help its million plus drug addicts. What I did not know at the time was that some of them had become terrorists responsible for the worst jihadist attacks in Europe this century.

I chose to live in Tangier, a formerly attractive city, famous in the 1960's for its hedonistic, partying lifestyle. By the time I went there it had lost its charm. Even the once fashionable portside buildings nestled into the rockface now looked decrepit.

My aim was to start Narcotics Anonymous (NA) for the drug addicts I had witnessed on the streets on visits there a few weeks earlier. In the following years I had many successes and almost as many failures. As time went by, I spread my efforts to include Alcoholics Anonymous (AA) as this was also much needed.

After a year I moved to Casablanca: in between I made numerous visits to Rabat, Marrakesh, Agadir and the Rif Mountains where I met addicts, alcoholics, drug dealers, doctors, psychiatrists and cannabis growers. As a result of these and my background, a picture emerged of the reasons for Morocco's drug problem and why it was so deep.

The more I discovered and the more people I met, the more I came to understand why my efforts often seemed so futile. At times they went forward in leaps and bounds, only to be followed by huge disappointments. Overall, at best, my progress was ten steps forward, nine and a half back.

However, in the back of my mind I knew it need not be like this. Both the NA and AA programmes work in every country where they were established. There are approximately a million Muslim drug addicts and alcoholics in recovery globally, and in France, Spain, UK, Netherlands and North America there are many Moroccans who are clean and sober.

What I came to realise was that Morocco's drug laws, policies and unrealistic treatment of drug addiction were the at the hub of their problem. This coupled with its depth, right down to its street children, led me to believe that the only way to solve it was to expose the issues in a way which would persuade the king and his government to make the essential changes necessary to put them right. How to do that was the question?

As is often the case in life, when the time is right, providence lends a hand. I was now wondering if that would ever happen in Morocco. I am pleased to say it and in a most serendipitous way.

****

It took just two minutes and thirty-eight seconds for Britain's minister of defence, David Smith, to give birth to a lifelong hatred when he met Mohamed Tahir, Morocco's new ambassador to London.

Coincidentally, that was almost the same length of time it had taken Levi Abrahams and Isaac Solomon to murder 47 and injure 109 Muslims at the Regent's Park Mosque the previous Friday, which was the reason for this abruptly convened meeting.

The previous night, the British prime minister had given an order requesting that the ambassador go to the Foreign and Commonwealth Office's headquarters at King Charles Street, Westminster at 10 a.m. to answer questions. This was immediately after the Director General of MI5, and Head of Britain's Counter Terrorism Command, briefed him as to the likelihood of an imminent Moroccan-led terrorist attack.

Mohamed Tahir, having taken up his post in London only four days earlier, viewed this as a bad start to a diplomatic relationship that had been festering for weeks. The relationship had begun to deteriorate when the previous ambassador made a huge faux pas at a function in the Moroccan embassy to promote tourism in his country. He was removed immediately after it was discovered.

In his 'Vision 2020' statement King Mohammed VI had said his aim was to boost Morocco's tourist numbers to 20,000,000. This would create 147,000 jobs and put it in the top twenty tourist destinations in the world.

The ambassador had been talking to Robert Pinkerton the owner of the UK's biggest private tour operator. They had been at university together and had remained friends ever since.

'How do you see opportunities for British tourism in Morocco in the next few years?' Tahir asked. 'You already have many visiting Marrakesh. It would be good if you could open routes to some of the other wonderful places we have to offer.'

'The signs are good,' Pinkerton replied enthusiastically. 'Our countries' relations have been at an all-time high since

King Mohammed invited Prince Harry and Meghan Markle to a state visit.'

'I agree,' the ambassador replied. 'The response to that was excellent.' Then he added, 'It wasn't like inviting Donald Trump to London on a state visit: a man better suited to run a brothel, the mafia, or start a world war. In just two years, his hatred of Muslims did immense harm to Arab-American Israeli relations, as well as Hispanic American.'

'I know,' said Pinkerton. 'And healing the wounds he caused will take a lifetime. The attitude Europeans have for America slumped to an all-time low when he moved into the White House. Many here think he should have been certified as insane.'

'God knows what he would have done if he had been re-elected,' said Tahir. 'There was already Palestinian, Iranian and Mexican blood on his hands. I dread to think what his narcissistic behaviour would have driven him to do if he had continued as president. He had already handed the reins of world power to China, and Putin must have been overjoyed at the way he split America. I believe he would have started World War Three if he had been given half a chance.'

'What I found astonishing is that many Republicans claim to be Christian,' said Pinkerton. 'Which does not say much for their understanding of Christ's teachings and those in the Bible.'

The ambassador switched the conversation back to Moroccan tourism and the country's progress, remarking on the high-speed train between Tangier and Casablanca and its solar energy site in the Sahara Desert, the largest green power production facility in the world.

Unfortunately for the ambassador and Morocco's diplomatic relations, a woman standing nearby had unintentionally left her phone voice recorder on. When she got home, she discovered what she had done and played it back. After listening to it several times, she realised who it was and put it on YouTube. Within twenty-four hours it had gone viral.

David Smith's family were not Jewish, but his wife's were. They had supported Donald Trump and hated almost anyone of Arabic origin. As her wealthy, politically inclined family had helped him rise through the ranks of the Conservative party, he was pleased to have the opportunity to put the boot in on their behalf.

After the briefest of preliminary introductions, he looked the ambassador in the eye and said, 'You have been ordered to come here because our security advisors believe there is the likelihood of an imminent attack by London-based Moroccans in retaliation for the Regent's Park attack. We are sorry for the incident and loss of lives of all who were there, including the twelve Moroccans, but we need to know as soon as possible where and when it will take place.'

The defence secretary's intention was to frighten the new ambassador so much that his response would be a compliant one.

In replying however, and without hesitation, Mohamed retorted, 'I came here because I was invited, not ordered. Had I been ordered, and known the reason, I would not have come. Morocco is a country of peace. It is not only our country that has terrorists; every country has them. America's recent approach to Israel and Iran has angered every Muslim country in the world. So why aren't the ambassadors of Saudi Arabia, Egypt, the United Arab Emirates, or any of the others here too?'

Smith had not expected such a response. After a momentary pause in which he hastily gathered his thoughts, he said, 'Your summons is based on recent intelligence, and the

Islamic approach of several eyes for one eye. In 2019, Muslims massacred nearly three hundred Christians in Sri Lanka in retaliation for fifty of them being murdered in New Zealand. As Moroccan jihadists are some of the most active, every indication is they will kill as many people as possible in revenge for the Muslims killed in London last Friday.'

Immediately going to Morocco's defence, the ambassador replied, 'I saw the video the terrorist conspirators put on YouTube. "In the name of God and long live Donald Trump!" is what those Israeli murderers shouted as they fired their bullets. Our King Mohammed VI and Moroccans value safety and life as much as any country, certainly more than terrorists like those do.'

The defence secretary may not quite have been put on the back foot, but realised that he was dealing with someone with the confidence and intelligence to tackle a potentially sensitive and delicate situation. But to see if he could break him, and to not give up, he continued in the same aggressive vein.

'We don't agree,' he said. 'The head of our security service received a damning ten-page exposé from a Briton who has lived in Morocco for the past few years. Much of its content is corroborated and summarised in an open letter he was going to release to the press before we stopped him. Our prime minister believes it is so important for your king to see it, he has instructed me to give you a copy.'

'I do not like your approach. Who is this person? What has he said that is so damning? Why isn't he here for me to question him?' The ambassador waved his arms in frustration.

For the next few minutes their dialogue went back and forth. David Smith first described the background and experiences the writer had outlined in the letter. Then he explained why the writer believed it was Morocco's drug policies that had created havoc and resulted in Moroccans' involvement in Europe's worst jihadist attacks, including America's 9/11. Next, he told him the writer's suggestion for remedying the causes and put forward an overall solution. The last thing he said was that the letter was courteous, so they had not tampered with the wording, though some things they believed were irrelevant had been redacted.

After giving the ambassador this information, the defence secretary stopped talking, seeming to think this would be enough to give him the upper hand and they could conclude their meeting.

But it did not. All it did was make Mohamed Tahir angry. He said, 'This is outrageous and undiplomatic! How do I know this man exists and what he says is true? Someone on your staff could have written the letter before you came here to put pressure on us.'

This heated reply raised Smith's tolerance level to at least that of the ambassador's as it implied underhandedness. He responded, 'All the facts are contained in two books this man has been writing on the subject and a synopsis for a documentary. If they get published, and the series is featured on television, it will cause huge damage to your country. Financially and politically.'

With that he paused and waited for a response. But the ambassador knew silence was sometimes a powerful weapon.

After a few moments David Smith continued.

'To prove its accuracy, I will read you an extract from it which describes some of Morocco's drug problems and their global consequences. You can decide for yourself if his claims are true. They come after an explanatory introduction. An attachment contains a summary of some of the causes.'

"I will listen, but do not expect me to approve your undiplomatic tactics or tone," the ambassador said, sounding pleased with his responses so far.

The defence secretary now took out the letter from its envelope. Before reading from it, he said, 'I will pick out bits that seem relevant. Stop me anytime if you have a comment or observation.' He began to read:

"'Your Majesty, ask yourself the following questions: Why are there thousands of drug-addicted children aged between eight and twelve living on Morocco's streets? This does not happen on this scale in other countries, so why in Morocco? Why is karkoubi, probably the most dangerous drug cocktail in the world, almost exclusive to Morocco?'"

'Stop there,' the ambassador interjected. 'We are doing all we can to put these situations right. But maybe your writer does not explain that.'

'He does, but he says that what Morocco is doing is wholly ineffective. If I read a bit more, you will understand.' Smith could barely disguise his enjoyment in exposing the wrongs of Morocco's drug situation. He went on:

"'Karkoubi is lethal, and its psychotic effect makes it easy for those who take it to be radicalised in prisons More than 65% of criminals in Morocco were on it when they committed their crime. Why is it the majority of jihadists involved in the Barcelona, Madrid, Brussels, London, Paris and Manchester terrorist attacks were Moroccan? Why was the only convicted criminal involved in America's 9/11 Moroccan? In the past sixteen years there were three lethal terrorist attacks by Moroccans in Casablanca and Marrakesh.'"

'But it was not only Moroccans who were involved. What else does he say?' the ambassador demanded.

'That a serial killer on karkoubi murdered fourteen people in Rabat and two female tourists were beheaded in the Atlas Mountains last year. Then he makes one of his most damning observations. He asks why there are more Moroccans who have recovered from drug addiction or alcoholism living in numerous other countries than there are in Morocco?'

Smith stopped and put the letter back in its envelope.

'If news of this gets out,' he said, 'your country, which thrives on the income it makes from tourism and illegal drugs, will be destroyed. Especially if there are more Moroccan-influenced attacks, which we believe there will be unless your king and government take the appropriate action. Is that enough to convince you to cooperate?'

His smugness showed.

While all this appeared to be like a bombshell to the ambassador, he did his best to conceal it.

He said, 'I have already told you my view. However, I will read it, and only if I deem it appropriate, will I or anyone else get back to you.'

Smith nodded. 'We want an answer within seventy-two hours. If we do not have one, we will take whatever measures we believe are best to protect our country. Do you have any questions?'

The ambassador had arrived accompanied by his PA, Ali Abadi, who had been quiet so far. Ali had more experience than the ambassador in dealing with British politicians, most of whom he found arrogant and self-righteous.

He now spoke for the first time. 'I have one, Minister. Does this mean Britain has had a spy operating in our country? If so, we would need to take advice before doing anything. We would also need to make sure the international community is aware; starting with the United Nations.'

This seemed to make the ambassador slightly more confident.

'I recall from my days at Cambridge,' he observed, 'that Britain does not take kindly to spies. Burgess, Maclean, Philby and Blunt, for example. And isn't it a coincidence that two of Britain's major contributions to the cinema are James Bond movies and John Le Carré's spy books? Perhaps you missed this, though, as you, like most of your colleagues and former prime ministers, were at Oxford, I believe?'

A neat parry, Smith thought, but he maintained his inscrutable expression.

'You will see from the content of the letter that no one was spying. The report was written by a man who went to live in Morocco for one single reason, to help your drug addicts, of which he says there are many. As he is an author, and as a consequence of what he discovered, he decided to write a book about his experiences.'

'You mean he was working for an NGO?' the PA asked.

'No. He was alone and paid for everything out of his own pocket. What he discovered he believes needs to be exposed because it is the cause of many of the world's drug problems and jihadist attacks. The letter summarises everything we believe you need to know.'

'But it is redacted, you said. Meaning you have taken out everything you don't want us to know. And as no one seems to have monitored what he was doing, it must mean he did not report to anyone. Not exactly the way to give its contents credibility.' Abadi looked straight into Smith's eyes. This was no longer going as well as the defence secretary had hoped. He now had an adversary, who, without having had time to think beforehand, was coming up with responses worthy of any politician.

'The latter is correct, but we know the book's contents are accurate. The facts that are pertinent have been confirmed by our consulate in Casablanca.' David Smith met his gaze.

'We need to see the books and the other document you mentioned. How can we do that?' asked the ambassador.

'I will send copies to your embassy. They each say the same using different writing formats.'

Not wanting any more awkward challenges, the defence secretary got up and put the envelope on the table between them, intending to mean that the meeting was over.

'I have another question,' the PA said, not getting up. 'Before we came here, I looked you up on Wikipedia. I understand you are married to Marian Goldsmith, the daughter of the chairman of the Conservative party. Is that right?'

If Smith had been a little agitated before, he was more so now.

'I am, but that has nothing to do with this,' he answered stiffly.

'Really? Well, I suggest it does. Her father gives a lot of money to Israel and has business interests there. He also gives a lot of money to the Conservative party. So, my questions are, do you think it is likely he and her family were pro Donald Trump's stance on Israel's illegal occupation of Palestine, and did you support that? Because it is clear to every other country this has added to the cause of many of the problems which have been brewing in the Middle East ever since.'

'I know what you are getting at and you are wrong. My family's political views have no influence on mine," the defence secretary answered, his face reddening.

Now it was the ambassador's turn to feel confident, so he responded with all the diplomacy he could muster: 'I find that hard to believe, and so will King Mohammed VI and the international community. The west is renowned for living as if money talks and having nepotistic influences in politics and business; just as Donald Trump did when he was president with regard his son-in-law.' After the pause that followed, Ali Abadi added, 'The twenty-two member countries of the Arab League and five international observers are already annoyed at the British support of America's anti-Muslim regime. We also need to know what was redacted. That usually means there is something in a document the protagonist or defender knows will influence an outcome.'

This time the ambassador stood up. He was now ready to leave too.

He said, 'You will get your answer when we are ready, not before.'

This latest direction of their conversation meant the defence secretary had a new card to play.

'The part that is redacted provides the solution which our advisers believe could work. If your country accepts that what is said in the letter is true, and Morocco is prepared to make the necessary changes, we will provide you with that information. However, as one of his suggestions is to get the help of the United Nations at the appropriate time, if you muddy the waters there now, you may not get their support when you need it.'

The ambassador paused before answering. As he did so, a smile gradually spread across his face,

'If there are issues that need changing, I am sure we have the right people to analyse what they are, and then make them. Today, I am more concerned about the spying issue, your denial of it, and your possible prejudice towards Israel. We will need to examine these further to understand if there is an anti-Muslim stance.'

Then he added a *coup de grâce*. He, too, had done some research on the British government.

'I am sure you know that not long ago, the Muslim Council of Britain demanded an Islamophobia investigation into the Conservative party. I don't think I need to say more.'

Although they shook hands, there was nothing warm in the act and no photographers to catch the disdain in their expressions. Each knew there would be unpleasant consequences to come. With no love lost between them, several new problematic diplomatic milestones had been put in place. The defence secretary went from what he had thought was a position of unassailable strength before he arrived to feeling that only a pyrrhic victory had been won. Conversely, the Moroccan ambassador and his personal assistant had gone from despair to believing they had won an important skirmish.

In reality, the ambassador knew deep down inside this was only a small victory in a potentially much bigger battle. And if that was not handled well, it could have major repercussions for Morocco internally and globally.

****

Soon after getting into their ambassadorial limousine to return to their Kensington embassy, the ambassador got out the envelope and looked at the words on the outside: <u>To His Majesty, King Mohammed VI of Morocco</u>

As he reflected on their meeting and wondered what the letter contained, his thoughts went from concern to satisfaction; on the one hand the paragraphs the defence secretary had read from the letter were damning, on the other, the answers given by his PA had clearly rattled David Smith. With these thoughts in his mind, he opened the envelope. Moments later he handed Ali Abadi the Twelve Causes of the drug problem in their country to read while he studied the letter.

Sire,

Warm greetings and all due respect to Your Majesty.

As our objectives to improve life in Morocco are the same, I am writing to suggest how you can achieve that in the best possible way.

Many of the over-riding problems are caused by Morocco's drug policies, financial greed, lack of proper treatment of drug addicts and poverty. As these are the reasons for major problems at home and abroad, correcting them will have positive influences on your society, help Morocco become one of the best countries in the world to live, remove issues that are off-putting to visitors, and make Moroccans feel equal to anyone anywhere.

Your Majesty, since 1984 I have been a regular visitor to your beautiful country. During visits in 2016, I was despondent to realise from many years' experience advising the pharmaceutical industry on business development, and thirty years helping drug addicts recover, Morocco has the worst drug problems of any of the many countries I have visited. I also discovered that Morocco's current policies do not help because the causes are not addressed, and drug addicts' underlying issues are not dealt with effectively. Sadly, this means nothing has improved since my first visit,

49

and globally Morocco's influence regarding drugs has got catastrophically worse, including influencing terrorist attacks and creating mafias.

To help Morocco's drug addicts and their families, in January 2017 I went to live there. My aim was to start Alcoholics Anonymous and Narcotics Anonymous in Arabic. These worldwide organisations have helped millions of alcoholics and drug addicts recover, including hundreds of thousands in Muslim countries. What is more, they are free. <u>But</u> they were not in Morocco!

To ascertain the facts behind the problems, over the next two years I met hundreds of Morocco's doctors, psychiatrists, psychologists, pharmacists and drug addicts in Casablanca, Rabat, Tangier, Marrakesh and Agadir. I made three visits to the Rif Mountains to meet cannabis growers, and met psychiatrists at addiction centres in Tangier, Casablanca, Marrakesh, Rabat and Agadir. I attended their AMA convention in Rabat in 2016. On every occasion I made notes and followed up with positive suggestions to individuals.

The more I discovered, the more I understood about the reasons for Morocco's internal drug problems, and why, in recent years, Moroccans have been the most frequent perpetrators of the horrendous jihadist attacks in Europe, America and in Morocco itself.

One of the biggest problems is the terrible stigma of being a drug addict, probably worse than in any other country. This is a direct result of your country's policies, so it is essential to put those right.

Your Majesty, ask yourself the following questions: Why are there thousands of drug-addicted children aged between eight and twelve living on Morocco's streets? This does not happen on this scale in other countries, so why in Morocco?

Why is karkoubi, probably the most dangerous drug cocktail in the world, almost exclusive to Morocco? This drug is lethal, and its psychotic effect makes it easy for those who take it to be radicalised in prisons, where more than 65% of criminals in Morocco were on it when they committed their crime.

Why is it the majority of terrorists involved in the Barcelona, Madrid, Brussels, London, Paris and Manchester jihadist attacks were Moroccan? Why was the only convicted criminal involved in America's 9/11 a Moroccan? Since 2003 there were three lethal attacks on innocent people by Moroccans in Casablanca and Marrakesh; a serial killer in Rabat on karkoubi murdered fourteen people; and in 2017, two female Scandinavian tourists were decapitated in the Atlas Mountains.

Why are there more Moroccans who have recovered from drug addiction or alcoholism living in France, The Netherlands, United Kingdom, USA, Canada, Belgium and Spain than there are in Morocco?

Your Majesty, Morocco's drug laws cause confusion at home and abroad. Cannabis and alcohol are everywhere, yet they are illegal. Morocco's 38,760 ton sales of cannabis resin make it the global world leader (source UN) and Diana Holding, a Moroccan private company, sells 30,000,000 bottles of wine annually. As more than 1,000,000 Moroccans are employed in these industries, is it that they are legal or illicit?

In February 2021, Morocco opened the door through a bill in parliament to legalise cannabis for medicinal purposes. This did not go far enough, but it was a step in the right direction. Based on the fact Morocco's Rif mountains are the largest cannabis-growing area in the world, and its climate and altitude make it perfect to do this, it should have *explored any possible legitimate purposes before. But as it did not, the hypocrisy of it being unofficially Morocco's biggest foreign-currency earner – US$10 billion annually – with 800,000 families in the Rif mountains dependent on it to survive, Morocco's policies have been a major cause of the mayhem surrounding its myriad of drug problems.*

Morocco's interpretation of the Qur'an on intoxicants does not make sense and is part of the problem: if God is all powerful, loving, omnipotent, and the provider of everything, God made the cannabis plant. As cannabis grows naturally in Morocco, why was its use as a medicine to aid mankind not supported before February 2021?

As addiction is a disease of the mind and body, addicts should be treated with understanding and love, not other drugs. They should not be imprisoned and ostracised by society as they are in Morocco.

Your Majesty, these are just some of my findings, but there are many more. Morocco needs to make significant changes to remedy them. So the sooner the appropriate changes are made the better it will be for Morocco's one million drug addicts, their families and all the countries influenced by its present discombobulating, hypocritical drug laws and policies.

Most importantly, Your Majesty, the solution can be achieved, and I know how to do it, which I am sure would be your goal if you knew it was possible.

Not all the reasons are Morocco's fault. Some are due to misunderstandings, misinformation by international pharmaceutical companies and American-influenced global drug policies, including the so called 'war on drugs.'

To achieve the best results, Your Majesty is called upon to instruct your government to appoint someone who understands the problems and solution, who has the right experience to oversee the changes. Someone who does it for humane, not financial or power-seeking purposes. Probably a foreigner who has no such biases.

Your Majesty, the proposed changes would be at no monetary cost to Morocco as the benefits will outweigh the negative costs of current policies. Your country will also reap many social blessings. It will become respected internationally, as well as help hundreds of thousands of Morocco's drug addicts go from unfailing despair to hope, uncontrollable drug use to abstinence, and from chronic unmanageability to responsibility.

Whereas, if there are more terrorist attacks committed by Moroccans, at home or abroad, the opposite will happen and your aim to grow your tourist population of ten million visitors a year to twenty will be thwarted.

There are many countries in the world that have seen the need to change policies to remove drug problems. It is their success that should be the role model for Morocco, not living in the past and blindly following America.

Yours faithfully,

A man who cares about Morocco's drug addicts, their families and all humanity.

Without saying anything, the ambassador handed Abadi the letter. He then read the causes.

12 Causes of Morocco's Drug Problems

Morocco loosely applies the world's drug laws, but in its case, because its past and present policies are hypocritical, they are discombobulating and cause more hardship than in any other country.

Morocco's government has not challenged the world's drug laws, even though it is the biggest grower of cannabis in the world and it is smoked liberally in many places there. It seems this must be because of the huge income cannabis generates for Moroccans at home and abroad.

Many Moroccans are badly educated, illiterate and extremely poor, so they use cheap, easily available drugs to lift their spirits and accept their circumstances. This suits the government's policy of pacifying them into not committing anti-social behavior, BUT it has a serious negative effect because it creates drug addiction.

Morocco has extreme ranges of socio-economic status, from the king at the top, drug lords, medical profession and government policy makers to its street sleepers. For anyone who understands addiction, the result of such division of rich and poor festers resentment, which is one of the main symptoms of social unrest and drug addiction.

Morocco has more than 1,000,000 drug addicts and alcoholics, none of whom are in recovery; each of these is tagged as a criminal and many commit every type of crime possible, as well as destroying their families and filling hospitals and prisons.

Morocco's policy is to pacify addicts by putting them on prescription drugs, instead of helping them recover using Alcoholics Anonymous and Narcotics Anonymous free programs that are successful all over the world.

Morocco's medical profession is complicit because it falls in line with the government's 'let's pacify them' policy.

Morocco's doctors' and psychiatrists' prescribing habits to treat addiction have led to confusion for its citizens, drug addicts, their families and pharmacists, causing more addiction problems as medical professionals are trusted to provide the most effective treatment for diseases.

Pharmaceutical companies providing drugs in Morocco incentivise doctors not to change prescribing habits by paying them financial inducements.

Morocco's health services are internationally known to be poor, which includes comparisons with countries in Africa and the Middle East. (The king, for example, goes to France for his health treatment!)

Morocco's interpretations of the Qur'an are inhumane and bizarre for two reasons:

(a) Addiction is a disease and recovery possible, but this isn't applied in Morocco.

(b) There are known medicinal benefits to cannabis, and more are likely to be found. A God of love and peace would surely not bless a country with the perfect geology and climate to grow cannabis if He did not want its people to use it for purposes that heal mankind.

12. Morocco's drug policies and attitude to drugs cause a terrible stigma of being a drug addict or alcoholic to anyone living there – probably the worst in the world – making recovery more difficult and harder for families to accept.

Slowly, Mohamed Tahir put the letter down, pondering on the causes and consequences described by the writer. He found it easy to see that Morocco's regimes, spread over many years, had created three obvious adverse effects. So as soon as his PA had finished reading the letter, he expressed his observations to him one by one. Ali Abadi agreed with his assessment and added a fourth. Their list read:

55

They have not helped drug addicts recover. In fact, they are detrimental and caused many of Morocco's worst problems.

They inadvertently created the widespread use of karkoubi, the 'drug of mass destruction', and the terrible repercussions associated with it.

The overall effects made Morocco itself sick, to the point where any more jihadist attacks committed by Moroccans would mean the world will point the finger of blame at its king and government's policies. Which at the moment is not the case.

Once the world knows the truth, there will be global demand for a reversal of our policies to fix the problems; while the opportunity to correct them before this happens will have been lost if the king does not act now. Whereas taking immediate action will save much embarrassment and bloodshed.

The more they talked about it, the more Mohamed Tahir and Ali Abadi realised that if the information they had just read and heard in the meeting with the defence secretary was made public, it would cause serious problems. Not least because, if there was a solution, why hadn't Morocco adopted it?

'You know the British better than me. What do you think we should do first?' Mohamed eventually asked.

'The fact this man was doing it voluntarily means he has no axe to grind,' Ali Abadi said. 'He only wants to help drug addicts. His conclusion must mean he found that in trying to do so, he was blocked, directly or indirectly, by people and policies. But you have spent more time living in Morocco than me. What do you think?'

'I believe most of what he says is true; his background and motives give it that credibility. But how do we explain this to our king? He will have a fit if this is aired publicly.'

'We focus on finding the solution. In the meantime we examine the American and other external influencers. As the writer says, much of it is not Morocco's fault.'

'That is good. Any other ideas?' the ambassador responded.

'Thank you. I'm pleased there is a way forward I had not thought of.'

'We also put as much blame as possible on the marketing tactics of pharmaceutical companies. There is so much bad news out there about them, especially American and British, that will be easy. It may mean some of our doctors and drop-in treatment centre managers were lied to and received back-handers.'

Abadi waited for the ambassador to respond.

'What worries me, though,' he said, 'is that the king's PR team always makes sure he has lots of promotional publicity and is photographed opening such centres. I saw this when he opened the Hasnouna drug treatment centre in Tangier. He and its head psychiatrist gave the impression it would help many addicts. But if the author of this letter is correct, none or almost none, have recovered.'

'I hope that's not true. If it is, it is bad news because that led to the opening of the others. If they are not working, and it is exposed, the king won't like it and will want to know why. Surely our psychiatrists know about the success of Narcotics Anonymous and Alcoholics Anonymous? I have heard them mentioned several times since I was posted to London,' Ali replied.

'So why are they not in Morocco when the writer says they are all over the Middle East?'

'I wonder which of Morocco's psychiatrists he met. Reda Oumainian is the former head of the Addiction Unit at Sale/Rabats's psychiatric hospital. I can ask him what he knows. Given his status as the most influential psychiatrist in Morocco, he might know who the writer of the letter is,' Ali suggested.

'A good idea. I know his father, Abdasalam Oumainian, the revered imam. I will ask him his view on the interpretation of the Qur'an and intoxicants issue. We need to know if the writer is right about Middle Eastern Islamic countries taking a different approach.' The ambassador began to feel a little more positive.

'Last year I read *Drogues, La Realite Marocaine* by Mohamed Ben Amar. It had little mention of the depths of the karkoubi problem described here. For me, that exemplifies the crux of Morocco's drug problems: no one wants to talk about them. The other headache is, who in Morocco benefits? Everyone believes it includes the police, state officials and God knows who else. As the writer says, our drug industry employs nearly a million Moroccans and the prospect of redeploying them has always been too unbearable to contemplate.'

Ali's observations threw more coals on the ambassador's formerly red-hot fire.

'That's the last thing I want to deal with right now. It's what and when to pass this up the line to the king I have to decide.'

A few minutes later they arrived at the embassy having travelled the rest of the journey in silence, both absorbed in thought. There were so many things to think about, not least being who were the Moroccan beneficiaries of its billion-dirham illegal drug trade? At the same time there was the dreadful thought that another Moroccan jihadist attack was about to occur in a major European city, or worse still, cities, or America.

Inside the building, just before they parted, the ambassador said, 'Contact Reda Oumainian, Mohamed Ben Amar and that psychiatrist at the Hasnouna in Tangier, then let me know what they say. Make sure you don't tell them the reason. Let them know the urgency, but not any detail. I will speak to Abdasalam Oumainian. Most important, don't say a word of this to anyone. We don't want any leaks, especially before the king is told. I want to know as much as possible first and have a better understanding of any solution.'

Chapter 4

The first thing Ali Abadi did when he reached his office was take out his prayer mat and point it towards Mecca. At the end of his routine prayers, he asked for guidance on Morocco's drug problems.

The meeting with the British defence secretary had seriously worried him. He had long been concerned about the role of Moroccans in terrorist attacks, having worked in the Madrid embassy in 2004 at the time his fellow citizens had been responsible for the jihadist attacks there that killed 193 people and injured 1,700: the most destructive such atrocity to date in Europe.

As the record of such attacks by Moroccans had become worse, he always suspected a challenge like this would arise when someone from a foreign country realised the extent of Morocco's role in radicalisation leading to terrorism.

The second thing he did was look up 'karkoubi' on the internet. Although he had known of its existence, living abroad for so long he knew little about its background or the devastating statistics related to it. Pondering the implications led him to deeper concern. He decided to email Reda Oumainian.

'Dear Professor Oumainian,

Excuse the directness of my request but I need to speak to you urgently about a problem that arose at a meeting today with the British defence secretary and our new ambassador to London.

Please call me as soon as you can, preferably before 15-00 today.

Your obedient servant,
Ali Abadi,
Personal Assistant to the Moroccan Ambassador in London

A little while later, he sent a similar email to Mohamed Ben Amar, but the wording was less direct; a third he sent to Dr Mohamed Drissi, former head psychiatrist of the Hasnouna Association in Tangier.

After that he sat back, reflected and waited. His thoughts went to two scenes he had witnessed in Casablanca a week ago, just before he returned to London after spending a family holiday in Essaouira on Morocco's Atlantic coast.

Near his 4* hotel on Boulevard d'Anfa, he remembered giving a wide birth to a group of street children arguing who looked conspicuously out of place in this fashionable part of the city. As he played it back in his mind he realised that each held a plastic bag from which they would inhale the solvents they contained. After that his mind moved to a scene in Casablanca's main kasbah near Casa Port railway station. It was the following day and he had walked through it on his way to catch a train to Rabat. It was eight in the morning and there were only a few people about, mostly men setting up and opening stalls.

Walking in front of him, swaying from side to side, was a boy aged around fourteen. After he had walked a few steps passed him, he looked back. Close enough to see the boy's eyes, he could tell that his mind was in cloud cuckoo land, the like of which he'd only previously seen in the worst street drug addicts and alcoholics. He, too, was sniffing something from a plastic bag, the smell of which Ali knew would be sickly and revolting.

At the time he had been repulsed, shocked by their ages and the state they were in. Now that he knew nothing

61

worthwhile was being done by the state to help them, even though there was a way that would, he was saddened. And as this he knew to be the case all over Morocco for many children, it was clear that their descent further into addiction could lead to karkoubi. As drug addicts will do anything to get money to buy drugs, the eventual outcome could be radicalisation into jihadism.

As he pondered, he thought about what his sister had told him the night before. She had rung to ask for his help with her son, Otmane. Aged twenty, he was about to go to university in Meknes. Earlier that day he had been physically violent with her and verbally abusive with his sister. She knew he had a problem with cannabis, and sometimes, alcohol, but he had never been like this before. Ali had replied that it might be nothing more than fear of leaving home and anger at her marriage breaking up a few weeks earlier. But, she said, she was sure it must be some new psychotic drug she had heard about.

Given what he had just read about karkoubi, Ali wondered if Otmane had taken that, and this was what had triggered his aggressive behaviour.

As he continued to reflect, a strange thought entered his mind: if the outcome of the meeting they had with David Smith meant the dark clouds that had descended over Morocco caused by its drug problems were removed, there could be a silver lining. Maybe, just maybe, he thought, it will be the awfulness of karkoubi and the seriousness of our drug problems which will be the catalyst to provide the alchemy needed to sort them out and prevent the terrible damage they are causing at home and abroad.

****

With nothing so positive in his mind, the first thing Ambassador Tahir did was email Abdasalam Oumainian. The second paragraph read:

'At the request of their prime minister, this morning I had a meeting with the British defence secretary, Mr David Smith. I left believing we may be facing an international crisis. As it would be better for me to explain my questions for you verbally, please call me as soon as possible. I need your advice before I contact our prime minister about it.
I look forward to hearing from you, etc.'

****

The first to respond to either of them was Reda Oumainian. He called not long after receiving the email, and after some introductory pleasantries, he asked, 'You said it was urgent, Si Abadi. How can I help?'
'I have just come from a meeting with the British defence secretary and our new ambassador to London, Si Mohamed Tahir. Some of it did not go well. Someone from the United Kingdom has been living in Morocco trying to help drug addicts, and what he discovered does not show our country's drug policies in a good light. He also claims that the Moroccans who committed a lot of the terrorist attacks in Europe may have been radicalised into jihadism while on karkoubi, specifically because of these policies.'
'That is preposterous,' Professor Oumainian replied briskly. 'In the past we had problems, but in recent years we have opened treatment facilities and the king is committed to helping as many drug addicts as possible.'
'It seems, the writer says, the issues go much deeper. Part of the problem is that our treatment centres are not run

effectively. It appears he has a lot of experience in this field and met many of our psychiatrists and doctors. Some of his views are based on what he learned from talking to them.' Ali said, trying to be as tactful as possible.

'Again, I think it is preposterous. But I would need to know more before I can comment properly. Why did you think I can help?' Professor Oumainian asked, sounding somewhat bewildered.

'I wondered if you know who this person is,' Abadi said.

'Without a name, I don't know. I meet a lot of people to do with drugs and addiction, in Europe, America and here. Do you have any other information about him?'

'He is involved with Alcoholics Anonymous and Narcotics Anonymous. Do you know these organisations?'

Reda closed his eyes for a moment and gave a slight wince; he now had a good idea who the man was. If he was right, he had met him three times and communicated with him for over a year. But for the past two years, because he had not liked what this man suggested his team do to get the best results, he had stopped replying to his attempts to communicate.

'I know both organisations and support them. I made presentations to our psychiatrists about them over two years ago and helped start a sort of Alcoholics Anonymous meeting in Rabat's psychiatric hospital soon after that,' Reda answered, hoping this would divert the conversation's direction.

'That's the first good news I've had since breakfast. How is it going? Do you have any results yet that I can pass onto the ambassador?' Ali Abadi asked.

'I am not directly involved. I would need to check with the head of the hospital. The professor in charge there took over and arranged for its administration. I was only instrumental at the beginning,' Oumainian replied, now deliberately distancing himself from it.

'Please do that and get back to me. I need some good news, because the ambassador will have to give a report to the prime minister and then, presumably, he will give one to the king. Another thing, what can you tell me about the drug cocktail, karkoubi?'

'Its side effects are horrendous. It is cheap and comes in the form of a pill, a benzodiazepine made in America which is crushed, then snorted or swallowed and taken with a cocktail of solvent, cannabis and alcohol. The pills are usually imported from Algeria or Spain where they are stolen using forged prescriptions.'

Reda Oumainian encapsulated his knowledge of the drug as fully as possible. Realising the seriousness of the direction their conversation was going, he believed that the more help he gave, the better it would be for him in the long term.

'David Smith told us it is almost exclusive to Morocco, and implied that Moroccans who take it are easy to radicalise. What are your thoughts on that?'

'That could be true, but I don't know. It is certainly the worst drug I have encountered in all my years helping drug addicts. And why it is exclusive to Morocco, I have never understood.' Reda Oumanian answered truthfully.

'He also said pharmaceutical companies give out misinformation which has exacerbated the problem in Morocco. Could that be possible?'

From the way Si Ali Abadi was putting his questions, Professor Oumainian realised he had done his homework, so answering honestly was the only way to respond.

'They do that all over the world. What is more, they often offer incentives to prescribe their products. Did this man say anything else?'

'He said American drug policies are a major part of the problem; especially the war on drugs,' Ali answered.

'In many ways I agree. The problem is, they are deeply embedded everywhere, so changing them in Morocco is difficult.'

'But some countries, the writer says, have changed them and their new policies are working. Do you know anything about this and which countries and policies they are?'

Ali no longer held back in the way he phrased his questions.

'I do, but I would need an update of the latest information. The world, including Morocco is moving towards legalising cannabis for medicinal purposes and some countries and states in America are legalising it for recreational purposes.'

'What are your thoughts on that?'

'This is off the record, right?'

'Yes.'

'I am probably for it,' Oumainian said. 'But my position as a prominent psychiatrist in Morocco makes it hard for me to express my view here.'

Ali guessed that the professor was probably wishing he had not made the call.

'I assume that is also because of the religious position we have in Morocco and your father,' he said, beginning to admire Oumainian's honesty.

'Yes, that does make it harder. But I am a medical man who took an oath; for me it is results that count. There are applications of cannabis proven to work for some medical conditions, and with all the global research that is going on, more that are positive are likely. So, professionally, I have to be in favour of legalising it.'

'Thank you for your help and honesty, Professor. I realise this cannot be easy for you. If you find out or think of anything else, please get back to me. I believe you have understood how important this is.'

After a slight pause, out of the blue, Oumainian responded, 'One piece of advice. Keep an eye on France. The French are the biggest users of recreational cannabis in Europe. Their government is debating legalising soon. If they do, it will have a significant influence on other countries in Europe, and as much of it comes from Morocco, there would be more demand. On the other issue, I will try to get back to you tomorrow, inshallah.'

'Thank you for that news. It is interesting. For your information, Ambassador Tahir is contacting your father about Islamic interpretations, which this man says is one of the causes of Morocco's drug problem.'

'You should also contact Mohamed Ben Amar in Montreal. He was an adviser when Canada legalised cannabis in 2018. I will send you his details.'

'I have read his book on drugs in Morocco and have done that. So, thanks again, you have been most helpful.'

As Reda Oumainian put the phone down, he shook his head, thinking as he did so, 'Why, oh why did I let that woman take over the running of the AA meeting? I should have insisted I did it for at least a year and made sure we used Blaine's experience to get it off the ground.' He remembered thinking at the time, that this man knew more about recovery from drug addiction and AA than anyone he knew. He had also liked the fact that helping addicts was his only motive.

Unfortunately, when he'd presented the idea to the other psychiatrists at the Sale-Rabat hospital, it was decided to do it in-house and change the name to AAA, 'Abstinent Alcoholics of Ar-Razi', at the same time changing the way it was administered.

Even at the time he'd believed this was a mistake, because as a doctor you don't change drugs or procedures that work, so why change a globally successful programme that always works when it is applied? As he'd often told his students, 'If it works, don't fix it.' But on that occasion, he'd allowed other people to make the decision.

He wondered where Richard Blaine was now. His advice could be helpful. He still had his details, and because of his commitment to helping Moroccan drug addicts, he would surely be pleased to hear from him.

****

Not long after Ali Abadi talked to Reda Oumainian, Ambassador Tahir spoke to Abdasalam Oumainian, Reda's father. Having been at university at the same time in Rabat, they knew each other and shared an interest in Morocco's historical literature. Whenever they spoke it began with a discussion about what they had recently read. But this time it needed to be different; it was Morocco's future that was at stake, not its past.

As soon as Mohamed Tahir answered, Abdasalam Oumainian said, 'Salaam alaikum, Mohamed. You mentioned an international crisis. What did you mean?'

'The British government believes there will be a retaliatory attack for the Muslims killed in London last Friday. They say Morocco has a bad record with regard to jihadist attacks, so they think it likely Moroccans living here could be involved.'

'Are there many Moroccans in the UK?' Oumainian asked.

'About 200,000. Mostly in London, with many in Notting Hill, not far from the mosque in Regent's Park where the attack happened. That is quite near St John's Wood and Golders Green where most Jews in London live.'

'I understand. So, how can I help?'

'Britain's defence secretary showed me a letter the writer planned to send to His Majesty King Mohammed. It was written before the attack last Friday and explains why Morocco's drug policies cause Moroccans to be radicalised to commit jihadist attacks. It was written by someone who lived in Morocco and who the British believe has the experience to know the causes and solution.'

'What is the problem then? If there is a solution, and the British know what it is, why don't they pass it on so we can implement it?'

'Some of the problem involves interpretations of the Qur'an,' Mohamed answered unhesitatingly, but knowing this could be a difficult subject.

'There is no way they would affect drug problems. If problems are caused by people on drugs, it is all the more reason to enforce Qur'anic law,' Oumainian responded.

'Our drug laws and Qur'anic policies, the writer says, are hypocritical and not based on humanitarian grounds. From what is contained in the letter, he has interesting arguments on both counts.' Mohamed closed his eyes and prayed for guidance.

'Interpretations of the Qur'an are the same for all Islamic countries. On this subject, verses 90 and 91of Surat Al-Ma'idah are clear.'

Presumably the word 'humanitarian' had annoyed Ahmed Oumainian as his tone expressed anger. However, the ambassador was ready for this.

'I have always thought like you,' he said smoothly. 'But some of the facts he reveals in the letter put a different slant on my previous interpretation. This is because he explains how Middle Eastern Islamic countries, such as Egypt, Iran, Saudi Arabia and UAE, have adopted programmes that help drug addicts and alcoholics to recover, whereas Morocco has not.'

Abdasalam paused, then said, 'I need to see the letter. Can you send it to me?'

'Yes, of course. Let's speak again after you have read it. But under no circumstances can you let anyone else see it before I know your answer and have had the opportunity to pass on my conclusions to our minister of foreign affairs.'

'I will do what you ask. But I am convinced I am right. It is just another attempt by westerners to put down Muslims.' The imam answered positively, though under the surface, Ali thought, he must have been disturbed as the situation was serious and its implications could not be taken lightly.

Chapter 5

Ali Abadi was a good man and rational thinker. He had studied philosophy, English and politics at university in Tangier, and later did a degree in English at SOAS in London. Although he had no doubt there was much about Morocco's traditions, religion and culture that caused it problems, his heart was still there. So anything he could do to improve the lives of its people he would go to any lengths to achieve.

Between the age of fourteen and eighteen he had attended the American school in Tangier. A dedicated pupil, while there he improved his English to a high level of fluency. Although he was sometimes offered drugs on the streets outside the school, only on a few occasions did he join others to smoke cannabis, some of whom, he knew, went on to become addicted, and at least one, a dealer.

Even though everyone knew drugs were rife all over Morocco, looking back, he was surprised to realise that his school did not have talks given by experts on the dangers of drugs, especially as it had almost exclusively Western influences.

He remembered frequently seeing children sniffing solvents from plastic bags within easy walking distance of the school, children who would definitely not have been taught the deadly consequences of where their drug-taking would lead. Like many adolescents, they were simply following the example of their peers. So his closest childhood friends would have done likewise had they not known better.

What Morocco needed, he concluded, was education about drug abuse throughout society. Probably the surest way to achieve that was for the contents of the letter to the king to be exposed. Otherwise, Morocco's drug policies that had gone on for generations would continue through to his children's children and probably their children as well.

This line of thinking caused him to turn his attention to the little he knew about the writer.

Would someone go to live in a foreign country with vastly different cultures at their own expense and write such a letter if they did not believe every word in it was true? And if it was true, it was important to find out who this person was as he could be the best person to put right Morocco's drug problems. As he had said, it needed to be an outsider with no ulterior motives. Otherwise, nothing would change.

By the time Reda Oumainian rang next day, Ali's aim was to establish the identity of the writer. If Reda knew who it was, his pride might make it difficult for him to admit it, especially if he had not been invited to be involved in starting the Rabat AAA meeting.

But more worrying was the suggestion that an outsider was the best person to sort out the country's drug problems. This would imply that Morocco's hundreds of psychiatrists, doctors and psychologists, including Reda Oumainian himself, had been wrong in their past treatment of drug addiction. In other words, they could not be trusted to correct the problems their doctrines had caused.

As Ali thought about such a slap in the face to a man who for years had been revered in his professional circle, he cringed at the prospect; it would challenge his ego to the core. A softly-softly approach therefore seemed necessary. But would that be possible given the sensitive nature of the issue, and could that achieve the best result?

'Do you have any news about what we discussed yesterday, Professor?' he asked, once polite greetings had been exchanged.

'I do, but I need more time to work on it,' Reda answered.

'What can you tell me now? I need as much information as possible to pass on to the ambassador,' Ali replied.

'I can confirm the AAA meeting is still running,' Reda said. 'However, it is too soon to say if it is working.'

'Why is that?' Ali asked.

'What I know from my experience in America researching AA, it takes time to get established,' Reda answered.

'How long do you think that will be?'

From the way Reda paused before answering this may have been a question he had hoped not to be asked.

'In other countries I think it's taken two to three years,' he eventually replied.

'It's already been going over two years in your hospital. So does that mean there are some former alcoholics in Rabat who are now abstinent? If so, do you know the number?'

Ali guessed that the professor was beginning to hedge.

'I don't know. I would have to check,' Reda answered hesitantly.

'But surely, given its importance, you have some idea?' Ali said. Then he added, 'What about other drugs? Would they be put on those instead? The writer says that parking addicts or alcoholics on other drugs is part of Morocco's problem.'

'Again, I don't know, I would have to ask.'

Ali could hear the professor's faint sigh.

'Please do. The writer implies that addicts in Morocco are always given other drugs to pacify them.' This time he made it sound like a challenge.

'Putting drug addicts on pharmaceutically tested drugs is part of the treatment of harm reduction all over the world,' Reda answered.

If he thought that this explanation of a global approach was going to put him off this line of questioning, he should think again. Ali gave a little smile as he replied.

'The writer mentions that. I will paraphrase what he says in his letter. That may help you understand why I need to know the answers. He says, "Drug substitution by itself does not work. It is the root cause of addicts' problems that need addressing. It is similar to the boy who put his finger in the dyke to prevent Amsterdam flooding, while all the time the flood defences were crumbling."' Ali quite liked the analogy.

'Harm reduction is a policy that is used everywhere. We adopted it for that reason.' Reda sounded defensive.

But Ali was not done. 'I will continue reading from his letter,' he said. '"Harm reduction may have seemed useful, but not when you look at the results and the big picture. Whereas, by dealing with the cause, Alcoholics Anonymous and Narcotics Anonymous have helped millions of alcoholics and drug addicts recover from all forms of addictive substances all over the world and stay stopped, including hundreds of thousands of Muslims in the Middle East and Asia." Then he says, '"But not in Morocco."'

Ali paused to let Reda respond, but he did not. So he continued. 'He implies that is because the pharmaceutical industry has brainwashed doctors into believing this is true as it benefits them financially. The evidence suggests he is right, and that harm reduction has not worked in Morocco. All it has achieved is to substitute one drug for another. Do you agree?'

This would be a hot topic for Reda. Ali's research had shown that he had supported the introduction of harm reduction in Morocco, including the use of methadone to treat heroin addicts. Now he understood Morocco's medical profession was looking at using two other drugs, Suboxone and Subutex, as opiate replacement therapies.

'Before we go further, I need to see the letter,' Reda said. 'I have an idea who this man is.'

'I hoped you would say that as I want to know too. I am happy to answer any questions you have about it, though,' Ali said.

'What name is it signed with?' Reda asked.

'There isn't one. He signs off saying he is an observer who cares about drug addicts and the people of Morocco. The contents suggest that is true. So if you tell me who you think wrote it, it would be helpful," Ali answered, thinking that this was probably the last thing Reda had wanted to do before he made the telephone call. Now he must know that answering the question was the only thing he could do, otherwise he would be seen as being obstructive.

'I had a meeting with a man called Rick Blaine two years ago in Rabat; it may be him. His commitment to help was impressive, as was his background. We got on well and I assured him I would start AA or NA in our hospital.'

'But then you changed that to start AAA, is that right?' Ali asked.

'Not exactly. I presented it to the psychiatrists who worked there and got some support. However, the way it went forward was not the same as Mr Blaine proposed and we lost contact.'

'Do you mean he stopped contacting you when he found out it was not AA that had been started?' Ali asked, picking up from his knowledge of Moroccans and the results to date of what had happened since.

'Again, not exactly. After a time, I stopped replying to his communications as I knew the AAA meeting was not run along the guidelines he'd suggested,' Reda replied.

'When did you last here from him?' Ali asked.

'I had some emails from him recently,' he said, clearing his throat.

'Did you reply?'

'No. They were more informative than needing a response. So, I didn't.'

Not wanting to rock the boat too much, Ali paused. Then he asked, 'Was that the only time you met Richard Blaine?'

'I met him on two other occasions. The second was when he was invited to the Association of Moroccan Addictologists' conference in Rabat in 2016. This was attended by more than a hundred psychiatrists and psychologists. He was asked to speak there about AA and NA's global experience, and what they could do to help Morocco's drug addicts, alcoholics and their families.'

'That's good. How was what he said received?' Ali asked.

Again, Reda Oumainian hesitated before answering. 'He did not speak. The organiser decided against it, I think at the last minute. I don't know why.'

As Ali digested this he realised that what would have been best had not been done. Why, he wondered? He needed further information, but maybe this wasn't the time to ask for it. Eventually he said, 'Thank you, Professor Oumainian. I realise this may not be easy for you, but I need to know the organiser's name. I have to know how successful that AAA meeting is and if it is being run efficiently. The writer says that if it isn't, it won't be effective, and lack of effective treatment, he says, is one of the causes of Morocco's drug problems.'

He suspected that Reda would be worried that if he passed on the organiser's name, it could cost this director, whom he had presumably supported, her job. Equally, he would also know it would be easy for Ali to find out from others who were there who she was. Obviously, he would try to protect his own position, and, as Ali had expected, his answer was laced with as many positives as he could think of.

'It is Professor Nazha Dalloul. She is the psychiatrist in charge of the hospital's addiction unit. When she took that job over from me, because of my experience advising on drugs and addiction in Europe and America, I did my best to pass on to her as much information as possible. I also maintained regular contact with her and the hospital, but left it up to her to contact me if she wanted my help. As I have got more involved with my UN, WHO and European roles, I had less to do with her and the hospital.'

'I understand, Professor. Thank you for your help. That is all for now. I will come back to you if I need anything else,' Ali said, ready to terminate the call.

'All I've ever wanted is to do the best I could for Morocco and its drug addicts are probably the people who need help the most. If you speak to Professor Dalloul, I would appreciate it if you do not tell her I gave you her name. We are still working together on some things and I would not want to jeopardise those.'

'Of course, dear friend. You have been most helpful. Rest assured I will do my best not to do that.'

Chapter 6

Most days in Amsterdam the streets are busy. But there is one day that attracts more crowds than any other: that is King's Day to celebrate the Dutch king's birthday.

It takes place on 27th April and features musical performances with people singing 'Het Wilhelmus', which describes the life of William of Orange and his fight for the Dutch people. Many people wear orange clothes, which is the national colour, but, as far as Yashine and his friends were concerned, there would be no better day to turn the city red.

Historically, this festive day passes peacefully with crowds everywhere, especially in Dam Square and on the canals. With many people high on cannabis and alcohol, blind to what might be going on around them, Yashine believed it was perfect from every aspect.

He and his brother had a laptop and mobile phone repair business; they also made complex computers specific to client requirements. The skillset they needed to do this meant that if they had the right materials, making the type of bombs that could be preset to detonate themselves would be easy.

Owing to his life on the streets of El Hoceima, Yashine mistrusted everyone. So at the ISIS offshoot's next strategy meeting, instead of making a detailed presentation of what he had in mind, he produced a more general idea. This was aimed to get approval, but also make a well-informed leak impossible. After all, compared to his previous criminal activities, this was by far the most serious, so being scrupulously careful was a major concern. He did not want to get caught before the group's planned day of reckoning.

After a positive response, he asked to be put in contact with someone who would be able to take his idea forward. Two days later he got an answer: he was to go to Belgium the following weekend and meet one of Europe's ISIS leaders. The only advice he was given was to wear simple western clothes and look as non-Arabic as possible.

The following Saturday, Yashine met his contact, Abdullah El Gullam, at Antwerp station. As they walked to a nearby café, Abdullah explained that their meeting was to ascertain the viability of Yashine's idea, and if it was decided to take it further, it would go to a higher level, outside Europe. After that it would need to be coordinated with other activities; but that was only if it was deemed suitable to helping ISIS achieve its global goals. So timing, he said, was all-important.

Because of the need for the utmost caution, Abdullah had chosen a café where they could sit side by side, out of view of cameras, facing a long mirror that would let him see what was going on behind them. As they sat down together he explained his choice in a way that emphasised their need for care at all times.

He said, 'We don't want to appear to be hiding, but at the same time we need to be cautious. From now on, that is the way we do it whenever we have any contact.'

This approach pleased Yashine. What also helped was that Abdullah followed up by describing himself in a humble way that made him feel he could trust him, at least for now.

'I am thirty-six years old and come from Saudi Arabia. I've lived in Europe since I was twenty-one, most of that time in Brussels. I speak French, Arabic and English; my American accent I picked up watching movies and US TV. Since I joined ISIS eight years ago, to look as inconspicuous as possible I often wear western clothes. Also, I like them.'

Yashine took in that he was wearing navy blue jeans, a plain grey open-necked shirt and brown leather gilet. He was clean-shaven and had short black hair. The impression his ensemble and appearance gave was that his aim to look as western as possible had been achieved.

'I understand. I wear western clothes, too, most of the time; also because I like them,' Yashine replied.

Abdullah then said that he was impressed with Moroccans because of the number of times they had been involved in terrorist attacks. He asked questions about Yashine's upbringing and the reason for his being in the Netherlands.

After getting satisfactory answers, he asked, 'Why did you join ISIS? Is it revenge you are after, or something else?'

'I was brought up in one of the poorest parts of Morocco. My family made a living growing cannabis, but never enough to provide all our needs,' Yashine answered.

'You mean you wanted more and now will do anything to get it?' Abdullah asked, at the same time indicating he understood.

'Yes. I used to see western visitors who had mobile phones, cameras and rented cars throwing money around on drugs and prostitutes. They treated me and my friends with disdain. I hated them. But I was too young to do anything about it. It was only later I realised I wanted what they had.'

Abdullah smiled, then asked, 'Why did you go to live in the Netherlands?'

'My mother's brother married a Dutch Moroccan and moved there. After that she arranged for me and my brother to live with them. When I saw how the cannabis we grew back home-made fortunes for Dutch drug dealers, I used my contacts to start importing it,' Yashine said.

'So, revenge and money made you a drug dealer,' Abdullah observed.

'I guess that's right.' Yashine looked down, ashamed of some aspect of that part of his life.

'I understand you are good with electronics and make a living out of it. Is that also right?' Abdullah asked.

'When I was in Casablanca, I worked at the Derb Gallef flea market mending phones and laptops. While I was there, I learned how to make computers. When Hamid and I had enough money from dealing in drugs, we started a business doing the same thing in Amsterdam. So far, that has gone well.'

Abdullah nodded his head. So far so good. Here was a man who had hatred in his heart, lived on the edge of life, and was a criminal with a good mind.

So, satisfied with what he had found out to date, he asked, 'Why do you think there have been so many Moroccans involved in terrorist attacks?'

'Much of Morocco is poor. So westerners with money stolen from us are loathed. There is also a big divide between the rich and poor in Morocco itself. The combination causes hatred, especially toward American politicians and its military, who flaunt a superior attitude and threaten anyone with bullying tactics who get in their way. There are many there like me who want to make a stand,' Yashine answered, surprised at the depth and intensity of his response.

'I come from a similar background,' Abdullah said, 'so I understand. No one likes a bully, especially one who claims that their God is greater than Allah.'

Growing in confidence, Yashine now said, 'There is something else. A few months ago, a friend visited from Casablanca. Before he arrived, I asked him to bring some karkoubi pills, a popular black-market drug in Morocco. As it can be packed in small boxes and looks like prescription pills, he was able to bring it without any problems. Have you heard of it?'

'I have. It is well known for making people do nasty things. I believe some Moroccan terrorists have been radicalised after taking it,' Abdullah answered.

Yashine was pleased he had mentioned it and especially with Abdullah's response. Earlier he had wondered if he should or not. Now he decided to go on, hoping that what he was about to say would convince Abdullah of his allegiance and suitability to the ISIS cause.

'That's what happened to me. I was in Oukacha prison in Casablanca for petty street theft. Almost immediately I arrived, I met an iman who introduced me to karkoubi. He was there because of the Casablanca bombs in 2003, as he had been responsible for radicalising some of the young Moroccans involved in that. Later, others he radicalised were behind attacks in Morocco and Europe, including Barcelona.'

'I heard about him.' Abdullah sat back, folding his arms. 'Now I understand your background, I am impressed. Is there anything else I should know?'

'A few months later, a former prison inmate of mine was visiting Amsterdam. I asked him to bring some karkoubi pills with him as I thought it would help me radicalise some Moroccans living here. As I said earlier, it is so easy to smuggle. He brought twenty boxes of ten foil strips. As each strip contains ten pills, it was more than enough for my needs.'

'What happened then?' Abdullah asked.

'People liked it and word about its effects spread. Then a dealer got to hear of it and approached me, asking if I could get more. It seemed karkoubi had never been introduced to the Netherlands before. After making some enquiries, I discovered from a contact in Morocco that someone in Spain was about to begin making it and his plan was to start dealing it in the Netherlands.'

'Was that true?'

'Yes. I found out who he was through my contact in Morocco and sources in Amsterdam's coffee shops. His name is Randy Cyriax. He was making regular visits to establish a network and I met him on one of them. As I speak English and am well connected, it was easy to convince him to use me. Within a few months I had sold karkoubi's benzodiazepine pills to hundreds of people, mostly Moroccans and a few Turks.'

Abdullah looked dubious.

He said, 'I have never heard anything good about this drug. I am sure if it gets into the wrong hands it could be dangerous. You should be careful.'

Yashine back-pedalled. 'As demand grew, to inflate the price Cyriax put controls on how much he shipped. What he did not realise was that this would lessen the likelihood of addiction to it, because addicts would switch to other drugs for their needs.'

'Relying on drug addicts in any way is risky,' Abdullah said, frowning. 'Whether its dealing or using, you are never dealing with reliable people, and the police are always on the lookout.'

'You are right, it would have been risky. Except Cyriax knew I had found out where he made it and how he transported it to the Netherlands. This meant I had some control over him. And as I held back from selling most of what I received and controlled who I sold it to and how often, he knew that if he rocked my boat, I could sink his.'

Yashine hoped this was the right bait to catch this very big fish.

'That sounds better. So, although Mr Cyriax makes it and ships it to the Netherlands, you have control of the whole Dutch karkoubi-users market. Is that right?' Abdullah studied him intently.

Proud of what he had achieved dealing in karkoubi pills. and determined to impress Abdullah, Yashine allowed his ego to take over.

'Better than that. I found out that not long ago he had a drug problem. If the police knew his background, he would not be allowed in the country.'

'That is better, but as I said, be careful, an addict dealing in drugs could be a dangerous ally. Now I want to know about your idea in detail. How much it will cost. What target do you have in mind? When would you carry it out? Who would do it? How would you do it? And lastly, what help would you need from ISIS?' Abdullah continued to stare at him.

'There are two targets, Dam Square in Amsterdam and Trafalgar Square in London, both on the 27th of April next year, timed to be less than one minute apart. The help I need from ISIS is to provide the explosives. Everything else I can take care of. I have the people to carry it out. My brother and I would make and store the detonators. I don't know how much it will cost. I will leave it up to you to work that out,' Yashine said, relieved he had dealt with the touchy drug subject.

'I like the idea of Amsterdam as it has never been hit, but the UK has been hit several times, so you can rule that out. Are you okay with that?' Abdullah asked.

'Yes. We will do whatever you say. Amsterdam is our main target anyway. It is just that two of my accomplices are from London,' Yashine answered.

'If this works, maybe we can use them and do London on another occasion. Now, I need to know who will plant the bombs. How do you know they can be trusted? And if they are on drugs, you must tell me. We have some good people in Holland we could use instead, including Moroccans, one of whom was involved in the Casablanca bombings in 2003.'

Good, Yashine thought. Abdullah had now moved on to practicalities.

'One is my brother,' he said. 'The others are two friends who are as keen to do this as I am. None of them are drug addicts. They know some of the details and can definitely be trusted. I can arrange for you or someone else to meet them if you need to. They answer to me unless you require otherwise.'

'I will get back to you on that. Now I need to know how you will do it.'

This was the moment Yashine had been waiting for, the make-or-break point in their meeting. It took him two minutes to explain the detail, twelve seconds for Abdullah to think about his response, and just a few moments for him to deliver it. 'It sounds as though you have thought it through,' Abdullah said. 'However, I need time to think about it, then make a report and channel it to the right people if I think it is doable. In the meantime, you are to act as if it will not happen. That means you do nothing more about it until you hear from me. Is that understood?'

'Yes, it is,' Yashine answered, disappointed.

'From now on you will not communicate with anyone other than me. I will give you a mobile phone which is only to be used for that purpose. You must turn it on three times a day for ten minutes at 08-00, 16-00 and 22-00, otherwise it stays off. There is one number stored on the phone titled, 'unknown.' If you need me, text that number but do not leave a message other than to say, 'Thinking of you.' I will then contact you at one of those times. Is that all clear?'

'Yes. Will the phone work in the Netherlands?' Yashine asked.

'It's on a Dutch Lebara rolling monthly pre-paid contract and already set up. It has never been used before. You don't have to do anything. Your friends must not know of its existence. In fact, the less they know from now on the better until you next hear from me.'

As he finished speaking, Abdullah got up, indicating the meeting was over. At the doorway to the café they parted.

All the way back to Amsterdam, over and over again, Yashine played the Dam Square scenario in his mind. But each time he got to the conclusion his spirit was dampened. He had deliberately not told Abdullah that the bombs would be set off remotely. This was not going to be a suicide mission. For the first time ever, he was enjoying life and wanted more of it.

Would ISIS be happy if the bombers did not give their lives to martyrdom?

Chapter 7

The first thing Ali Abadi did after his conversation with Reda Oumainian was to look up Rick Blaine on the Internet. After several hits and misses, he found a website and newspaper articles which contained enough information to convince him this man knew what he was talking about. This also helped him conclude that Blaine, or someone like him, would be the best person to sort out the mess Morocco was in with drugs and addiction. But he would know from his experience of Moroccans that convincing the country's psychiatrists and authorities that an outsider would do this better than anyone they could appoint internally would be a huge hurdle to overcome.

For a person to admit they are wrong, pride makes it difficult, but for people like psychiatrists, doctors and politicians, right up to the king, in a country bristling with low self-esteem regarding drugs, and the super-egos of such people, could be impossible. The best approach, he thought, was to track down Rick Blaine. Then, through him, if appropriate, find a way to expose the situation by putting as much of the blame as possible on outside influences such as America and the pharmaceutical industry. If that could be done, perhaps it could work.

With this in mind he sent an email to the address on Blaine's website. '… we have several interests in common; especially your experience helping drug addicts in Morocco. I would like to talk to you about this on the phone, or we can meet if you are in London. My number there is 07977 280456.' He signed it Ali Abadi, Moroccan Embassy, London without reference to his role there.

The next thing he did was look up the Alcoholics Anonymous and Narcotics Anonymous websites, followed by 'harm reduction' and 'methadone.'

'Alcoholics Anonymous is a fellowship of men and women who share their experience, strength and hope with each other that they may solve their common problem and help others to recover from alcoholism. The only requirement for membership is a desire to stop drinking.

There are no dues or fees for AA membership; we are self-supporting through our own contributions. AA is not allied with any sect, denomination, politics, organisation or institution; does not wish to engage in any controversy, neither endorses nor opposes any causes. Our primary purpose is to stay sober and help other alcoholics to achieve sobriety.

Next he read, 'Narcotics Anonymous, is a non-profit fellowship or society of men and women for whom drugs had become a major problem. We are recovering addicts who meet regularly to help each other stay clean. NA is a program of complete abstinence from all drugs. There is only ONE requirement for membership, the desire to stop using. Our program is a set of principles written so simply that we can follow them in our daily lives. The most important thing about them is that THEY WORK.

There are no strings attached to NA. We are not affiliated with any other organisations, we have no initiation fees or dues, no pledges to sign, no promises to make to anyone. We are not connected with any political, religious or law enforcement groups, and are under no surveillance at any time. Anyone may join us, regardless of age, race, sexual identity, creed, religion or lack of religion. We are not interested in what or how much you used or who your connections were, what you have done in the past, how much or how little you have, but only in what you want to do about your problem and how we can help. The newcomer is the most important person at any meeting, because we can only keep what we have by giving it away. We have learned from our group experience that those who keep coming to our meetings regularly stay clean.'

The simplicity of the words and each fellowship's singular purpose to help alcoholics and drug addicts impressed Ali. The fact that they accepted anyone from anywhere, of whatever faith, at no cost, surprised and appealed to him.

After reading numerous websites describing harm reduction and its objectives, he understood why it had not worked in Morocco. In some cases, the wisdom of drug substitution was challenged, whereas the results of NA and AA proved beyond doubt that complete abstinence for a drug addict or alcoholic should be the objective.

As far as methadone was concerned, as soon as he realised it was a substitute opiate, he understood why it may not work effectively, especially as he now knew from the letter that in Morocco heroin addicts are put on it for life. And as America had a self-confessed killer epidemic stemming from over-prescribing opiates, he failed to understand how it was that this and other drug substitutes were so widely supported. He asked himself why there had been resistance by the Moroccan medical profession to AA and NA.

To see if he could find an answer, He re-read Rick Blaine's letter.

'... because the causes are not addressed and drug addicts underlying issues are not dealt with effectively... '

When he added this to his conversation with Reda Oumainian about harm reduction, he began to understand.

Ali had studied philosophy at Cambridge University. Some of his favourite philosophers were the pragmatists, and it was America's John Dewey whose five different stages of the reasoning process now entered his mind.

First, when habitual patterns of action are proven unsuccessful, an analysis of what is wrong must take place. The second is to extract from the results the causes in order to find a problem-solving solution. Third, the use of intellect and successful experience to find probable answers. Fourth to apply reason to these, and fifth, test the results.

It seemed to Ali Abadi this process had been adhered to by Mr Blaine, who had no ulterior motive because he was only trying to help Morocco's drug addicts. But as he made contacts with the country's medical professionals treating drug addiction and alcoholism, and addicts and alcoholics themselves, he had inadvertently come across a host of other problems that influenced the direness of the situation. Then, by applying his business experience, knowledge of drugs, addiction and his own recovery, he was able to discover the reasons, then the potential solutions for much that was wrong.

After extracting the causes, he had sought a solution based on this personal and global experience. Once he had some answers, he had set upon a course of action that he hoped would work. What he had then come to realise was that the best way to implement it was to gain the King of Morocco's backing, and the most effective way to do that would be to expose it in the media, otherwise nothing would be done.

And why not? Ali Abadi thought. If that is the only way it will work, and there is much to gain, and nothing to lose, whereas leaving the situation as it is it, it will get only get worse.

In the last paragraph of his letter to King Mohammed VI, Rick Blaine had pointed out that there were many countries in the world which have had success by changing their drug policies. So the next thing Ali did was ascertain which they were and what their success had been.

Using the question, 'Which country has had the most success changing its drug policies?' top of the Google list was Portugal.

The headline of the first entry read, 'Since Portugal decriminalised all drugs in 2001, there have been dramatic drops in overdose deaths, HIV and hepatitis infections and drug-related crime.'

This begged the question, if that was the case, why had the rest of the world not followed suit?

Reading further, Ali discovered that before the year 2000, because of drugs, especially heroin, dirty needles and lack of proper treatment, Portugal had developed the highest rates of HIV and hepatitis B and C in Europe; in addition, crimes and overdoses caused by drugs were common.

It seemed to him that Portugal's decriminalisation policy was based on three things:

a) There is no such thing as a hard or soft drug, only healthy and unhealthy relationships with them.

b) An addict's unhealthy relationship with drugs conceals the underlying reasons why they abuse them.

c) The eradication of all drugs in society is impossible.

Ali read on with growing interest. In 1997 approximately 45% of Portugal's reported AIDS cases were among intravenous users, and by 1999 nearly 1% of its population was addicted to heroin, while its drug-related AIDS deaths were the highest in the European Union.

After discussions in Portugal's Parliament, in 2001 decriminalisation of drugs came into effect. As a direct consequence, blood-borne and sexually transmitted diseases and overdoses dramatically decreased. As targeting drug use became an effective HIV prevention measure, it was decided to treat the possession and use of drugs as a public health issue. So instead of a criminal record and/or prison sentence, addicts would receive a fine and/or a referral to a treatment programme. From then on, money saved from taking individuals through the criminal justice system was spent on rehabilitation and get-back-to-work schemes.

In the following eighteen years, drug use diminished among the fifteen to twenty-four age group, drug-induced deaths decreased steeply and now Portugal has three overdoses per million citizens, compared to the European Union average of 17.3. HIV infection has steadily reduced and become a manageable problem, and there has been a similar downward trend for cases of hepatitis B and C.

The policy was complemented by allocating resources to the drugs field. This was done by expanding and improving prevention, opening residential treatment centres, the use of outside resources such as NA and AA, and helping with social reintegration.

Next, Ali looked at the Portuguese websites for Narcotics Anonymous and Alcoholics Anonymous. On NA's he found there were 144 weekly meetings spread across the country and AA had only a few less. As the result, in a country with a population less than one-third the size of Morocco's, for more than thirty years NA and AA had helped thousands of Portuguese drug addicts and alcoholics recover, while in Morocco the success rate was almost non-existent!

Further research revealed that Portugal had established numerous treatment centres that operated alongside NA and AA. The European Union's head office for drugs and addiction chose Lisbon for its head office, and Portugal's prime minister at the time of its decriminalisation was Antonio Guterres, secretary-general of the United Nations.

Ali concluded that when it comes to drugs, rehabilitation and changes to policy, without doubt Portugal was the best country in the world to follow.

His next step in his quest to find Morocco's solution was to establish which country has the best results for recovery from drug addiction. The result astonished him, because it was big, and it was a Muslim country.

He learned that because of Iran's 1,900 km border with Afghanistan, this Islamic country probably has the worst opiate problem in the world. It was estimated that four million of its seventy million people are opium addicts: a similar percentage to that of alcoholics, prescription and illegal drug addicts in the West. As he looked for the reason for Iran's problem, he discovered it was partly because it lies on the drug trafficking route from Afghanistan to Turkey and Europe, with an estimated 140 tons of heroin entering it annually.

Similar to the USA, overdoses in Iran were a leading cause of death, second only to traffic accidents, many of which were caused by drivers under the influence of opiates; and half the prison population of 220,000 were drug traffickers or addicts.

Sadly, Iran's lack of understanding of addiction meant its laws had sanctioned more executions per capita than any other country in the world, and over half those executed were drug traffickers. But the drug problem there being so vast, and the country's thinking so wayward, exposed the futility of its draconian measures. This made it obvious that only a major change of policy would remedy the situation.

In 1990, two brothers from California started the first meeting of NA in Iran. Thirty years later, there are more than 500,000 members of NA in recovery spread all over the country and more than 25,000 NA meetings a week. In

2012, a sports centre there hosted an NA convention which had 24,000 former Iranian drug addicts attending.

So, for Iran, recovery from drugs had been onward and upward ever since. At this rate of growth, hundreds of thousands more would soon benefit, as would their families and society in general.

If the NA approach was adopted by the Iranian Government as its primary source of recovery from drug addiction, Ali concluded, these statistics would rise considerably, as its effect would reach many more of its four million sufferers. And by applying the same logic that would do the same for Morocco's drug problems. The only difference being that Morocco needed AA as well to help its four hundred thousand alcoholics, in addition to NA for its million addicts hooked on cannabis, prescription drugs, heroin, cocaine and karkoubi.

As he reflected on the information he had accumulated, he had an extraordinary revelation. On one hand, through NA and AA, America had given the world a solution to opiate and all other drug addiction, yet it still had the worst record of opiate overdoses of anywhere in the world. On the other hand, Iran by applying NA to help their opium addicts recover had excellent results. Yet these two countries' politicians were forever playing dangerous mind games with each other over nuclear arms, even more lethal than drugs, that could result in millions of pointless deaths.

He deduced from the evidence he had that the over-riding problems with drugs were caused by politicians, aided by the pharmaceutical industry. And as America was in constant conflict with Iran, if the world were to know the facts, a more sensible approach could be forced on them that would help, not hinder, as it currently did, the world's drug problems. After all, that was surely in every country's best interest.

In disbelief at the absurdity of this scenario, Ali returned to John Dewey's reasoning process. As soon as he did, obstacles he had not thought of before manifested themselves which were exclusive to Morocco. These started with its partly dictatorial leadership, and as that meant the king, his first thought was that it would be insurmountable. Then he remembered one of his favourite expressions: 'The impossible we can do; miracles take a little longer.'

With an annual allocation of US$300million, Morocco's monarchy received more public money than any other country's royalty; that was 18 times more than the Queen of England. King Mohammed VI had at least one royal palace in every major city in Morocco, and one near Paris, the costs of which were huge, especially for staff, clothes, cars and the other luxuries he adored. Forbes magazine estimated his personal wealth at US$6 billion and he owns 80% of Morocco's economy; from agriculture to motor vehicles, banks to mining, supermarkets to food.

So why does he need public money that could be put to much better use to help drug addicts? Ali wondered. Especially when he knows he rules over the fourth poorest country in the Arab world!

Ali already knew these figures and facts. He also knew that because inequality is rife in Morocco, it has a specific word, hogra to describe the anger, rage and humiliation experienced by individuals and communities that have been deprived of their basic human rights. This was made clear in demonstrations in Rabat and Casablanca at the time of the Arab Spring, which was based on a feeling of exclusion and an undercurrent of public discontent caused by unemployment, corruption, rising prices and the holding of political prisoners. Even though on the positive side the king had recently devolved roughly half his powers to a prime minister to appease this.

Was it any wonder drugs are used to pacify our people? he mused.

After pondering on this, he reflected on the new information, concluding that if this money were spent funding the rehabilitation of drug addicts, as it was in Portugal, it would save Morocco billions of dollars and benefit its society. And if there was a way for the king to be seen to have introduced such a policy, his stature as a leader and benefactor of the poor, at home and abroad, would be boosted. Especially when Ali recalled that in 2010, the whistleblower Wikileaks produced documents alleging the high level of corruption in Morocco involved the king.

As a Moroccan diplomat working abroad, Ali knew that an international view of Morocco concerned the lack of openness its authorities allowed its media. And as freedom of the press is highly regarded in democratic countries, when it is denied, it leaves foreigners asking, 'What has Morocco got to hide?'

This image was not helped in 2016 when the acclaimed American documentary maker Richard Ray Pérez was expelled from there, as well as his team, because he had pointed to the lack of freedom of expression in Morocco. While Reporters Without Borders, the international non-government organisation whose aim is to defend the freedom of the press and protect journalists, claimed that similar issues had continued to exist since King Mohammed VI took the throne.

Ironically, most visitors to Morocco came away saying that it was a lovely country, with many wonderful features and mostly hospitable people, some of which plaudits had been helped by efforts made by the king.

One of these was in 2017 when he removed the *lèse–majesté* laws. Before this it had meant it was a criminal offence to speak badly of him, his family or his policies, with prison sentences of between one and five years for offenders. The problem now was that the legacy lingers as Morocco's monarchy's uninterrupted rule goes back to the 13th century.

Dictatorships and ruling monarchies that have been passed on from generation to generation are criticised as they clash with those who believe democratic government, not autocratic rule is best. Their view is that human beings need to live in environments where they can think and speak freely, which is also better for fair societal relations. This would mean Morocco's approach was, and had been, wrong for centuries to many who live there and observers in the rest of the world.

Other issues that did not help King Mohmmed VI and Morocco's image were the giant photographs of him adorning buildings and streets, and his picture were frequently on newspaper front pages: foreigners would conclude he had a big ego and Morocco still had an almost autocratic leader. But worse, his palaces were surrounded by people living on the breadline, while his renowned self-indulgent lifestyle meant the claim he was a direct descendent of the Prophet Muhammad did not stand up to altruistic scrutiny. However, as this claim has been passed down since the 17th century, for a Moroccan to oppose it would be tantamount to blasphemy.

So, unless he changes his way of life and makes the government do the same, he would not command the respect he presumably desired. As Confucius said, 'In a country well governed, poverty is something to be ashamed of. In a country badly governed, wealth is something to be ashamed of.'

King Mohammed IV ascended through lineage, not on merit, to Morocco's throne upon the death of his father. With good reason, the French press christened him 'King of the Poor.' Fifteen years later his personal wealth had grown from an estimated US 500 million to a staggering US$ 5.8 billion, an increase of more than 500%. While the conditions of Morocco's many poor did not change at all.

Surely a king who cared about his people would want them to have at least a modicum of his vast wealth. So, it was no wonder the world found a speech he made in 2014, asking, 'Where has Morocco's wealth gone? Who is benefitting from it?' hilarious and hypocritical, prompting a plethora of sarcastic responses. Especially when it was well-known that his many palaces' daily running costs, paid for by the state, were US$ 1,000,000, plus there was his excessive expenditure on lavish designer clothes, luxury cars and his collection of the world's most expensive watches.

After an early education in Morocco, he had attended universities in Belgium and France studying political science and law, where he gained a PhD. After that he returned to Morocco and became president of the Moroccan High Council of Culture; next he joined the military, becoming Commander in Chief of the Royal Moroccan Army, nepotism in the extreme and not good for his or Morocco's global standing.

As the New York Times reported, he enjoyed a reputation as a playboy with a fondness for fast cars and nightclubs, while the Guardian reported that Wikileak's disclosures showed corruption spread across all levels of society, right up to the highest in Morocco. There had been rumours he was homosexual, (a serious offence against Islamic tradition) since this was believed to have been maybe part of the reason he secretly divorced his wife, Princess Lalla Salma, who had hardly been seen in public since. His lifestyle, behaviour and the way he dressed suggested he would be equally at home as a non-Muslim or hippie.

Ali had often wondered privately if these facts would worry a psychologist or psychiatrist as to the king's mental state. In his studies of philosophy he had learned that morality and lifestyles are keys to being respected by a leader's public and material 'fixes' were renowned for being part of underlying mental issues.

After reviewing his discoveries on the internet, and recalling his experience when he'd lived in Morocco, he concluded that if some of what he feared was true, such a monarch would not be the right person to take Morocco through this current crisis. He also conjectured that getting the king to change his behaviour and attitudes to put matters right would be no more important than Morocco itself doing the same. But with the power, arrogance and egos of its rich businessmen, politicians and medical profession deeply embedded, the factors causing Morocco's drug problems that need changing would not be easy to put into practice. The only solution he could think of was similar to Rick Blaine's: international exposure of all that was wrong in Morocco. While doing it saving as much face as possible was the answer, Ali thought.

He started to figure out an answer. What he came up with pleased him: the king gets Morocco's Permanent Representative to the United Nations in New York, ambassador Omar Hilale to explain Morocco's situation to António Guterres the Secretary-General of the

99

UN. Given what Guterres did to solve Portugal's drug problems, he would be likely to back it. As Hilale created and presides over the Group of Friends against Terrorism, he would be the perfect person to do it. He then points the finger of blame at the history of what the king inherited from his father, America's drug policies and the shenanigans of the world's pharmaceutical industry. After that, the king gets Morocco's medical profession to fall in line and put in place the best-known policies.

The international community, seeing the seriousness of Morocco's aim to put right something not all its own making, might then forgive the King and Morocco. This could remove what had earlier seemed immovable obstacles and mean that what is needed for Morocco to put its drug problems right materialise.

Chapter 8

Those who have been to Amsterdam will know that cyclists outnumber cars on the streets manyfold. Almost 70% of the population travel to work or school by bicycle; it is estimated there are over 880,000 bicycles, more than one per resident.

To Yashine this meant that just as starlings flock together to hide from preying hawks, and sardines hide in massive shoals to avoid being eaten by predators, the best place to hide bombs in Amsterdam was in bicycle frames.

The first thing he did when he arrived at Amsterdam Central station was walk to Dam Square, his aim being to check the location of bicycle stands. The most frequently used and best positioned he found was behind the 't Nieuwe Kafé at one end of the square, furthest from the Monument. In other parts surrounding the square there were more sparsely parked bikes, all perfect for his idea.

After taking photographs of the ideal locations and bicycles perfect for converting into bombs, he headed home happy, knowing that if ISIS gave the go-ahead, he and his fellow jihadists could do the rest.

As well as learning how to make computers and mend mobile phones in Morocco, in his youth in El Hoceima Yashine had learned to make bicycles out of spare parts he found on rubbish dumps. After making one for himself, then another for a friend, others asked him to make one for them until he ran out of parts. At the same time, to bolster his income, he turned to male prostitution with foreign visitors. What he had learned during his short lifetime was that he was technically clever, liked to have money, and the only way to achieve the results he desired was to do as much as possible himself.

Today, this meant that when Yashine looked at an electric bicycle, what he saw was a normal pedal cycle with its frame filled with explosives. He reasoned that if four of these were strategically placed around Dam Square, each with an identically timed device linked to a mobile phone, he could cause the devastation his revenge demanded for the degradation caused by the westerners who had violated his country, family, mind and body.

Best of all was that his knowledge of phones and technology meant that he could trigger them simultaneously and remotely, even from another country, even from Morocco!

On his train back to Haarlem, Yashine called his brother and asked him to arrange a meeting that night with Mahi, Nabil, Nadia and Mariam at their home. Between leaving Dam Square and arriving there, all he thought about was what to tell them and what to leave out. Soon after his friends arrived, and the usual banter and laughter settled, he began to speak.

'The meeting with my ISIS contact, Abdullah, went well. I outlined our ideas, which he seemed to like, except that we are only to hit Amsterdam, not London as well.'

'Did he say why?' Hamid asked, glancing at his girlfriend, Mariam.

'The reason he gave was that London has already been attacked and as a result there is stricter security there. Whereas the Netherlands has not been attacked, so is more vulnerable. It is also more complicated hitting two venues at the same time,' Yashine answered.

'That makes sense. We can do London another time,' Nadia, his own girlfriend said.

'He was also concerned about our involvement in drugs. I assured him none of us are addicts and there have been no problems with the police.' Yashine paused, waiting for any response.

Hamid asked, 'Was he okay with that?'

'I think so as he did not pursue it,' Yashine replied.

'Did you tell him about karkoubi?' Mahi, the eldest of the six, asked.

'Yes, and I'm glad I did. He knew of it and was interested when I explained how we have used it to fund our operation.' Yashine remembered that part of the conversation with satisfaction.

'That's good,' Mahi said. 'So what happens next?'

'He is making a report and will get back to me. I told him the only help we need is for ISIS to provide the explosives and detonators; the rest we can do.'

'How will you communicate? That's always risky,' Nadia observed.

'It is. So he has put in place a system which for the time being is between him and me only. Anything else?' He looked around the group.

'Does he know we will not be suicide bombers or near the scene when it happens?' Hamid asked.

This was not the direction Yashine wanted to go. He gave what he hoped would be a deflective answer.

'No. And from the way our discussion went, this was not the time to tell him,' he replied.

'But that could be important for ISIS. They may want to use similar strategies to ours in future,' Hamid responded.

'There will be a better time to tell them. So, if there is nothing else, let's enjoy the rest of the evening.'

Yashine said this hoping that would be the end of his briefing. What surprised him was that only Hamid seemed in favour of finishing. The others seemed agitated and gave every sign that they did not want to stop. Wondering what to do, he put forward his main argument.

'You may not have understood what Hamid meant. If my plan works, the complexity of the equipment and devices we use can be used again if we are still alive. If we are dead, that knowledge goes to the grave with us.'

Mahi was the first to answer. 'The reason I joined you on this mission was to give my life for what I believe in. If I don't do that, I will be betraying Allah.'

'Yes.' Nabil, Nadia and Mariam spoke firmly, making it clear this was how they thought as well. The women had always been hard line since they were radicalised under the influence of the power of karkoubi back in Casablanca.

To try to combat their discontent, Yashine said as persuasively as he could, 'I understand your concerns, so you will have a choice. What will happen is that the four bombs will explode at the same time in Dam Square. If you want to be there when that happens, it is up to you. If you don't, you can leave the device you are responsible for, and be somewhere else when I press the switch that detonates them. The problem is, if you are seen hanging around, it may look suspicious, so you would need to go somewhere else for a few hours, then return.'

'As we don't know the details of your plan, you need to tell us what they are and how it will work. That will help us make our decision,' Mahi said.

'Abdullah told me only to do that if ISIS gives us the go-ahead. He thinks the less you know at this time the better. After they make their decision, I may need to change some of it if they don't approve what I proposed today,' Yashine answered.

'Don't you think they will be put off by us not being martyrs and dying for Islam?' Nadia asked.

'In that case, let's wait for their response before we decide what to do. The important thing is they liked what I said today. I'm sure there will be more questions if they want to pursue it.' Yashine tried hard to bring the briefing to a close. As they all respected Yashine, especially the fact he had been invited to meet ISIS and that his meeting seemed to have gone well, it was agreed they would wait until he had heard from Abdullah.

Exhausted from his efforts and the excitement of the day, all Yashine wanted now was peace. So after hugging each of his co-conspirators, he went to his room. But the meeting had stirred up fire in Nadia and she wanted to know more about his plan and what Abdullah had said. So within minutes of his lying on the bed, she was in the room too.

Standing by the side of the bed, looking down at him and clearly angry, she said, 'You didn't answer my question in the meeting. Don't you think ISIS will be put off if we don't die for the cause? I want to be a martyr and that's what I thought following your plan would achieve. We don't understand why you've changed it. I'm sure ISIS wouldn't like it if they knew. Martyrdom has been the hallmark of all jihadists who have dedicated themselves to do the will of Allah.'

'You were there,' he said brusquely. 'You heard what I said. We wait for ISIS's response. Once we have that, if it is positive, I will tell Abdullah. Then they can decide if they want Hamid and me to carry out more attacks along similar lines. What you and the others do is up to you.'

'If you are not prepared to die for the cause, your attitude is wrong,' Nadia answered venomously.

'No, it is your understanding of ISIS that is wrong. They do not demand jihadists are suicide bombers. That is how extremists and the media interpret it. ISIS suggests it as the ultimate sacrifice.'

Yashine had known for some time that Nadia's extremist views would be a problem. This was why he had not told her that if Abdullah's response was negative, he and Hamid would still carry out the attacks on 27th April next year. The plan he had masterminded did not need the help of anyone else, except to plant the bombs. It was the impact of doing it under the banner of ISIS on the world stage that made him want to do it with their blessing.

From the moment he'd hatched his plan after his radicalisation in Casablanca's Oukacha prison, Yashine had spent hours studying the making of bombs, detonators and devices used in successful terrorist attacks. From India to Gaza, Vietnam to the IRA, he discovered that over and over again bicycles had been used to deliver explosives, or as the explosive device itself.

His other searches meant he knew that all he required would be the right amounts of triacetone and triperoxide (TATP) to make what are known as 'Mother of Satan' bombs, both of which are easily available. All he then needed was the money to do it, and as the cost was quite small to buy the bicycles and other things, his deals in karkoubi would pay the maximum US$ 12,000 he required.

In Yashine's view not even the goal was complicated. It was only ever going to be the people who helped him that could cause problems. And this already seemed to be the case.

Chapter 9

Yashine's first bicycle bomb took him less than one week to make from start to finish. Once he had bought the bicycle, and components that would turn it into a bomb, the rest he found relatively easy.

Although he had not heard from Abdullah, as he was going ahead with his plan regardless of the ISIS decision, he decided to make one. After that he would find a way to test it, which would help him know the overall cost and its effectiveness.

Having researched the market, he decided 26" electric mountain bikes were best for his purpose. A search on eBay located a five-year-old Carrera in reasonable condition for 190 euros, which was perfect. After that, online shopping to buy the components for the bomb and a second-hand smart phone meant that in six days he had all the materials he needed. All he had to do then was test it to make sure it worked and remove all possible identification marks.

After some location and geological research, he chose as his experimental site an old cement quarrying area called Sint Pietersberg near Maastricht. As there were tunnels and caves everywhere there, he was sure he would find a spot that met his needs.

The first problem he encountered was the weight of the reconstituted bicycle. Even in its original form it had been quite heavy, but with its frame and battery packed with explosives, it was more so. He would have to make sure he never had far to carry it, and as it no longer had a battery, he never had far to cycle.

After a few test rides to make sure it functioned normally and he could handle the weight issue, he took it to Maastricht by train the following Saturday afternoon; that way he avoided a lot of weekend walkers and cyclists who went there at that time of the year in the morning.

After putting on a helmet with a powerful built-in light, he set off an hour before dusk. Except for having to be exceedingly careful to avoid potholes, the three kilometre ride there was easy, and in another half kilometre he found the perfect deserted place to hide the bicycle.

He had already booked into a hostel near the railway station, so after setting the timing device, he walked backed to Maastricht excited and very pleased with himself, knowing that if it worked, he had the means to achieve his objective in Dam Square.

After a takeaway supper alone in the hostel, just after ten he set off in the direction from which he had left the bicycle bomb. Once he reached the edge of the city, he found a spot where there was little traffic noise. There he took out the mobile phone tethered to the bomb device, set it, and for the next few minutes acclimatised his hearing to the sounds around him. Once he was familiar with them, and the directions from which they came, he was ready.

But he need not have been so meticulous. The explosion was so loud, if he had been nearer the city centre, he would still have heard it. He even saw a faint flash of light as it exploded.

Amazed, delighted and bemused, all at the same time, he retraced his steps as quickly as possible back to the hostel. Within seconds he heard a police car siren, and when he saw it approaching, quickly got out of the way. This was followed by two more vehicles, a fire engine, then an ambulance, causing him instant fear as he thought he may have done something wrong. But his fear slowly subsided as he remembered there were no identifiable traces on any of the components and that he would be on a train to

Amsterdam early tomorrow morning. And all this had been achieved for under 600 euros.

As Yashine knew he would need money to buy the detonators and explosives, if ISIS did not provide the equipment for the attack, the first thing he did when he got to his home in Haarlem next day was check his stock of karkoubi. Randy Cyriax had not answered his most recent request, so his stocks were relatively low. He believed this was because Cyriax was applying the tactic of holding back supplies to raise the need, and therefore the price.

Since he dealt with Cyriax directly, he called him from his spare phone, knowing he may not answer if he saw who it was. Aware he might need the money he made from dealing in karkoubi to pay for the bicycles, as well as the explosives and detonators, he had to make sure his request was successful. On the fourth ring Randy answered.

'Hello. Who is this?' he asked bluntly.

Yashine had planned what he would say, and as he knew never to trust dealers, especially one whom he knew was a drug addict, he got to the point quickly.

'Hi, Randy, it's Yashine. I have some good news. I've just returned from another part of The Netherlands. When I was there, I met someone from Norway who offered me four times the price I pay you for the karkoubi ingredient you supply.'

'Did you say Norway?' Randy asked, sounding confused.

'Yes. He was in Casablanca recently and tried it there. He now wants it for himself. The problem is he goes back to Oslo next weekend and I don't have enough stock,' Yashine lied.

With his mind buzzing from the drugs, insatiable greed, and remembering that Yashine knew his drug-using background,

Randy paused. Then he said, 'I'll see what I can do. How much do you need?'

'500 strips of ten.'

'How much in euros is that?' Randy asked, his voice slurred.

'20,000, but it must be here by Friday. I also need two hundred strips for my needs at the usual price as I have virtually none left.' Good so far Yashine thought, let's hope Cyriax is not too much off his face to register what I said.

'It isn't a problem. I'll bring it myself,' Randy said, so excited he pressed the 'end call' button at the same time.

This did not faze Yashine. He wanted Randy to think this was the easiest money he would ever make. Even in his mind's drug-fuelled state, he would know that selling 500 strips at four euros a pill, and 200 strips at two euros a pill, that cost less than 0.5 euros to make, packaged and distributed in the years ahead, karkoubi would make him a fortune.

Yashine finished the call glowing inside. If he got 500 strips of ten karkoubi pills at four euros each, he could sell them for five and make 5,000 euros. In addition, the 200 strips he got at two euros would make him another 6,000 euros. But his warm feeling did not stop there. He believed Randy had only agreed because of the hold he had on him and very soon he would use that to insist they went into partnership. If they did, he had projected that it would make enough money to keep him the rest of his life in a manner beyond anything he could have imagined growing up in the slums of El Hoceima. Being a suicide bomber was out of the question.

As it transpired, this line of thinking worked out well. Three days later, Abdullah responded saying ISIS had approved the plan. However, they insisted he stop dealing in drugs.

They would fund his idea and provide the explosives and detonators he needed.

On the same day that Yashine received this information the Maastricht police made an ambiguous statement about the explosion the previous Saturday night: 'Our findings so far are inconclusive. It may have been explosives left there from the old mining days,' This left him with a choice he had not expected.

On the one hand he could go forward with the backing of an organisation that spread terror whenever it was mentioned in connection with jihadist attacks, but who may not support his refusal to die as a martyr stance; on the other, he could go ahead relying on his own ability, source it himself and live a rich, happy life.

What he told Abdullah was that he would discuss it with the others and report back to him, only saying this as he knew he would need the support of at least his brother to carry it out.

Chapter 10

My first action when I received Ali Abadi's email was to search the internet with his name. What I found excited me, so I decided to follow up his request, knowing it would be the first time I had contact with a Moroccan diplomat who might be able to influence my project. What was more, Abadi was in London where I felt safe; and as PA to the ambassador, together they would be in direct contact with personnel higher up Morocco's political chain.

Whenever Ali Abadi's private phone rang and the number came up as 'unknown', he did not answer it, taking the view that if it was someone he wanted to speak to, they would leave a message he could answer when and if he wished. On the morning I rang, he was driving, so he was able to hear me on his speaker as I left a message. As soon as I said my name, he pressed the answer button.

'Hello. This is Ali Abadi. Did you say you are Rick Blaine?'

'Yes. I received your email and am ringing as you requested.'

'Thank you, Mr Blaine. I am driving to Heathrow airport, so I can talk now on my hands-free phone if that suits you.'

'That's fine. You said you are interested in my experience with regard to drugs in Morocco. How can I help?'

'I'm the personal assistant to Morocco's London ambassador. I believe you know Reda Oumainian, whom I spoke to recently about Morocco's drug problems. He said he met you last year and that I should talk to you.'

'Yes, I know him. In what context did he say that?'

'He indicated you may be the best person to help with a dilemma we have,' Ali answered, which surprised me, given Oumainian's recent lack of support.

'That's very flattering as he is highly respected in Morocco regarding its drug problems. In what way did he think I can help?' I said.

'Morocco has a dangerous drug called karkoubi that can make its users wreak havoc on societies and families. Are you familiar with it?' Abadi asked, knowing, of course, that if I wrote the letter I definitely was.

'Yes.'

'Are you also familiar with the problems it has caused in Morocco?'

'Yes, but the problems your country has with drugs are not just with karkoubi and they have not only been confined to Morocco,' I answered, making sure I expressed my greater concern.

'What do you mean? I did not think Karkoubi existed in other countries.' I guessed that he had only got some of the answer he'd hoped for.

'You are right. karkoubi is used almost exclusively by Moroccans, but some who took it were probably radicalised there and went on to commit jihadist attacks abroad. That was what I was referring to, and as you must know, Morocco's drug-trafficking network is one of the most established in the world.'

'I understand. Is there anything else you think I should know?' Abadi probed.

'Morocco's drug problems are deep. Karkoubi is only one of them, and I believe the tip of the iceberg. But I still don't understand why you say you need my help. You have people living in Morocco who know the problems first-hand.'

Abadi must have decided the only way forward was to put his cards on the table.

'The ambassador and I were at a meeting in London recently and shown an unsent letter addressed to King Mohammed. It contained an analysis of what the writer perceived are some of the reasons for Morocco's drug problems, which may be getting worse, and offering an outline of a solution. What the ambassador asked me to find out is, who wrote the letter and what is the solution?'

'Why ask me?' I answered, stalling.

'I asked Professor Reda Oumainian, our country's leading expert on drugs and addiction for his thoughts. He did not shed light on the authorship of the letter, but told me about your efforts to help drug addicts in Morocco and thought you might be able to help with a solution.'

Ever since I had begun writing my contrary views on Morocco in two previous books, I knew there would be people there who would not want them published. Reda Oumainian would be one of them. Now, I wondered, could this man about whom I knew nothing be trusted, or was he on a fishing trip for something sinister? I decided it was wise to choose the latter.

'I am sorry, but I cannot help you. I left Morocco last September when I had done all I could. I came to realise that everything that needs to be done must be by Moroccans; as an outsider who did not speak Arabic, I faced an insurmountable wall.'

'That is interesting because it is the opposite to what the writer suggests,' Abadi responded diplomatically.

'Why, what did he or she say?' I asked. I could not remember the precise wording of my letter to the king.

'That the best person to advise on the solution is probably a foreigner because they would have no biases or ulterior motives. Which sounds right, would you not agree?'

I recognized that Abadi's response was designed to be as sensitive as possible to this delicate situation. And as he had spoken to Reda Oumainian, who had suggested he speak to me, I was beginning to realise this could be the golden opportunity I'd dreamed of. However, once more I paused. The way the conversation was going was feeding my desire to help, but I could not see how to capitalise on that without compromising my position.

'Let me think about it,' I said. 'If I come up with a way I can help, I will let you know.'

Ali Abadi decided now was the time to throw what he presumably hoped would be winning dice.

'The British government is worried there will be a terrorist attack in the United Kingdom in retaliation for the mosque attack in St John's Wood. Their defence department has asked us to do all we can to help prevent this because their intelligence says it is most likely it will be led by Moroccans.'

So that was why Reda Oumainian had suggested I might be the right person to ask for help. Although he knew what some of the solutions were, he had not supported putting them in place because he knew it would rock some of Morocco's deeply embedded laws, religious and cultural issues, the benefits of which went to the top of its government and possibly the king. But I could do it if I was given the opportunity.

For the first time in more than a year I had the thought that this could be the opportunity I had been waiting for. But milliseconds later I had another which seemed to make more sense: let it happen. If it does, it will be the perfect time to expose the situation, then Morocco will have to do something about it.

But Ali Abadi was no fool and his ploy had worked. My conscience and desire to help won. The prospect of such an attack and potential loss of lives was the only consideration that mattered. So, seconds later, I responded, 'The only reason I would be willing to help is to save the lives of Morocco's drug addicts and help their families. If I could be sure my suggestions would be carried out, I am willing to consider it. But first I need to know who, other than Reda Oumainian, knows you are in contact with me.'

'No one. Not even the ambassador. He knew I was contacting Professor Oumainian, but he does not know what he told me.'

'Keep it that way. I need to remain anonymous in all but our communications. However, before I do anything, I need you to assure me you will do your utmost to make sure there will be no danger to me or my family. If I ever suspect this is not the case, I will not have anything more to do with you, or anyone else from Morocco.'

'I understand and give you my word,' Abadi answered. He did not have a choice. He would know that westerners in general do not trust Arabs.

'That isn't enough. I need something in writing along that line on embassy paper.'

'I can do that, but I cannot speak for Reda Oumainian. As he is not a government employee, he is not sworn to secrecy in the way I am.'

'Tell Reda Oumainian to ring me. I will deal with him. I have an idea I think he will like,' I answered.

'Anything else, Mr Blaine?' Ali asked, clearly pleased the conversation had finally gone in a satisfactory direction.

'I need to talk to Reda before we take this further. I don't know him well, but I do know I don't agree with the strategies he and Morocco's medical profession use to treat drug addicts. I would need to know I have his full support as he and his family have a lot of influence in Morocco,' I said.

'I will get him to ring you as soon as possible, and I will make clear how important it is he listens to you,' Abadi answered, his positive reaction tinged with dismay. He would know how arrogant such people can be.

After we finished our conversation, I thought about what might transpire as a result. I recalled how I had come to see Reda Oumainian as an ego-driven, ambitious man who had not stood up for me at the Moroccan psychiatrists' conference the previous year. And more recently he had not replied to my emails or texts, even though he had previously promised his support. In other words, I no longer trusted him. But I knew a lot about people's pride, especially when it comes to psychiatrists who deal with addiction; their arrogance often prevents them doing what is best because they think they know better.

Pondering on this gave me an idea for how I could use Oumainian's character defects to my advantage.

****

In the event, I rang Reda Oumainian that afternoon. Before we opened the subject of drugs, I said, 'I need to record this conversation as I may need to refer to it again. You will understand why by the time we finish talking. I hope that is all right with you.'

'I understand. In that case, send me transcript,' he replied, then added, 'Ali Abadi made it clear this is a delicate situation and we are to work together on this for the best possible result.'

'Thank you. Also, for the kind words you used to explain my efforts to start NA and AA in Morocco to him. When we spoke today, I knew from what he said I still have your support, and if that is the case, by doing what I have in mind, together, we can achieve much of what we all want to accomplish.'

Oumainian, I assumed, may be sceptical because he knew his recent behaviour towards me had been less than cordial. Although he seemed to like me when we first met, and said he admired what I was doing, this had clearly not been the same for his colleagues. As a consequence, his ambitions and position meant he subsequently sided with them. So I was pleased when he responded, 'You said "together" and "we". Please explain, as I do not understand.'

'You have the experience of dealing with drug addicts in Morocco and the respect of the medical professionals there who treat them. I don't have either. Also, you speak the language and are well known for your work with the UN, WHO and Council of Europe on drugs. I don't have these either. But what I do have that you don't is experience of using drugs and recovery in Alcoholics Anonymous and Narcotics Anonymous. It is the overall combination of these that will be the formula for success Morocco so desperately needs,' I answered.

He could not argue with this rationale.

'I remember and agree. You have personal experience of years of drug abuse, besides being a business advisor to the pharmaceutical industry, and first-hand knowledge of recovery with AA and NA. Please go on.'

'I also have something else, which from Ali Abadi's point of view is more important. He believes I know the solution to most of Morocco's drug problems, whereas you and your colleagues don't, or if you do know, you have not applied them.'

I deliberately worded my response to challenge Reda Oumainian. I wanted him to understand that I would be in charge.

'I find that hard to believe. I agree you and the organisations you represent know a lot about treating drug addicts. But our problems are much deeper than that. You wouldn't understand them even if you lived here twenty years.'

Oumainian said this more sharply than I expected. He may have been thinking, how can a foreigner know how to rid my country of a scourge that has grown over many years? And how can I explain it to my colleagues if he does?

I responded, 'I have written two books on Morocco's drug problems and the solution. If you read them you will understand why I believe this is true. If after that you agree, I will guide you through the processes that will get the best results.'

I paused deliberately. What I was about to say was the bait I hoped would catch a very big fish in Morocco's ocean of drug problems. The hook's bait I was going to use was Oumainian's ego and ambition.

'We will do this in such a way that you get all the credit. That is because of the positions you hold, and if my name is attached to it, I will be breaking the tradition of anonymity essential to the success of NA and AA.'

Now, it was Oumainian's turn to pause. It seemed my aim to capture his attention may have worked.

He responded, 'I understand why you need to remain anonymous. But how do you know your idea will work? I know there are things Morocco has done wrong, but to think one man knows how to fix our drug problems seems ambitious.'

'If I was in your shoes, I would think the same. The answer to the problems you will get by reading my books.'

'I hear what you say, but I still think it is implausible,' Oumainian answered.

'Trust me, it isn't. That is the way it has to be for this to work. It is the culmination of all I have ever done in life, so my heart and soul is in it. You will understand this when you read the treatment I wrote for a documentary covering the problems and solution.'

'Has the documentary been made?' Oumainian asked immediately, no doubt concerned that if it had, it might contain information he would not like.

'It is shelved for the time being. The way forward starts with King Mohammed. He is involved in the major decisions and what Morocco needs here requires his blessing. Before today, I believed the best way to get that was to expose the situation. Hence the reason I wrote the books and aimed to make a documentary.' I knew that what I said may come across as threatening.

'Send me the documentary treatment. I will read it and get back to you.' Oumainian said, having grasped that it would give him an opportunity to be part of the solution.

But I was not finished yet.

'I need a letter from you first, confirming that you will not mention my name to anyone at any time regarding any of this. I will have it drawn up so that it is legally binding and protects me in every way. Ali Abadi will be the only other person who knows, and he has already agreed to put the same in writing.'

Reda Oumainian would be aware that given our history, I would not trust him to simply give his word. He also knew I would do as much as possible to help drug addicts. And if I believed this was the best way to do it, I would not put that in jeopardy. To make sure he had positive thoughts if he followed my idea, I planted in his mind a seed that would wholeheartedly capture his attention. I said in as affirmative tone as possible, 'There is another interesting possibility. If Morocco gets this right and the knock-on effect influences other countries to follow suit, the Nobel Peace Prize committee would view such a humanitarian act favourably. They already know the excellent results achieved by AA and NA. If Morocco used them and applied the right policies to put its drug problems right, their committee could well award this much-revered prize to the people who initiated it, including the king.'

After a pause, Reda responded. 'That is something I would not have thought of. I am like you; I just want to help Morocco's drug addicts and their families. Send me a draft and I will read it. If I am happy with it, I will sign it.'

For me, my ploy had worked. I replied, 'Thanks. I have one made out. I will send it now and we can talk again tomorrow. I will copy Ali Abadi.'

'Don't forget to send a transcript of this conversation. I may need to refer to it,' he said.

'Two last things. The project needs a code name and I need a pseudonym. I suggest for the former 'Hat-trick', and for me, 'Jack Reynard'. Is that okay with you?' I asked.

'It is, but remind me in writing,' Professor Oumainian agreed.

With that we said our goodbyes and ended the call. I was optimistic. I guessed that Reda Oumainian's mood was not quite the same.

****

Less than hour after my phone conversation with Reda Oumainian, I emailed a Non-Disclosure Agreement (NDA) to him and copied Ali Abadi. My covering letter read:

Dear Prof. Oumainian,

As discussed in our phone conversation today, attached is a Non-Disclosure Agreement. Please sign it and email a copy to me.

As soon as I receive it, and a similar NDA from Ali Abadi, I will send you the two books and documentary treatment I have written. These outline my view of the reasons for Morocco's drug problems at home and abroad and what I believe is the solution.

When you have read them, if you agree, I will work through them with you until such time as it is clear that Morocco has put in place the practices which will correct its past and current damaging policies. Once these are established, Morocco's medical profession and politicians should be able to take them forward from there.

The name of the project is 'Hat-trick' and my pseudonym from now on is 'Jack Reynard'. Please refer to the project or me by these names in future. For legal purposes the NDA is in my real name and subject English law.

Yours sincerely,

Rick Blaine

After reading it twice, Reda Oumainian telephoned Ali Abadi. On the third ring, Abadi answered.

'Hello, Reda. I was expecting you to ring.'

'Have you seen it? I cannot sign this. I have no idea what this man is going to suggest. Do you?' Oumainian answered angrily.

'No, and I understand your frustration when it is an outsider telling us that what we are doing is wrong. However, I think we both know from talking to him he knows a lot about this subject, and most importantly, he comes at it from a different angle to us because we grew up in the Moroccan system, which means we have biases that he doesn't have,' Abadi said.

'I have spent my working life helping drug addicts and my qualifications have taken me to the top of my profession. I cannot believe an outsider knows more than me about Morocco's drug problems.' Abadi's words had not pacified him.

'I agree, but there are differences, and the situation is desperate. And we have nothing to lose by listening to him. His experience is all hands-on and he has no personal agenda, other than to help drug addicts. Ours is steeped in our culture, drug laws, religion, and in some cases, our livelihoods,' Abadi reasoned.

As Ali Abadi said this, Reda Oumainian recalled what Rick Blaine had said, that he would be his intermediary and beneficiary of any success Morocco achieved from following his suggestions. He had to admit that there would be aspects of Rick Blaine's solution he would agree with.

So. not wanting to shoot himself in the foot, he said, 'What do you suggest I do?'

As Oumainian's tone had softened, Abadi replied, 'If there are things in the NDA you don't like, you can suggest changing them, then agree to it. Once you have read the books and documentary summary, you will have a better understanding as to whether his ideas would work. If you think they could, we find a way to go forward with them. I will stand by you either way, and make sure the Moroccan ambassador in London supports you as well.'

'Is the NDA you are signing the same as mine?' Reda asked, feeling more at ease and remembering how success could enhance his political aspirations.

'It is virtually the same, except it includes non-disclosure to anyone in Morocco or at the embassy.'

'Are you okay with that?'

'I have to be. This is politics and the situation is extremely serious. I am sure you know from your father what that means to Moroccans.'

Oumainian interpreted this as meaning there could be an element of flexibility in interpretations, especially as it was only subject to English law.

'Thank you, and yes, I understand. I will do it later today and copy you as he requests. Now you have explained the situation, I will probably sign it as it is.'

'Good. That way there is a better chance of addressing Mr Blaine's fears. Also, we are all trying to achieve the same result. I know from experience, Moroccans who live abroad are fed up with the reputation we have regarding drugs. Another terrorist attack where Moroccans are involved will do much to worsen their situation. I am sure from my meeting with Britain's defence secretary, his government would do all they could to make that happen. Before their prime minister took office, he had made it clear he suffers from Islamophobia,' Abadi said, emphasising this prime minister's known position.

'Several times when I have been at the UN or WHO, I have felt ashamed of what some of my countrymen have done in the name of what they called martyrdom. If this helps stop

Moroccans doing such things, I am for it. Such violence has nothing to do with the teachings of Islam,' Reda replied.

The passion with which Oumainian said this surprised Ali Abadi. 'I am with you all the way on that,' he said. 'As a diplomat representing our country abroad, I have had several awkward instances where I felt the same.' He paused, then said, 'I have one other question for you about Mr Blaine. From your knowledge of him, do you think he will have credible ideas?'

'When I met him, I told him how I believed starting AA and NA in Morocco was the answer to some of our problems and I would support starting them at our hospital. The problem was, I did not get the backing I'd hoped for, so I had to compromise. If his other ideas are as good, I look forward to receiving them. I will let you know what I think once I do.'

'That is encouraging,' Ali Abadi said, sounding pleased. 'I will keep an open mind until then. What do you think about his views on karkoubi?'

'Karkoubi terrifies me. Given Morocco's international illegal drug network, its cheapness and effect on users, I am amazed using it has not reached France, Spain, the Netherlands, United Kingdom or America. If that happens, it could open a whole new Pandora's box of drug trafficking and hatred towards Morocco.'

This response by Morocco's leading authority on drugs encouraged Ali Abadi to express his major concerns about karkoubi.

'I agree. If the rest of the world knew about the devastating effect it has had on crime in Morocco, it could influence tourists to stop visiting. Also, we are trying to establish Morocco as the best country in Africa for international businesses to open offices; the karkoubi effect could prevent that. But how, I am asking myself, did we get in this mess? Why don't other countries have the same problems?'

'Many times, I've wondered that too. Every country has problems with drugs; ours just seem worse than everyone else's. I pray Allah forbid the karkoubi Pandora box is opened anywhere else, because it will inevitably be blamed on Morocco.' Oumainian sighed.

'Our job is to make sure we find the way to stop that box being opened. I just hope Mr Blaine's ideas will help us do that.'

Chapter 11

Had Ali Abadi and Reda Oumainian known what was happening at the same time in Amsterdam, they would have felt far worse about the future effect karkoubi would have on Moroccan public relations: because not all Muslims and Moroccans thought like them.

In particular that day, Abdullah El Gullam of ISIS, Yashine and Hamid Abu Zoubeir, the bicycle bombers from Amsterdam, definitely did not, and others spread more widely would also be planning to harm those they branded 'Western infidels'.

The plan Yashine had proposed to Abdullah in Antwerp, except for one proviso, had been accepted by the controllers of ISIS in Europe, and that proviso had to do with karkoubi. As Abdullah told Yashine this on the phone, waves of defiance flooded the latter's mind, but expressing them at this time he decided would not be in his best interest. Instead he said, 'The karkoubi issue will not be a problem. All of it comes through me, so I control it.'

What Yashine was doing was buying time. He knew that if he spurned ISIS support without checking with the others, it could jeopardise their backing him; especially Nadia and Mariam, which indirectly meant Hamid, as he was besotted with Mariam whom he had asked to marry him. But Yashine had misread ISIS's intentions. They had a much bigger plan for karkoubi, which Abdullah's reply partly clarified.

'When I come to Amsterdam tomorrow, I will explain everything. Do not say anything to your friends or brother before then, not even that we are meeting. I will see you at Central Station at eleven and we will walk to Dam Square. I need to see the target for myself. After that I will have a better understanding of your idea and will tell you what our plans are for karkoubi, which we believe you will like.'

Surprised by the suddenness of the meeting, and slightly confused, but realising ISIS must be prepared to go forward with his plan, Yashine replied,

'That's good for me. I will be there. Anything else?'

'Not for now. I will ring you when I am nearly there, so you can tell me where to meet you.'

The next day, when Abdullah explained ISIS's idea, Yashine was initially overwhelmed. Never could he have imagined such a scenario even in his wildest dreams. To begin with he would have thought it was partly insane, but as Abdullah talked him through it, it made more and more sense. In fact, by the time they parted, Yashine believed it could take ISIS from being a serious threat to security wherever it operated to having a massive impact on a more global scale.

'What do you mean, ISIS wants to take over my role dealing in karkoubi?' Yashine exclaimed when Abdullah first mentioned what they proposed.

'I told my friends at ISIS how karkoubi is sometimes used in Morocco to radicalise your countrymen. Then I explained what you told me about your supplier and how you are his only dealer. Once they assimilated this, they realised that when these are combined, it represents the potential to radicalise more people, and at the same time provide a way to raise funds for ISIS through drug dealing.'

'It is too complicated. I don't like the sound of it. Randy Cyriax is a drug dealer, an addict and British. That is not a healthy combination for ISIS to do business with,' Yashine answered, feeling insecure.

'You are doing it, aren't you? So why not ISIS through you?' Abdullah reasoned.

'You mean without Cyriax knowing it is ISIS?' Yashine asked.

'Yes. Once we have established that it works, later we can decide what to do. The main thing is to radicalise as many new people as possible; just like you and your friends were. The more there are we can trust to carry out our plans, the better. There are far too many who talk the talk, but don't have the courage to walk the walk.'

Remembering his desire not to die a martyr, Yashine cringed when he heard this. But then he realised it meant ISIS needed him even more going forward. As this had been his main worry, he began warming to this new idea.

'I am beginning to see the logic,' he said a little cautiously. 'But I am still concerned about Randy Cyriax's mental state. How do you propose I deal with that?'

'To begin with, you continue to work with whatever arrangement you have with him, always remembering from now on his real partnership is with ISIS through you. This means that anything you do or say, you have to bear that in mind, and never mention ISIS by name to anyone. Do you understand?'

'I think so, yes,' Yashine answered, though he still did not understand why this made sense from ISIS's point of view.

Noting his hesitancy, Abdullah said, 'I suspect some of this is hard to understand. If you tell me what your position with him is right now, I will try to explain better.'

'I recently made an order based on generous financial terms to accommodate what I perceive I will need in the next few months. To make sure he complied, I created a fictional character from Norway who wants to deal in karkoubi there.'

Yashine said this as brazenly as he could. He was not going to tell Abdullah money from this was to pay for the trial run he'd made in Maastricht a few days ago and the possible future need for bicycles and bomb-making equipment if he chose not to use ISIS.

'Was he receptive to that?' Abdullah probed, knowing the world of drug trafficking was fraught with dishonesty.

'Yes.'

'Do you trust him?'

'No. I had the impression he was high on drugs when he agreed.'

'If that was the case, he may be desperate for money. Is that likely?' Abdullah asked.

'No. He and his family are loaded with it. I have done some checking and they are worth more than a hundred million euros.'

By now they had reached Dam Square. On the way, Yashine made comments about the number of bicycles and how easy it would be to hide the ones he would use in the cycle racks he had designated as the most effective.

As they walked around the square, he pointed to the four racks he would use, taking selfie photos in front of each. As by now there were thousands of people in the square doing the same, this did not stand out. At the same time Yashine reiterated how, for the same reason, his bomb-rigged bicycles would be even less conspicuous on 27th April, when hundreds of thousands would be celebrating the king's birthday.

As they walked back to Central Station, Abdullah expressed his pleasure at what he had seen and the thoroughness and simplicity of Yashine's plan. As they parted company, he asked casually, 'Do you know anything about the recent explosion in Maastricht? It sounded as though a lot of explosives were used. One of my colleagues asked me to ask you.'

130

'No. As far as I know that is all the police have said. As no one was hurt, it did not make much news,' Yashine answered, equally coolly.

'If you hear anything, let me know,' Abdullah said.

'I will,' Yashine answered calmly. Had he had time to think about it, his answer may not have been quite as casual.

With that they went their separate ways, Abdullah to report back to ISIS, Yashine to reflect and decide what to do.

Twenty-four hours later Yashine discovered a recent UN report by specialist monitors warning that the recent pause in terrorist violence may soon end and a new wave of attacks was likely. When he coupled this with America's recent threat to send ISIS fighters detained in Syria by US-backed forces back to Europe, he perceived the strength of ISIS would escalate to well beyond what it has been for some time.

This new information gave Yashine hope, but it also worried him. The good news was that more attacks would mean more deaths of those he hated, but these announcements meant it was likely more security forces would be put in place. To get a consensus view among his fellow conspirators he convened a meeting.

First he described the time he had spent with Abdullah and what ISIS proposed, then he put forward the new information and what he thought it meant. After that he asked them their thoughts on how they should proceed, telling them that when it came to such important decisions, it was important to have each of their views as what they thought overall was most likely to prove best.

After discussing all the issues, they were split fifty/fifty; three for going forward with ISIS, three for going it alone. This was resolved by Nadia, who proposed they begin with

ISIS, and if there were any hiccups, they did it alone. Before that, due to her disappointment about ISIS not supporting the attack in London, she had been in favour of doing it themselves.

Much to Yashine's surprise, three days later, Abdullah rang saying he needed to meet him again in Amsterdam. 'We have discussed your plan and want to bring the date forward. If the number of people in the square when we met is typical of any Saturday, we don't see the need to wait until next year.'

'Our thinking was it would cause more of a sensation if it was on an important public holiday; there would also be two or three times more people in the square that day,' Yashine replied.

'Your thinking is too local. ISIS's aim is to be a global force for Islam. This is not about a single city or country; we want the whole world to recognise the purpose of ISIS. Do you understand?'

'I do now. I had not thought of it like that,' Yashine answered, pleased his group had agreed that working with ISIS was the best route.

'At the moment security in the Netherlands is more relaxed than Europe's other major cities, which is why we think Amsterdam is perfect as our next major target. But if there are attacks elsewhere before next April, it would be tightened.'

'That's because so far the Netherlands has not been targeted,' Yashine said, this tallying with his own views.

'That's right. We are concerned that because there are many Moroccans living here, a lot must go back and forth to Morocco and some may have similar hostile ideas that could harm our plans; someone in the Mocro-Maffia for instance. We are ready now and the possibility is that if we don't target the Netherlands soon, someone else could do that, which could ruin it for us. In the past, the name ISIS bred fear and that's what we want to return to. The recent loner approach of mentally unstable shooters and bombers is not one we want attached to us. Ours is an honourable cause, a crusade against heretics.'

Overjoyed by what Abdullah said, Yashine's response was simple: 'You said you want to meet. When do you have in mind?'

'Tomorrow, same time, same place. I want to see how busy Dam Square is in the middle of the week.'

'That's good for me. I will see you then.'

On both occasions when they had met previously, it had seemed as if they were on an equal footing, each one checking the suitability of working with the other. This time, from the moment they met at Central Station, Abdullah made it clear that he and ISIS were in charge. Even before they left the station concourse he began to establish this.

'My leaders believe there are some things you need to know. In the past few years, the white supremacist attacks in America and New Zealand have infuriated our leaders and new members have poured in, while Donald Trump's racist rhetoric and pro-Israel stance created a platform for us to justify defending Islam and Muslims. This means we need to do something big urgently to show the western infidels that our troops are as ready as ever to fight for our just cause. That means your idea in Amsterdam has gone to the top of our priority list of upcoming attacks in Europe.'

Yashine was delighted. He replied, 'That's fantastic. What do you want me and my friends to do?'

'As ISIS has been quiet in Europe recently, we want you to work out the earliest date you can be ready, and that

133

cannot be too soon. Our terrorist attacks are a means to generate attention to the teachings in the Qur'an by inflaming hostilities, and we only achieve that if we act at the right time, in the right places. We believe that the recent lapse in our activities means the time is right for the bloodiest attack possible, and one of the best places to do that today is in the Netherlands.'

Abdullah had replied to Yashine's question without hesitation. Now he paused, waiting for him to respond.

'I will need to check with the others, but I believe I speak for them when I say that as soon as we have the detonators and explosives, we can be ready within four weeks maximum,' Yashine replied, now brimming with enthusiasm.

'The sooner you meet them the better, then let me know what they say. You can have the weapons you will need in about ten days. We already have a cache of arms in the Netherlands.'

'Because of the urgency of your wanting to meet me I arranged to meet them tonight.'

"Good. Now let's go to Dam Square. There are a few things I need to check.'

****

By the time Yashine met his co-conspirators, a few hours after his meeting with Abdullah, he had changed his mind as to what he wanted to do.

'I spent four hours with my contact from ISIS today,' he told them. 'We have been given their green light, but my thinking now is we are better off doing it by ourselves. The more people who know our plan, the more likely it is someone will talk. We don't need them or anyone else to provide what we need, only money, and I will get that from selling karkoubi; most importantly we will have control of the timing and locations, which we won't have if ISIS are in charge.'

'But the ISIS name gives it clout and our attack in Amsterdam will add to the global fear already associated with them,' Nadia countered immediately.

'My idea is that we would post something in the media that suggests we are one of many offshoots of ISIS. That would imply that ISIS has widespread splinter groups, which should foster even greater fear,' Yashine said. Having expected this response, his answer was already prepared.

'In my opinion, there would be greater benefit being part of a bigger organisation, so I agree with Nadia,' Habib echoed, adding, 'What do you think, Mariam? You have always been on the side of doing whatever would have most influence.'

'I understand Yashine's point of view. He has met ISIS several times. If he is sure he can do it without them, I can see the benefit of that,' she said, surprising Yashine and the others. Then she asked, 'When would ISIS want to do it?'

My contact said he will get back to me on that. My view is that we should strike now when the days get dark early and there are still crowds around. Also, I've had another thought. I want one of the targets in Dam Square to be Madame Tussauds. It is open until 8 p.m. and has queues outside until six. It is opposite the Royal Palace, so if bombs go off at two-second intervals, as well as one at each end of the square, the result would be chaos as well as the carnage we hope for.'

'My God! What an idea! I would want to film it,' Mariam said.

Nabil now spoke for the first time. 'You are a genius, Yashine, and Mariam's idea is fantastic. If a film of that was posted on YouTube, it would have the most viral impact of all time.'

'Do you really think you can do it?' Nadia asked, coming around to Yashine's thinking. 'The idea of us filming it from the top of one of the high buildings in the square blows my mind.'

'I only thought of it today when I was there and saw the crowds; Mariam's idea is the icing on the cake,' he answered, loving their enthusiasm and this new idea.

'What about cycle racks. Are there any nearby?" Habib asked.

'There is one near enough in each case for our needs,' Yashine replied.

'Am I right that as ISIS knew most of your plan, they realised we would not be suicide bombers?' Nadia asked.

She was sharp, Yashine thought. 'We did not discuss it,' he said. 'Because of the nature of their strategy, that question didn't come up.'

'It sounds to me as if we have a new plan that is the best one yet,' Mahi said. So far he had made little contribution to their discussions.

'Do we all agree?' Yashine asked.

A show of hands and nods of heads said they did unanimously so he had only one more thing to establish.

'I can have everything ready in three weeks. I propose we plan our assault for three days after that.' He wondered how quickly they would realise what day that was.

'That's the 31st of December,' Habib said.

'This gets better all the time!' Nadia said. 'There will be huge crowds everywhere and most will be drunk or high on drugs. There would be pandemonium when the bombs go off.'

Another show of hands said they were all for carrying out the attacks themselves on that date. As soon as that was done, Nadia said, 'As you four guys are planting the bombs, Mariam and I won't have anything to do. I suggest she and I find suitable places to live stream the attacks on our phones. This would ensure the world sees what their hate policies towards Islam have caused.'

'That's brilliant, Nadia. I cannot think of a better way that shows my love for our cause,' Mariam said. 'It will be our way of achieving martyrdom.'

With the others giving the idea their full support, the meeting broke up with each believing their attacks had the potential for achieving the most widespread publicity possible, at the same time causing a huge amount of harm.

A hectic three weeks followed. First Yashine sold all his karkoubi stock to buy the bicycles; then he waited for Randy to arrive with the drugs he needed that would pay for the explosives and detonators. This meant he had to find new cusJackers who would pay higher prices.

The meeting with Randy started badly. He demanded more money than the four euros a pill he had previously agreed. So Yashine reminded him that was eight times the cost of making them and shipping. Then, with him still demanding more, Yashine reminded him that it was he who would go to prison if he was caught. After more resistance he carefully pointed out that the only way he could get a light sentence was if he revealed his source. Although Yashine knew this would leave a sour taste, it was worth it to make Randy agree.

Buying the explosives and detonators was easy. He had already bought triacetone and triperoxide to make the bicycle bomb he used in Maastricht, so he returned to the same store for what he needed to make the bombs.

Without another hitch, for the next seven days, Yashine and Hamid worked day and night to make the four 'Mother of Satan' bicycle bombs. After that they told their co-conspirators and waited.

Chapter 12

When Mohamed Tahir summoned Ali Abadi to a meeting two days after they had met the British defence secretary, he was not hopeful any progress had been made. His conversation with Abdasalam Oumainian had not been fruitful, so he saw no reason why Abadi's contact with his son would have gone better.

'I spoke to my imam friend,' he began. 'For the questions I asked about Islam and drugs, his answers didn't help. How did you get on with his son? I imagine it was the same.'

'To begin with he was like that, but by the time we finished speaking a second time, he was expressing views that were encouraging. This was probably because he sees at first hand the awfulness of Morocco's drug problems and is familiar with the success of solutions in other countries.'

'That does sound better, I needed some good news. So far, settling in London has not been easy. I had hoped the United Kingdom would be straightforward compared to the countries I have worked in before. Anything else?'

'My news is better than that. I tracked down the author of the letter to the king and spoke to him.'

'That really is good. You should have told me sooner. How did you manage that? Was it useful?'

'Very. I would have told you, but it is complicated. He is sending me the two books he has written on the subject. As each contains the problems as well as what he thinks is the solution, we will have something to consider.'

'We will need to have him checked out by our people. He could be a spy and there may be an agenda that could be damaging.'

'We cannot do that. The reason it is complicated is that his number one demand is that he remains anonymous and I have to sign a non-disclosure agreement before he will send me the books. I also had him talk to Reda Oumainian, who has to do the same.'

'That is unreasonable. It is a highly dangerous important situation and for one man to make such demands of a country is out of the question,' Mohamed Tahir answered, applying the authority of his ambassadorial position.

'In that case, we will have to drop it. He has given me his reasons and they make sense. He is a member of Alcoholics Anonymous and Narcotics Anonymous and anonymity is an essential aspect of their traditions. He is also concerned as to his personal safety and that of his family. In my view, neither of these can be argued with. If I were in his position I would want the same.'

Ali Abadi realised he was voicing an opinion which may not go down well with the ambassador.

After a slight pause, Tahir said, 'I don't like it. What do you suggest we do?'

'I have thought about it and don't think there is a problem in agreeing to his terms. We need to see the books, and if what he says is as good as he claims, I am sure we can figure out a way to adapt them without mentioning him. Reda Oumainian has also agreed to sign an NDA.'

Abadi offered his carefully worded conclusion based on the importance and delicacy of the situation.

'I need to think about it and get advice from Morocco. Anything else?'

'British politicians have lost a lot of credibility in recent years. Because of a recent report saying drug crime is escalating, to improve their prime minister's image he told the British people he plans to establish more prison places, expand the police force, and make national security a priority.'

'Drugs, fear and crime are political tools used by all Western politicians. They all say they will do the most for the people's welfare, which no one believes anymore. If you have any other thoughts, let me know.'

The ambassador expressed the experience he'd had in France and the USA where he had worked previously, expecting the conversation to end there. But there was something else Abadi needed to tell him.

'I was at a function at the Dutch embassy yesterday. There are a lot of Moroccans living in the Netherlands, so someone from here is often invited. At one point, I was talking to their ambassador's PA who I have got to know well. He told me their country recently considered raising their terrorist security alert level after an unexplained bomb went off. But, because it was in an isolated place and no one was harmed, the government and media played it down. But the size of it, and fact that the Netherlands has never had a major terrorist attack, has caused the police to fear their country may soon be a target. Given the circumstances, if it was not an accident, they think it may have been a test or prank by a loner or small terrorist group.'

'Why didn't they raise it if that's what they think?'

'It was at an old mining site and could have been explosives left there when it closed. It had been very hot that day and they think something could have caught fire and set it off. A recently planted man-made device, though, is still their main line of thinking,' Abadi explained.

Mohamed Tahir nodded thoughtfully. 'In case there is something else, keep in touch with your contact there,' he said.

'He also mentioned their concern about the rise of the Mocro-Maffia.'

'I am not surprised. We are all worried about that.' Mohamed said.

'As it happens, it is my brother's birthday on 31st December, so I am visiting him in Amsterdam for a few days. He has lived there thirty years and most of the people he knows there are Moroccans. I will get his thoughts without telling him the reason.'

'A good idea and well timed. I had a letter today from David Smith, the British defence secretary. His tone is still hostile. I need to respond as the situation worries me. I will send it to you, so you can help with my reply when you have more information.'

'Let's hope nothing else bad happens,' Abadi said. A recent British prime minister's anti-Muslim rhetoric and Donald Trump's past actions in Israel and the Middle East stirred things up, so that Muslims in every western country will be even more targeted unless we can put a stop to the extremists' activities. The problem is, their behaviour angers those already radicalised and makes it easier to persuade new ones to join, so more attacks are likely, not less.'

'And that is all for political gain. Nothing whatsoever to do with what's best for the people they serve and the world we live in,' Mohamed Tahir added.

****

The following Friday Ali Abadi flew to Amsterdam. Before boarding the airplane, he noticed that several of his fellow passengers looked North African. When he was near enough to hear them speak, he realised they were Moroccan. He also noticed that security at both Heathrow and Schiphol was higher than usual, which he assumed was because it was in the middle of a major holiday period. Plus, he noted there were more armed police in Amsterdam than in London.

That evening, after supper with his brother Ahmed and his family, he asked him what it was like being a Moroccan living in the Netherlands.

'I am so used it, I hardly think about it,' his brother answered.

'But it is not like Tangier where we grew up," Ali said.

'It isn't, but as I have lived here so long, it's not something which crosses my mind much. Why do you ask?'

'I find living in London is very different. But I have a disjointed view as I spend half my life working with and seeing Moroccans. The rest of the time I mix with foreign diplomats and live by British laws and standards,' Ali said.

'I don't spread my wings wide,' Ahmed said. 'I do much the same things every day. Most restaurants I go to are Moroccan and my neighbourhood has many people from our part of north Morocco living here. The only difference is, for the last twelve years I have lived in a big house in the wealthier part of Slotervaart.'

'What about crime and drugs? Are there average problems here?' Ali asked, moving into the area he really wanted to know about.

'Slotervaart used to have a bad reputation, but crime rates have dropped. We had a Moroccan mayor not long ago who targeted that. The worst things now are youths putting potatoes in car exhausts or stealing oranges from street traders. And everyone turns a blind eye to these. That's about it.'

'And drugs?' Ali asked, hoping for some useful information.

'I don't know that scene. But because of the number of Moroccans living here and our central Amsterdam location, rumour has it Slotervaart is one of the hubs for cannabis trafficking,' Ahmed answered.

'Have you heard of karkoubi? It's a drug cocktail we have in Morocco that's causing problems.'

'No. But I will ask my sons. They are often offered drugs at university. What is it?'

Ali described the facts as he knew them about the karkoubi drug cocktail and the concern the UK government had regarding terrorist attacks linked to it. He explained that it was impossible to say that radicalisation was a direct consequence of using it, but the thinking was that it was often used for this purpose, especially in Morocco's poorest communities and the prisons.

Ali waited for Ahmed to return from going to ask his eldest son if he had heard of it.

'Mohamed says that about a month ago someone offered it to him for the first time. He was told that if he took it, it would raise his feeling of manliness. I am pleased to say, he refused it,' he told Ali, sitting down again.

'Did he say if it was a Moroccan who offered it to him?'

'Yes, it was someone from Haarlem who used to live here. They grew up together.'

'Has anyone he knows taken it?' Ali persisted.

'I don't know. I will fetch him, so you can ask him yourself,' Ahmed offered.

Mohamed was twenty-three years old and studying to be a doctor at the Faculty of Medicine at Amsterdam University. He was at the end of his second year. Because he had spent all his life in the Netherlands, and dressed and spoke like a European, he came across as one, but his dark skin and jet-black hair gave away his origins. His mother and father practised the true teachings of Islam and had brought up their children to do the same. To Mohamed, non-violence, honesty, spirituality and love were the principles he lived by.

'You told your father you had been offered karkoubi. I thought it was exclusive to Morocco, but it seems that is no longer the case. What can you tell me about it, Mohamed? I would be interested to know,' Ali asked as unthreateningly as possible.

'I have been offered it twice,' Mohamed answered. 'The first time was a month ago, the second was last week. Both times it was by the same person. I know him and his brother because we went to the same school when they lived near us. They are older than me, but we were friends at that time.'

'What do you know about the effects of the drug?' Ali asked.

'I know what it's made of, and that to get the full effect, you take it with alcohol. It makes users feel powerful,' Mohamed replied concisely.

'Do you know anyone who has taken it? If so, what effect did it have?'

'I don't, but he told me this was his fifth shipment and he got it from Spain. Also, that it was exclusive to him.'

This was not the answer Ali had expected. He said, 'You said he got it from Spain. I thought it was exclusive to Morocco and Algeria.'

'It was, but not anymore it seems. It would be easy to make anywhere once you know the ingredients. Then all you need is a laboratory.'

'Anything else?'

'He and his brother were in prison in Morocco two years ago with Mounir el-Motassadeq, who was involved in the

145

9/11 New York attack. I am told they were radicalised there. When they came back to Amsterdam last year, they had changed a lot.'

'Have you seen them regularly since then?' Ali hoped not.

'No. They come from the Rif region and mostly mixed with people from there. I think he only contacted me about karkoubi in the hope I would introduce him to medical students who are well known for experimenting with drugs.'

'What is his name? I won't contact him now, but it might be useful at some point,' Ali asked, wondering if Mohamed would give it.

'Yashine Abu-Zoubeir, and his brother is Hamid,' Mohamed answered without hesitation.

'Thanks, Mohamed. That is most useful. I appreciate your help.'

'It's a pleasure, Uncle. Let me know if I can help further. I only have a slight knowledge of this drug, but what I do know is all bad.'

Ali could now relax. 'So how are your studies going, Mohamed?' he asked. 'Your father says that you are a star student!'

Chapter 13

The next day Ahmed Abadi took Ali to the Mamouche, one of the most revered Moroccan restaurants in Amsterdam. Before this they had spent the afternoon at the highly popular Rembrandt exhibition at the Rijksmuseum, and before that visited Madame Tussauds with Ahmed's family.

It was the 31st of December. As the day went on, more and more people appeared on the streets. When Ali commented on this, Ahmed explained it was like this every weekend throughout the year, but as this was New Year's Eve, there were more than ever out and about.

Ahmed had booked the restaurant for six. They were not interested in being caught up in the parties that would be everywhere later. Arriving a few minutes early, they ordered mint tea and an assortment of Moroccan appetisers, including squid and quinoa tagine, a Mamouche specialty. As they had not seen each other for a year, for the next two hours their plan was simply to catch up.

Within minutes of placing their order, there was a huge bang, followed by another, then two more almost simultaneously. The windows in the restaurant shattered as crockery, cutlery and bottles on tables fell to the floor and smashed into smithereens.

Ahmed and Ali instinctively scrambled under their table, braced their bodies, and clasped their hands above their heads. Amsterdam had suffered its first-ever terrorist attack.

****

Because every day is always busy with cyclists in Amsterdam, the evening before the attack, Yashine and his three male co-conspirators each took a normal bicycle to

Dam Square and left it chained to one of the bike racks he had chosen as the perfect position for their assault, ensuring that each bicycle filled with explosives would be in the right place the next day. Also, they would have instantly available transport to make their return journey.

The following morning, at different times, they went to Yashine's home where he had made and stored the bicycle bombs. They then cycled different routes to Dam Square. Once they had left the bicycles in their designated places, they sent a text to Yashine confirming it. He then took the last bicycle, aiming to leave it in the place near Madame Tussauds where he had left his normal bicycle yesterday. When he got there, he found that his bicycle had disappeared, presumably stolen overnight.

Since he could hardly report this to the police, he retreated to the side of the Madame Tussauds building, making sure his face was never in view of a nearby camera. There he waited for someone to remove a bicycle so he could use their space. A few minutes later a young woman arrived who did exactly the same, except she waited next to the cycle racks.

By the time a man turned up to move his bicycle, Yashine had grown tense. So instead of politely telling the woman he had been there before her and waited a short distance away, he spoke to her harshly and pushed her out of the way when she began to argue. As it happened, the man moving his bicycle was Moroccan, and as it is common for Arabic men to treat women with disrespect, dealing with the situation was relatively easy. Yashine left more or less contented that his mission had been accomplished.

After checking the positions of the bicycles left by his friends, and satisfied all was in order, he got on a bus to Schiphol airport, aiming to arrive before 16-00. Without telling anyone, the previous evening he had changed the plan for himself. He booked a Royal Air Maroc flight at 18-40 to Tangier and that was where he was now heading.

All the way to the airport, the wrongness of what he was doing to his brother and friends caused his anxiety levels to rise and rise. He hoped that once he was on the other side of airport security, his fear would lessen, and he would calm down.

For convenience all he carried was a small, light backpack. To make travelling as simple as possible, he had chosen to wear a ski jacket with lots of pockets. He had two mobile phones, each with its own sim card. To make sure the settings on both were still correct, as soon as he was in the terminal he went to a toilet, checking again their battery strength and clock times. After that he headed for security.

At the entrance he knew there would be bins to deposit items that could not be taken through the barriers. Having carefully wrapped the phone that he had synchronised to detonate the bombs in toilet paper, he deposited it in one of them. Then he walked through security, now even more nervous but satisfied all was in order.

Once through, every minute for the next hour seemed like an eternity. Three times he had to go to the toilet and on the last occasion the sight of blood on the toilet paper frightened him even more. The answer, he decided, was something to calm him down. He knew alcohol would do that. But could he dare risk it as it might impair his judgement? He decided he could. Anything was better than the frenzy that was going on in his head.

As he stood at the bar waiting to order two large vodkas, he had the shock of his life. A firm tap on his shoulder caused him to freeze and his hair to stand on end.

'Hi, Yashine, do you remember me? I'm Nadia's friend from London, Fatima. We met in Casablanca last year.' The gorgeous young woman beamed at him, clearly pleased to see him.

Never in his life had Yashine been so afraid. 'I'm sorry,' he said, knowing she must have been surprised by his reaction. 'I thought you were someone else. Of course, I remember you.'

In the instant before he knew who it was, he thought he had been spotted by a security guard depositing the phone in the bin. Or, his Muslim beliefs told him, it was a messenger from Allah come to chastise him for ordering alcohol.

As his heart stopped racing and his mind cleared, he managed to say, 'I was about to order coffee. Would you like one?'

'That would be lovely. But what are you doing here? I thought you were with Nadia in Amsterdam.'

This time on the back foot for another reason, Yashine had to think quickly. But now his mind was clearer, he was able to respond. 'An issue with my family in Tangier came up this morning and I need to go there urgently. That's why I am travelling light.' He pointed to his bag. 'If I have to stay more than a few days, she will join me and bring more of my things.'

'I hope it's not serious,' Fatima said.

'I will know more when I get there,' he said, relieved he had got out of this tricky situation. Also, for at least the time being he was not obsessing about the situation in Dam Square.

'How are Hamid and Mariam? Are they still together?' she asked.

'Yes. We see a lot of them. I was with them earlier today before coming here. So, what are you going to do in

Tangier? Do you know anyone there?' he asked, trying to change the subject.

'My uncle and aunt live there and have invited me to stay for two weeks. I travelled via Amsterdam yesterday as I had to see my sister who lives here.'

'Maybe we can see you in Tangier if Nadia comes. She would like that,' Yashine said, feeling safer.

'That would be great. They live in Asilah, which is quite near. There are trains every day, so I am sure we could.'

For the next forty-five minutes they talked, with Yashine frequently looking at his watch. After a while, Fatima asked quizzically, smiling at the same time, 'Are you a nervous flyer? You are always looking at your watch. And the way you reacted when I touched you means you must have been wired up.'

First embarrassed, then realising this was also an opportunity, Yashine responded, 'I am. In the time before take-off, I always worry. Once we are in the air, I'm better.'

'You are silly, Yashine. I will be there to look after you. Maybe we should ring Nadia. I am sure she would be pleased to know I am looking after you in your hour of need.' She winked, giving a seductive smile.

This was the last thing Yashine needed. He didn't want anyone, especially Nadia, to know where he was. He laughed, then replied in a similar flirtatious manner, 'I think she might be jealous. She knows I find you attractive. Ever since we met, I hoped I would get to know you better. Now I have that chance, I don't want to spoil it. Let's enjoy our time together. I will contact her tonight.'

'Okay. When you speak to her, give her my love. I really like her,' Fatima answered, happy to talk but deciding not to flirt anymore. Yashine seemed to need little encouragement in that department.

A few minutes later it was announced it was time to go to their boarding gate: it was now 17-45. As Yashine wanted to be alone for the next thirty minutes, he made an excuse about needing the toilet and said he would meet her at the gate. He stood up quickly, giving her little time to respond. just managing to say, 'Don't worry. You will be all right.'

Having already established the direction to go, and how long it would take to get there, he knew his timing was perfect. Eight minutes later he was in the nearest toilet to the gate, three minutes after that he had everything ready.

The first thing he did was send a signal to activate the phone he had left near security. Once this was done, he set a pause of two minutes before that phone sent signals one second apart to each of the four devices in Dam Square that would trigger the detonators hidden in the bicycles. His only concern after this was that he would not know if they had exploded until he reached Morocco.

****

'What the hell is going on?' Ahmed said, moments after the four explosions that caused hm and his brother to drop to the floor.

But Ali did not answer. He was too busy asking himself the same question and saying silent prayers. A short time after the fourth explosion, he started to get up. As he did so, he said, 'Are you okay, Ahmed? I am sure those were bombs, and not too far away.'

'I'm sure they were too. Let's get out of here. There may be more,' Ahmed agreed.

'I have to see what's happening. We've been dreading terrorist attacks in London for weeks. If that's what it was, I just hope Moroccans had nothing to do with them,' Ali said, deeply concerned.

'It was from the direction of the Royal Palace and Dam Square. I will come too. I know the way,' Ahmed answered, Ali's composed attitude making him feel more assured himself.

Almost immediately they stepped outside the restaurant the sound of police sirens, fire engines, ambulances and shop alarms that had been triggered could be heard in all directions. Streetlights were not working and the sound of people screaming in the distance could be heard; many were running in both directions. Already whatever had happened was causing more chaos to any city in the Netherlands since the Germans bombed Rotterdam in the Second World War.

Ali and Ahmed walked as quickly as possible, but were slowed down by the darkness and people coming towards them. At the flower market, about halfway there, they were stopped by police on one of the bridges. After asking what had happened, they were only a little wiser. It was clear no one knew, except that it was probably four bombs in, or near, Dam Square.

****

The flight to Tangier was two-thirds full. As there were two empty seats next to Yashine's aisle seat, Fatima asked to move alongside him, next to the window. This was bad news for Yashine as he wanted to keep his phone on to see if there were any announcements relating to Dam Square right up to take-off. Because he was so agitated, he turned it to silent.

After settling in, Fatima sent a text to her sister. The reply she received minutes later told Yashine all he needed.

'It seems there has been a bomb attack in Amsterdam.'

As Fatima read it, her mind raced back to Barcelona where she had been staying when terrorists struck there. A moment later, she thrust the phone into Yashine's hand and said, 'Oh my God, read this.'

He scanned the message quickly.

'It's terrible,' she said. 'God forbid it isn't Moroccans. I am sick of being tarred with a brush that applies only to a handful of sick extremists. I was in Barcelona when they struck there.'

Momentarily Yashine was lost for words. He was angry at her response, but knew he had to say something in the same sympathetic way. Otherwise his beliefs would be in the open and the flight to Tangier horrendous.

As excruciating fear flooded back to him, he turned almost white. He ventured to say as carefully as he could, 'I know how you feel. Sometimes on trains and buses I see people looking at me as if I am a leper.'

Just then the captain announced over the loudspeaker, 'I am sorry but there has been an incident in Amsterdam. It means our take-off time has been put back forty minutes. I will let you know if this changes.'

'That's all I need. I just want to get away from here,' Yashine muttered.

'Don't worry, we can't have an accident when we are grounded,' Fatima said, attributing his words to his fear of flying. 'I will keep my phone on until we take off and ask her to keep me updated.'

For the next few minutes Fatima did not help Yashine's anxiety as she talked about her experience in Barcelona and other recent bomb attacks in Europe where Moroccans were involved. He remained silent until she received another text. She read it out to him:

'It was in the centre of Amsterdam and there were several bombs. Probably a lot of people were killed and injured.'

This time more fear entered his mind, exacerbated because Fatima remarked, 'I wonder if we will take off at all.'

'I need to go to the toilet,' Yashine said, heading to the nearest facilities.

A few minutes later, Fatima received a third text from her sister.

'It was in Dam Square and there were four bombs. It seems a lot of people were killed and injured. Is your flight still leaving?'

'That's terrible,' she replied. *'I've met a Moroccan friend, so I'm travelling with him. He is devastated too. We are delayed until at least 19-15. I assume we will take off then.'*

By the time Yashine returned, Fatima had mulled over the texts and what he had said. Considering his responses, she thought he seemed to take their flight being delayed personally, even implying that their delay was more important than the bomb attacks.

As soon as he returned and sat down, she said, 'I've had another text from my sister. She says there were four bombs in Dam Square and she believes a lot of people are dead and injured.'

This time she listened more closely to his response and watched his face and body language.

'I am not surprised. I just want to get to Morocco. I have never felt at home here,' he said, a sheen of sweat on his forehead.

'What do you mean, you are not surprised?' she asked directly. 'But you do care about any deaths, the people who are injured and their families, I hope?'

'Of course,' he said, aware that she had scented something odd about his behaviour. 'I have this issue in Tangier on my

155

mind. If I don't get there tonight, it might be too late. ('PLEASE shut up and stop questioning me, Fatima!' a voice screamed inside his head.)

'Do you mean someone is very ill and might die?' she asked.

This time he could not hold back his emotions. 'That's right. Now please stop, Fatima, I don't want to talk about it. This is turning into the worst day of my life.'

But Fatima didn't stop; she was getting angry too.

'Well, you are not alone in that. Everyone in Amsterdam and most of the Netherlands will be saying the same. Especially those who've had loved ones murdered by terrorists. And why haven't you contacted Nadia? Surely you want to know if she is all right?'

That was too much for Yashine. He answered angrily, desperate to shut her up.

'Of course I care about Nadia. I called her from the toilet. She was with our friends and they are all alright. Now stop talking. I have just been sick. I am a nervous wreck.'

For the next few minutes, they sat in an uncomfortable silence. Then the captain came on again. He said, 'I am very sorry, but we have been grounded. All flights from Amsterdam have been stopped indefinitely. As soon as I have more information, I will let you know. In the meantime, stewards will serve complimentary refreshments.'

Immediately Yashine got up and headed back to the toilet. He could not stand the anxiety anymore. This time he did turn his phone on and waited until he was connected. As soon as it was, it signaled he had received ten messages: four from his brother, three from Nadia, one from each of the others, and one from Abdullah. They all said more or less the same thing, except Abdullah's.

His friends mostly said, *'An amazing result. Where are you?'*

But Abdullah's read, *'I heard the terrible news on the television. I hope you and your family are not affected. Please confirm you are all right. My friends and I will do anything we can to help.'*

Yashine wished he had not turned the phone on. It had turned from being the best day in his life to the worst. If Hamid and his friends found out what he had done, they would know he had betrayed them, and Abdullah could turn ISIS against him as well.

As he knelt on the floor with his arms on the toilet seat, he faced the wall and prayed out loud, 'Please, please, Allah, have the aeroplane take off or find me an answer to my problem. I did this in your name. Now I am the one suffering.'

By the time he got back to his seat, he had thought more about Abdullah's and the others' texts. As the bomb attacks had been so successful, maybe the wording of Abdullah's meant he was offering him an olive branch of protection. But why would he do that? How can I find out? he asked himself.

Just before he sat down, to stop Fatima going on from where she had left off, he made as if he was talking on the phone, speaking in Dutch to make sure she did not understand. Once he was settled, he sighed, put his head back and closed his eyes. He did not want any more interference to his terror-ridden state of mind.

Not long after, an answer to his earlier prayer came in the opposite way to that which he hoped. The captain announced, 'The incident in Amsterdam means that no planes are being allowed to leave here tonight. You will need to disembark. Your luggage will be sent to the baggage reclaim area. There you will be given a choice. Either you can return to your homes or you will get a voucher to stay in a nearby hotel. For those who still want to go to Tangier, our aim will be to leave as early as possible tomorrow. But at this time, I cannot guarantee that or when it will be.'

Desperate for inspiration, Yashine kept his eyes closed: This is the end of the world for me, he thought. It's Allah's punishment for my not choosing to die as a martyr. But why? I don't understand. The result of the attack was perfect. He gave me the skills and desire to do it. So why is he punishing me like this? I could do it many times more for him if he rescues me now.

His thoughts were interrupted by Fatima, who had calmed down. She said, 'That's an easy choice for me, I will stay in a hotel and go tomorrow. What will you do Yashine?'

Yashine, too busy with his thoughts, tried to listen for an answer to his questions to Allah. With no answer forthcoming, he replied with the intention of stalling Fatima, 'I am not sure. I need to speak to my family in Tangier. Then I will talk to Nadia again and decide after that.'

By now he realised that for the next few days security at Schiphol airport would be at least doubled, so the chance of his getting caught could be greater. He decided that if he took a bus into Amsterdam now and stayed in an Airbnb, he could contact Nadia and the others and persuade them that keeping away from him would minimise the likelihood of them being associated with him; especially desirable if his links to ISIS came to light. In addition, a night to reflect and study developments would be good.

Less than an hour later the passengers were ushered off the plane and told to wait in the same gate area they had used before boarding. Once there, a roll call was taken, after which they were escorted to baggage reclaim. There they received their luggage, and one by one, were offered a hotel room and given expense claim forms to cover compensation for their missed flights.

Once outside, Yashine boarded a number 197 bus to the centre of Amsterdam. He found an Airbnb near the Vondelpark perfect for his need and used the internet to book it. This at least helped his state of mind because he was now free of Fatima, and there was nothing on the news he now followed closely to suggest the police had any idea who had carried out the attack, although ISIS's name was mentioned. This helped him to conclude that his decision to carry out the attack independently had been a good one.

His new mood also helped him with his call to Nadia. As soon as she answered, he had his prepared words ready. He began by saying, 'Hi sweetheart, how are you? It is hard for me to talk because I am on a crowded bus.'

'Where are you? We've been worried sick you were caught, or something else happened.' She sounded almost tearful.

Yashine's immediate reaction was to laugh. Desperately, he tried to hide this from her and any listener nearby, realising the tension he was feeling. After that he replied, 'I know how you feel. I can't wait to be with you and have you in my arms. The flight from Warsaw was delayed. I think there was an incident in Amsterdam or something.'

This confused Nadia. But guessing it was because he needed to be cautious, she answered, 'I think I understand. I assume there are people who can hear you. Is that right?'

'Yes, that's right, darling.'

'Put what you want to tell me in a text,' she said. 'That way I can forward it to the others.'

Yashine now had the answer he had hoped for. Delay was what he wanted. He replied, 'A good idea. I'll do that soon.'

The call ended, Yashine composed what he thought was the perfect text. Then, reading it twice and editing it, he pressed send.

'There are a lot of police in the city, and I suspect they are stopping anyone who is Arab-looking. I will ring later and tell you where I am. Don't tell the others until we have spoken. Just tell them all is well, and I will see you all soon.'

She replied, *'I understand, and they will too. It was a wonderful result. I can't believe how well it went. We have booked our ticket to heaven.'* This was followed by what were to her appropriate emojis.

Nadia's text worried Yashine. Given its timing and insensitivity to the situation in Amsterdam right now, he realised that in some circumstances it could be incriminating. So he deleted it from his phone, along with every other message between them. After that he did the same with each of the other bombers, just in case there was something significant there too. After that he sent a bland reply to Abdullah to see what he had to say.

'Thanks for your offer of support. At the moment, my family and I are fine. What help did you have in mind? It would be useful to know in case we need it later.'

Not long after he got an answer.

'We can do anything you want. All you have to do is let me know and I will make sure your wishes are carried out. Your friends here love and admire you. We want only the best for you and your family.'

Yashine deleted this, along with the others to and from Abdullah.

Chapter 14

Jan Walvis was head of 'Dienst Speciale Interventies', the Dutch counter-terrorism equivalent of SWAT. The evening of the attacks in Dam Square, he was at home with his family. As the Netherlands had never had a serious terrorist attack, the likelihood of such an event was seldom on his mind. This meant he had not thought of such a disaster happening as he happily drank several glasses of nouveau Beaujolais at lunch that afternoon, followed later by schnapps.

When his number one officer, Chief Commissioner Martin Kuyt, rang with news of the terrorist incident, his first thought was that he hoped it would be minor, but as soon as he knew it was not, his second was that the amount of alcohol he had consumed meant he needed a driver to take him to the scene. And although this would mean a delay in leaving, it would give him time to think and clear his head; plus he could make phone calls en route.

On the way to Dam Square he was tempted to listen to the radio to get the latest news. However, he decided that as he had no direct experience of such an incident, it was better to remember all he had learned from his visits to Paris, Brussels and Barcelona after their attacks in previous years. Also, as the journey would take at least forty-five minutes, he had time to telephone Marcel Droulers, his friend and former head of the Belgian equivalent unit in Brussels, to ask his advice. By the time he arrived in Dam Square his head was clear and he had enough information to lead the enquiry.

The first thing Martin Kuyt had told him was that there were at least one hundred fatalities and many injured. The preliminary analysis suggested there had been four bombs, each placed in densely used parts of the square. After hearing this, and surveying the scene near Madame Tussauds where he was parked, he went to the Royal Palace, as from the top of the building he knew he would get the best possible view of the overall situation in the square.

Dam Square is more rectangular than square, and the Royal Palace is no longer lived in by the king and his family. It is situated near the centre, and during the day, because it is open to the public, invariably crowds gather in front of it, so Jan was not surprised this was the scene of one of the attacks. From a top-floor window overlooking the square, he was able to ascertain the extent of the damage.

In a very short time, he realised that as well as the many people being treated by medical personnel, and the scores of police officers, there were bicycle parts scattered everywhere, something he'd also noticed as he had walked across the square earlier. This, plus the sight of four small craters, reminded him that bicycles had been used for carrying explosives in the Vietnam war and by the IRA in the UK. It prompted him to say to Martin, 'I want to see each of the cameras that filmed proceedings prior to the attacks that focused on nearby bicycle racks. Get as many of those and close-ups as possible. After that, check for similarities of the types of bicycles, who put them there, and at what times in the twenty hours prior to the explosions. Check to see if there are any common threads. My hunch is that there will be. The explosives may have been attached to the bicycles or in their frames and handlebars, also there may have been small pieces of metal and nails used as shrapnel.'

Catching on immediately, Martin said, 'If that's the case, we might find they were left at the same time by several individuals, or one person spread over several hours. Either way, what the cameras show will be useful. I'll get onto it right away. Because of the size of the frames that would need, we are probably looking at mountain bikes.'

'Or electric, because of their extras. And make sure the media don't find out. If we are right, the last thing we want is mass hysteria relating to the million or so bicycles and cyclists we have in the city,' Jan said.

'Or in the Netherlands. There are twenty-three million. That's more than one per person,' Martin pointed out.

Back in the square, in front of the palace, Jan picked up several charred remains of bicycle parts and broken nails. After examining them, he handed them to Martin, saying, 'I want as many of these as possible collected from each scene and keep them separate. Then get forensics to see if any of them were in contact with explosives. I also want to know what type of device could trigger this. I assume it would be a mobile phone, and if that is the case, is there a way its location at the time can be traced and does that phone still exist? Now I need to prepare something to say to the press.'

Fifteen minutes later, Jan was standing in front of more than a hundred journalists, television cameras and photographers. Although he was used to speaking in public, he had no experience of anything to do with bomb attacks, or of anything on such a large scale. So, determined to say as little, and be as accurate as possible, he quickly made some notes. Reading directly from these, he said, 'At this time, there is very little I can tell you. That is partly because it is too soon to comment, but also we have too little information about the attack or who the victims are. As soon as we have more information, we will let you know. In respect of the victims' families, I will not answer questions and request that you do not speculate on the reasons for the attack or who the attackers were. Be assured we will do all we can to catch them as soon as possible. Thank you and good night.'

A babble of questions arose from the media. But Jan was ready for that and had already turned his back on them and was walking towards the middle of the square.

****

At about the time Jan Walvis gave his press statement, Ali Abadi was on the phone to Mohamed Tahir in London. As soon as the ambassador answered, Ali said, 'I am in Amsterdam. You have probably heard of the latest terrorist attack here about an hour ago. I was near enough to hear several bombs go off, but I don't have any details. I tried to get closer, but the police have cordoned off a large area with Dam Square in the middle.'

'Isn't that where the king's palace is?' the ambassador asked.

'Yes, but he and his family don't live there anymore. As it was New Year's Eve and early in the evening, there would have been tourists everywhere. I was there earlier today with my brother's family.'

Tahir sighed. 'Let's hope Moroccans are not involved. We have a good relationship with the Netherlands, especially with its ordinary people since our king paid an informal visit there in 2016.'

Ali did not answer. He remembered how that visit had disturbed his brother as he and many others thought King Mohammed's brief stay in Amsterdam had more to do with hedonism than anything else.

'What are your plans now?' Tahir asked.

'To stay here at least until the weekend. The more I find out the better. I am staying with my brother who speaks Dutch and is well connected. If I find out anything, I will let you know.'

'And vice versa. If you have even an inkling there is a Moroccan connection, you must let me know immediately. I am sure the British will want to know who the perpetrators were too. I don't want them knowing before me, and if it is Moroccans, I will need to let our prime minister know before they do.'

Even as these words came out of his mouth a spasm of fear went through his body, exacerbated, he knew, because of his previous meeting with the United Kingdom's defence secretary.

Chapter 15

As soon as I heard the news of the Amsterdam bomb attack, I went on the internet: first to book a one-way flight the following day to Amsterdam, then to do a search of the websites that would give me the most accurate up-to-date news. I also studied the videos and television news pictures taken in Dam Square at the time and immediately after the bombs went off.

The more research I did, the more I became convinced that the attacks' timing and location meant it could be the work of Moroccans based in the Netherlands. And if it was Moroccans, would it provide the perfect opportunity to expose all I knew and force Morocco's leaders to change their drug laws and policies?

At the same time, as I was doing my research, David Smith, the defence secretary was talking to the prime minister about the attack. They finished their call with the PM ordering him to call the Moroccan ambassador to summon him to another meeting, this time at No 10 Downing Street later that day. But his first call was to me.

He cut straight to the chase. 'I have spoken to the head of MI5 and the prime minister. We need to know if you think the attack in Amsterdam was carried out by Moroccans. In your letter you make it clear you expected more attacks. Our question is, is this likely to be one of them?'

'Right now,' I replied, 'I don't know. But by this time tomorrow I will. Last year I went to Amsterdam to start Narcotics Anonymous for Moroccans who live there. I know several of them quite well and one of them should know the answer, or they'll have a contact who does. I have booked a flight to Schiphol tomorrow morning.'

Seemingly pleased with my response, Smith said, 'Do you need support? We have our embassy in the Hague, and consulate in Amsterdam.'

'No. The people I talk to will be former drug addicts, so they were once criminals. The last thing they will do is talk if they think I am on some sort of policing mission,' I answered.

'I understand. You know that world better than me,' he said.

'And I know Moroccans,' I agreed.

'Indeed, you do. Contact me as soon as you know something. Anything else?'

Smith's friendliness opened the door for me to make the one request I had always hankered for.

'There is. You know from my letter to King Mohammed that the drug situation in Morocco is horrendous and affects many other countries. When the time is right, I want our government to do all it can to expose this. In exchange for your word to do that, within twenty-four hours I will give you chapter and verse of everything I learn about the bomb attacks.'

He would know from my years of commitment to helping drug addicts that I meant what I said. So, because he needed my help, and realising it could enhance his standing if there was a positive outcome, he replied, 'I cannot commit to anything. However, if you get the kind of information we both hope for, and Moroccans are involved, I will do everything I can to help you. After all, it's in everybody's best interest, including Morocco's.'

At nine o'clock the following morning, Amsterdam's Schiphol airport reopened. Some of the early planes to land were KLM's City Hoppers from London's City airport. I was on the first of them.

I had booked into the American hotel, an easy walk to Dam Square. In the taxi from the airport to the hotel I called five of my Moroccan contacts in Amsterdam and arranged to meet each of them, most especially Nasser Mubarak, who worked at a drug rehabilitation centre. He was the best-connected former Moroccan drug addict I knew living there. Over coffee Nasser confirmed my suspicions: as there were so many Moroccans living in the Netherlands and Amsterdam, the attacks were most likely committed by one or more who had links to ISIS. Then he told me something I did not know that made me doubly convinced.

'In the past few weeks, we've had addicts at the centre on karkoubi. Who the dealers are I don't know, but it should be easy to find out. My assumption is that it is trafficked from Morocco via Spain and France along established cannabis routes.'

'If karkoubi is here, I am not surprised Amsterdam's had an attack. If we can trace who sells it and where it comes from, we might get some enlightening answers,' I said, hoping the net was closing.

'Although I don't like pointing the finger at my countrymen, I know we have to try to stop karkoubi reaching Europe. I took it in Morocco, and on one occasion, I became so angry I threatened my mother and sister with a knife. If I had taken more, I am sure I would have used it,' Nasser said.

'Just the thought of that drug spreading is horrific. We have to do all we can to stop it,' I replied.

'I trust you, so I won't ask you what you have in mind. But I need to be sure that if I give you any names, you will do all you can to protect the Moroccan community here. As you know from the success of NA, not all Netherlands-based Moroccan drug users are bad people. The probability is there are only a handful of people involved, and they may not be Moroccan. The vast majority of Muslims I know who live here are as peace-loving as you and I.'

I was convinced Nasser said this to make the best case he could for me to remain open-minded. I answered, 'I give you my word. Our interests are the same, to help drug addicts recover, and this awful situation may be a vehicle to help us do that.'

We concluded our meeting soon after, agreeing to meet or speak on the phone that evening.

During the rest of the day, I met my other Moroccan contacts in Amsterdam. Each knew about karkoubi being available there, but because they all attended NA and were clean of drugs, none had any direct contact with it. From what I learned, I ascertained it had only been there a few months.

When Nasser came to my hotel early that evening, he was so excited that at first what he said did not make sense.

I know where it comes from, who the dealers are, how much it costs and how long it has been here. Most importantly, I know where I can buy some tonight if I want to.'

Slow down, Nasser. What do you mean, where 'it' comes from? I assume you mean karkoubi? And surely it comes from Morocco?'

No. The main karkoubi ingredient here is made in Spain and shipped to Amsterdam once a month in fruit containers,' he answered.

Are you sure? It would mean the whole of Europe is under threat if it's true,' I said. This was not good news.

It's true. I was as surprised as you are. I don't know the exact location it's made, but I can probably find out. Users pay up to five euros a pill; in Morocco it costs one.'

'That means there is a big enough price difference to attract other suppliers. With the profits that would provide, it will attract the mafia. Ever since I heard about it, I have dreaded something like this would happen. God forbid it is not too late to stop it. If Amsterdam's Mocro-Maffia gets hold of it, it could start a drug war.'

I was now more worried than I had ever been. AuJackatically, I leaned back in my chair, closed my eyes, and prayed for guidance. After a few moments, much to my surprise, Nasser expressed his concerns with all the passion only a Moroccan who loves his country and countrymen could.

'Why, oh why, did our king and politicians let this happen to our wonderful country and people? Why haven't they done something about it? They know the tragedies karkoubi has caused. The king claims to be a direct descendent of the prophet Mohammed, but if Moroccans are involved in this, because it's the policies he presides over that allowed it to happen, no one will believe that. We have known this was likely ever since Madrid and Barcelona, and all the other attacks in between where Moroccans were involved.'

To take in what he said and depth of feeling with which he had said it, I thought for several moments. Then I said, 'Your king has done much good since he inherited the throne, but Morocco's problems with drugs and poverty are massive. Unfortunately, due to lack of understanding of their causes, the measures in place haven't improved them. This is mostly because they were not dealt with by people with the right experience, and some may have their own agendas. Now it is only radical reforms that will address the issue. I still hope Moroccans aren't involved, but given what we know, I don't think that's likely.'

170

My mind wandered to thoughts I'd had many times since I had gone to live in Tangier.

Maybe, this is God's way of revealing the path to resolve Morocco's drug problems. Every cloud has a silver lining, and if that were to happen here, the butterfly effect could have wondrous repercussions; after all, that is what He has done for many addicts and their families in other countries. So, why not now Morocco?

I did not say this out loud. Instead, I suggested we met again tomorrow and to ring each other if there was any new news.

Chapter 16

As well as a permanent webcam, Dam Square has an abundance of cameras covering it. To examine every moment of the footage of each for the twelve hours before the bombs went off, Jan Walvis ordered a team of officers, led by Chief Inspector Ilsa Lund, to examine them.

Jan's non-racist principles would have prevented him from telling CI Haggar to look out for anyone of Arabic origin acting suspiciously, but in this instance there was also another reason he found that difficult. Although Ilsa had lived in the Netherlands all her life and was a most accomplished police officer, her parents were Moroccan. However, this was precisely who Ilsa believed her team should be looking for and what she would say to each of them individually after she had given them the same instructions.

Ilsa loved Morocco and her heritage. She knew it well having visited it many times to see the rest of her family who still lived there. At home she had learned Darija, the Moroccan Arabic dialect, and although her parents practised Islam, she did not. Until the age of eighteen, she had worn a hijab, but since then she only wore one on special Muslim occasions. On visits to Morocco, she enjoyed wearing a mixture of traditional Moroccan and European clothes. So, other than her jet-black hair and medium dark skin, most of the time she looked and sounded European, while deep in her heart was a love of Morocco and Moroccans.

From an early age she had wanted to be a policewoman. The fact that she was highly intelligent and worked hard meant she quickly rose through the lower police ranks. Nine months ago, aged thirty-five, she had become the youngest female chief inspector in the Dutch police force.

The main fear Ilsa had in her job had always been that because of the rise of the Mocro-Maffia in the Netherlands, and Moroccan involvement in global terrorism, some of her countrymen would commit a terrorist attack in Holland which she would have to investigate. As there are 400,000 Moroccans living in the Netherlands, and there had been no such attack there to date, she believed the odds of there being one was a distinct possibility. And if that were to happen, it would tarnish the reputation of the many good Moroccans who lived there.

'I don't think we are looking for suicide bombers,' she told her team. 'My view is this was a well-planned, coordinated attack using bicycle bombs, detonated from elsewhere. It has ISIS, one of its cells, or some similar terrorist group written all over it.'

Several times, in the next few hours, each person examining the camera videos thought they had found something of interest. But after scrutiny, only one incident seemed potentially interesting. This was when a minor scuffle broke out at one of the bicycles stands just after one o'clock, a peak time for tourists to be in the vicinity.

The footage showed a woman who had been waiting for several minutes being prevented from parking her bike in a newly available space by a man who seemed to have just arrived. He had pushed her out of the way and taken the space. As he seemed to threaten more physical force when she argued with him, a man and woman passing by verbally intervened, but as another space became available the issue was resolved and the altercation ended.

Other than that, on the rest of the video footage there seemed nothing significant.   This   was   reported   to   CI

Haggar, who watched the bicycle fracas several times in slow motion, then still by still.

The first thing she noticed was that the man seemed to know the location of the camera overlooking this particular area as he always kept his back to it. The woman, though, did the opposite and would be easily distinguishable. This was because she often faced the camera and her multi-coloured hair and yellow luminescent cycling vest would make her easy to identify, especially as the words   'Stay   Calm: Just Do It' were boldly printed on the back.

Another camera picked her up moments afterwards going into a nearby coffee shop, where she stayed until she returned to move her bicycle two hours later. From the naturalness with which she went there, CI Haggar thought there was a good chance she could be a regular and known there. So she delegated two officers to go to the coffee shop with photographs of the woman and find out anything they could about her.

Next, she reviewed the man's movements from the moment he came into view of the cameras. Once he had put his bicycle in the rack and secured it, he removed the battery and saddle bag. He then took something out of a pocket that he seemed to fit under the saddle. As removing batteries and saddlebags was commonplace to prevent them being stolen, it was the man's other action that seemed unusual. To most people it would have gone unnoticed.

'From now on we are looking for someone parking similar or identical electric mountain bicycles to that of the man's, any time between 12 and 14-00. Anyone you see doing that, let me know immediately, especially if they seem to put something under the saddle.'

In the next hour and a half, the team discovered there had been four electric mountain bicycles parked in that time which looked identical to the one parked by the man. But as none had the person who left them put anything under the saddle bag, it was assumed there may be no connection and it was merely coincidental.

Further study of the video stills revealed that the bicycle in question was an Ancheer, one of the cheapest on the market. A member of the team had one and recognised it. He pointed out there was no need to use the battery in Amsterdam as it is flat, so anyone using one would only need to use pedal power. He added that electric mountain bikes in Central Amsterdam were very rare, so for four to be left there in such a short time was unusual. When asked where he'd bought his, the answer was unhelpful as it was on eBay from a man in The Hague.

Based on this line of thinking, Haggar ordered them to fast forward each of the appropriate cameras to 17-30. Each camera's video recordings were then scrutinised to see if any bicycles had been moved in that time. After that they checked to see if they were still there just before the bombs went off at 18-00.

After assessing the results, she asked for the best possible close-ups of each person who had left these bicycles, especially their faces and clothes and anything that might show their ages and who they might be. She also told them to check body language for signs of strange behaviour, anything that seemed odd; were they in a hurry, on their own, which direction did they go when they left the square?

There had to be some things they could work with to ascertain who they were.

At the time her colleagues were looking at individual camera footage, three of her team were also watching the square's permanent webcam recordings. To begin with they were too overwhelmed by the horrendousness of what they saw to do proper analysis, but after replaying them several times, especially in slow motion from the moment the first bomb went off to the fourth, they had a clearer understanding of what had happened. The one problem was that the webcams only took film of portions of the square at any one time. They had to manually piece together the film sequences needed to make the bigger picture effective.

Once this was done, the result was amazing, but not as helpful as Haggar hoped. This was because the many people coming and going in every direction, plus cyclists, trams and vehicles, were not involved in the attacks, though they were the main contributors to the awfulness of what was to happen when the bombs exploded. Finally, dust and debris blocked out much of what took place, and afterwards the square was littered with rubble as well as body and bicycle parts, while several of the best-placed cameras had stopped working.

As soon as Haggar had assimilated everything she could, she called her team together. She did not need a script; given how angry she felt it was easy for her to know exactly what she was going to say.

Her first order was to check what the webcams that were available showed in the four hours before the attack and after. With regard to the latter, her hope was that someone involved had returned to the scene to witness the devastation they had caused. People who did this sort of thing were renowned for revelling in such glory.

Then she said, 'Take close-ups of the bicycles to check if they are rentals. If not, find out who stocks those particular bicycles and if anyone sold one or more recently to a single cusJacker. Spread your wings all over Amsterdam. We don't know where the assassins live or if they were here temporarily. I suspect the former, but if it was temporary, they had probably been here for at least a month. For something like this to work, I am convinced at least one of them is local, speaks Dutch and knows Amsterdam well.'

She paused for thought, then added more venomously, 'We are going to get these assassins, whoever they are. I grew up in Amsterdam and love my city. If the killers are still here, I want them behind bars and suffering as much as possible, as soon as possible. We need to do this quickly. Show the world Dutch people are not men and women who sit around looking at windmills, smoking pot, growing poppies or painting masterpieces all day. We have the courage and determination of Anne Frank. No one comes here and murders our citizens without paying for their crimes in the most punitive way.'

By now she was so steamed up she ended with a rousing rallying call, shouting and raising her arm, 'Let's get the bastards. I want hourly reports and if you find anything that seems important, let me know immediately. I will have my phone on 24/7, so you can contact me any time.'

One of her officers handed out lists of the bicycle shops in each of Amsterdam's seven districts, while she directed them to work in twos and carry out interviews of as many shop staff as possible in every type of bicycle shop.

CI Ilsa Lund's enthusiasm and anger were not lost on her colleagues, most of whom felt the same. All were Dutch, most had grown up in Amsterdam and loved the city and their country as much as she did, so, when they left the briefing, they were in tune with her feelings and attitude.

In the time before the shops closed for the night, nearly half the cycle shops had been seen. Most sold electric bicycles, but none sold the model that featured in the photographs, and none had sold more than one of any type at a time. All they could do now was wait until the other shops opened the following day.

****

Just before entering the coffee shop near Dam Square visited by the woman in the yellow vest, Bianca van Dyck, the older of the two officers, said to her colleague, 'I know this place. I used to come here with my brother when I was a student twelve years ago. If it's the same owner, he will remember me, so let me do the talking.'

The coffee shop, although it was quite dark inside, looked the same as it had on her numerous previous visits: oblong wooden tables facing inwards along both sides of a room with four to six young people sitting at each smoking cannabis, drinking coffee and talking. Most seats were taken, which meant the aroma of cannabis filled the air, bringing back pleasant memories to Bianca.

The man serving at the counter was Pieter van den Broek, who recognised Bianca immediately.

'What a lovely surprise! Why have you stayed away so long? Everyone always comes back to see me sometimes, but not you!' he exclaimed with genuine pleasure.

Bianca had always liked Pieter and was delighted he remembered her so fondly. Then, recalling the reason why they were there and the seriousness of the situation, she answered, 'It is good to see you, too, Pieter, but I am with the police now, and that's why we are here.'

'I was told you had joined. I suppose you are here about the bombs. What do you want to know? I will do anything I can to help,' Pieter replied.

Bianca showed him the photograph of the woman in the yellow vest and asked, 'Do you recognise this woman? She came here around one p.m. yesterday.'

'I do,' he said without hesitation. 'Her name is Eva de Jong. She used to help me sometimes. Now she comes here to see friends.'

'Do you know where I can contact her?' Bianca asked.

'Yes, but she won't have had anything to do with this. She is a vegan. The last thing she would do is harm an insect, let alone people,' Pieter said.

'We hope she can help us, that's all. Something happened to her before she arrived that might be useful,' Bianca replied gently, to reassure him.

'I have her number on my phone and her address will be in our office records. I'll get them for you,' he volunteered.

Once outside, Bianca relayed this information to CI Ilsa Lund, who responded, 'Text me her address and I'll meet you there in twenty minutes. Do not contact her before I get there.' At Eva de Jong's home, she replayed in her mind lessons based on her counter-terrorism training at the Hague Centre for Strategic Studies the previous year. There she had learned that when it comes to terrorism, the perpetrators are so sophisticated that what seems obvious and real is not always the truth.

'I will do the talking,' she told Bianca as they waited for Eva de Jong to open the door. 'I'm going to ask her open questions, so she isn't led by what we think we know. Is that understood? You only come in if I ask you to at the end.'

'It is. My father used to say that it is often better to take the cotton wool out of your ears and put it in your mouth!' Bianca replied.

'I am going to word my questions in a way that I hope means she will bring up the issue with the bicycle, not me,' Ilsa said.

The door opened, and after a brief statement and show of their identity cards on the steps, Eva invited them inside. By the time they were seated in a simply furnished living room, Ilsa had noticed that Eva seemed nervous, more than most people she called to see at their homes in her line of duty. As a result, she began by saying in a quiet tone, 'We are making enquiries about the bomb attack in Dam Square. We know you were there for a few hours before it happened and wondered if you saw anything suspicious.'

Eva shook her head. 'No, I didn't. I went to see some friends in a coffee shop where I used to work near the square, that was all,' she answered hastily.

'Did you see anything, or did anything happen to you that was unusual?' Ilsa probed, still gently.

After a few moments, Eva answered. 'Well, there was one thing, but I don't imagine it has any relevance.'

'What was that?'

'I had been waiting for a place to put my bike at a stand in the area I always use. Then, as someone was about to move their bike, a man came and pushed me out of the way and took my space,' Eva replied.

'Did you speak to him?'

'Only to say I had been waiting therefore the space was mine. But he swore at me in Arabic, then said in Dutch he was in a hurry and that the space was his.'

'Did the person who was removing his bicycle try to help you?' Ilsa asked.

'No, he didn't. I think they might have known each other. They spoke in Arabic. In fact, it was Darija, a Moroccan dialect. I lived in Casablanca for a year and got to know the accent.'

'Did they look Moroccan or Arabic?'

'They looked North African. I find it hard to tell the difference. But I did not get a good look at them, I was too afraid. I know what such men can be like to women. As soon as the one taking my place became aggressive, I deliberately avoided eye contact.'

'Would you recognise them if you saw them again?' Ilsa asked hopefully.

'I am not sure. I was so frightened, I tried not to stare.' Eva answered timidly, clearly not enjoying being reminded of all that happened less than two hours after she had left the scene of the most horrendous terrorist attack in Europe since the recent Barcelona atrocity.

'This is very helpful, Miss de Jong, and thank you. It would be good if you come to Centrum Amstel police station this afternoon between three and four o'clock and look at some photographs. I will also arrange for you to see the incident with the bicycles which was caught on camera. It may remind you of something; especially your idea that they knew each other.'

As soon as they were outside, Bianca said to Ilsa, 'Let's hope we have the face of the other man on the video. I looked at it several times and cannot recall if we do. I was too focused on the man who took Eva de Jong's space.'

'To begin with, I was the same,' Ilsa said. 'But the third time I watched it I noticed the two men had a brief verbal exchange, and the second man, for a moment, I think was in full view.'

'I hope you are right,' Bianca said. 'That would be good.'

'If we can find the man who took that stand, and that other man, we may have some of the answer. I had the impression that although she was scared, she would help us as much as possible.'

Back at Centrum Amstel, the first thing Ilsa did was go through the video of Eva de Jong's bicycle incident. When she got to the part where the altercation occurred, she paused and went through it frame by frame. To her delight, she was right: they had a full-frontal image of the second man, who was almost definitely of Arabic descent.

Armed with this information, Ilsa telephoned Jan Walvis with an update. He told her to contact the Live Facial Recognition unit at the Dutch national police headquarters in The Hague where he had once worked.

The woman she spoke to there, told her to send the photographs to them and they would check through the 1.3 million people on their database to see if one of them was the man in question. Less than an hour later the answer came through.

'We don't have a record of him. Our database only covers people suspected of committing a crime which would have a jail sentence of at least four years. As it is considered by many to be invasive of people's privacy, we are restricted in its use.'

'In that case, what do you suggest?' Ilsa asked, frustrated by this information. 'It's very important we interview this man as soon as possible. We think he will have vital information to help with our enquiries regarding the bomb attack.'

'Ask your boss who he knows at the American embassy. The US government has much more on this. They have something called "Iarpa Janus" which the CIA uses.'

'Thanks. I will.'

As she ended the call, she remembered she had heard of this and that it was named after Janus, the two-faced Roman god. There was a contact who might be able to help.

Ilsa had been to private functions at the US embassy when she'd worked in The Hague ten years before. At one of these she had met, and soon after, had an affair with the senior attaché to the ambassador. His name was Thomas Reynard and the affair had ended eighteen months later when she moved to Amsterdam, and he went back to Washington.

After checking the time difference to make sure he would be up, she sent Jack an SMS message asking him to ring her.

'Hi Jack, it's urgent. Contact me as soon as you can. I need your help with a work issue. I hope you are well. Ilsa'

As she scrolled through previous texts and photographs between them on WhatsApp, memories flooded back, and she realised how much she had enjoyed their all-too-brief relationship. By the time he replied, she was wishing they were still together, and that their work had not torn them apart, as now she was single, forty years old and had not met anyone she liked as much in the years since they'd parted.

'Will call in ten minutes,' he replied a few minutes later.

Ilsa brought her thoughts back to the matter in hand. Her emotional issues would have to wait. She remembered that Americans like Jack went straight to the point; so, when he rang, she knew there would be no preliminaries.

'Hi Ilsa, it's good to hear from you. I got your message. What's going on? You said it is urgent.'

'It's good to hear from you too. I'm sure you've heard about the terrorist attack in Amsterdam. Well, there were two witnesses to something that happened before who may be able to help with our enquiries. Our police only do face recognition of people with serious criminal records, and we don't have any for one of them, a man. I believe your Iarpa Janus system may have something as it has many people of

Arabic origin in its bank. If I send you what we have, can you help?'

'Is this official or unofficial?'

'Unofficial and official. I'm leading the enquiry, but human rights groups here say Face Recognition banks are invasive. So you can decide. What I will say is we need it badly and my boss told me to find out who he is.'

'Send me the photos and I will see what I can do. Anything else?'

Ilsa's answer was an auJackatic 'No', but even as she said it, she was wishing she could add, 'I have missed you.' But this was police work and in her world that always came first.

'I will get someone onto it right away and get back to you. Do you have any other information? It would help if you can narrow it down,' he asked.

'Probably Arabic of Moroccan origin. We have a lot from there who live here, over 400,000, so he is probably one of them. We don't suspect him of anything, but he was in the right place at the right time to have seen something.'

'That helps.' Then to her surprise, he added, 'Let's catch up when I am in Amsterdam. I was going to contact you and let you know I plan to come there. It would be good to see you.'

'Let me know the dates. I will make sure I have some free time,' she blurted out, overjoyed.

'I haven't fixed them yet, but it will be soon. All you have to do is say you are single, would like to see me, and I will be there. Who knows, I might even be able to help you with your case. You will recall I was at the US embassy in Rabat before I went to The Hague.'

'My God, I had forgotten that' Ilsa said. 'Yes, I am single, and it would be lovely to see you.'

'Great! I'll book my flight and hotel right now.'
Ilsa longed to say he could stay with her, but she resisted. The memory of the last time they had been together and the tears that flowed stopped her. Earlier that week he had told her his time living abroad was over, and he wanted to settle in the country where he thought his heart was. He'd asked her to go with him, but she had declined. At that time, her career was foremost in her mind.

Chapter 17

After completing an identity sketch with a police forensic artist of the man who took her space at the bicycle stand, Bianca van Dyck asked Eva again about his voice.

'As I told you, it all happened so fast, I don't remember. I just know he spoke in Arabic to the other man, and in Dutch to me. I am sorry, but that's all I can recall.'

'When he spoke Dutch, did he have an Arabic accent? It could be useful to know if he had lived here all his life,' Bianca asked, encouraging her to remember as much as possible.

'I think he had, but I am not sure. His aggressive attitude frightened me, so I was more concerned for my safety. Some Arabic men can be quite violent with women, I remember from my time in Morocco.'

Bianca made no comment. 'Let's look at the video of the incident again,' she said, 'and see if it reminds you of anything you haven't already thought of. I will start at normal speed. Tell me to stop or slow down whenever you want to.'

When it reached the point just after she was pushed, Eva asked Bianca to replay the last few frames slowly, then frame by frame. The more she looked at it, the more she came to think the men may have known each other. At the time she had been distracted because she had been using her phone, but now she remembered the one whose space she was going to take had spoken to the other man before he pushed past her.

Bianca watched it closely several more times, wondering if the encounter could have been pre-planned; and if it was, were they involved in the bomb attack?

Having this particular bicycle in this precise position was presumably important to the terrorist attack. She called Ilsa.

As soon as Ilsa Lund arrived the three of them watched this part of the video together. After discussing this possibility, Ilsa told Eva she could leave and thanked her for her cooperation. Then she told her not to speak to anyone about it, and if she thought of anything else, to contact her immediately. Lastly, she asked her if she had any questions.

'Only one. Do you think they can trace me? I live alone, and after a bad experience with a man who attacked me in my flat in Rabat, I have been nervous at night. I was fortunate then because at the time I was dog-sitting for a friend's two dogs who frightened him off.'

"From the video footage, I don't think either of them looked at you enough to recognise you. But if you have any doubts, go and stay with someone for a few nights. Also, buy a different cycling vest. Your yellow one is very distinctive. Whatever you decide to do, make sure you let me know where you are. Officer van Dyck will take you home and you can take her number as well.'

Soon after Bianca and Eva had left, Ilsa received a text from Jack.

'I have some of the information you want. Ring me as soon as you can.'

That took less than two minutes. The information from Eva de Jong and the wording of Jack's text triggered an adrenalin rush through Ilsa's already excited nervous system.

'What took you so long?' was Jack's reaction. 'I thought Moroccan girls like you play hard to get.'

Ilsa laughed. 'Yeah, well, this is different. Anyway, I'm a Dutch citizen. We thrive on punctuality. I just had some good news from a female witness and hopefully you have some too.'

'I do. Your man is well known to our people. He travels a lot and we have kept a file on him ever since he left Casablanca two years ago.'

'Excellent. What do you have? Name, age, address?' Ilsa asked.

'Name and age, yes, address, no. Last known was when he returned to his former home in El Hoceima when he left prison in Casablanca. He stayed there three months, after that we know he went to the Netherlands. So I am sure you have something on him. He has been a criminal half his life and Interpol must have a file on him as well,' Jack answered.

'Thanks. I will check it out with them. Anything else?'

'I am arriving in Amsterdam tomorrow night. I told my boss the situation and he agreed I should leave pronto. I did not tell you I was seconded for nine months to Homeland Security last year. When it comes to terrorism, the US will go to any lengths to nail anyone who might threaten us.'

'Wow, that's quick and great news! Let me know your flight time and I will try to meet you at the airport,' Ilsa said, overcome.

'For security reasons I have to fly to Volkel Air Base which our air force uses for missions like this,' Jack said. 'If my flight is on time, I will get into Amsterdam in the morning in time for breakfast. I am staying at a small hotel I know near the Rijksmuseum. We can meet there.'

'Okay; send me details. Given the way this is going, I am hopeful we will know more about who the terrorists are very soon.' Ilsa said. 'So far, it looks as though they are

Moroccans who might have links to ISIS or another jihadist group.'

'Do you have any other ideas? I am wondering about links to drugs, since the cannabis smoked in Amsterdam's coffee shops is almost exclusively Moroccan,' Jack said, keen to find out all he could before he arrived.

'Our police recently found out a drug cocktail called karkoubi is being used here; it is widely used in Morocco, but here it seems its main ingredient comes from Spain. It is believed it has sometimes been given to young people to radicalise them. Now it has reached the Moroccan community in Amsterdam.'

'I remember it from my time in Rabat. A man murdered fourteen people there after taking it. But you said Spain. When I was there it was exclusive to Morocco.'

'It was, but now it is here as well.'

'I had never heard of it until I lived there. Just the name of it terrifies many Moroccans,' Jack replied.

'If it spreads to Europe, there is no knowing where it will end.' Ilsa said, expressing the view she knew was held by her colleagues in the drug squad.

'It used to cost one euro in Morocco. How much is it in Amsterdam?' Jack asked.

'I'm sure it would be several times that amount. But I understand that is only because supply has been limited.'

'That could be because the supplier is trying to set a high price to establish a more lucrative market.' Jack answered, applying his knowledge of drug dealers.

'That's worrying because then other dealers and the Mocro-Maffia would step in.' Ilsa said.

This was the introduction Jack needed to tell Ilsa something else. 'What I am about to tell you is confidential. The British government has received a letter from a man who lived in Morocco for two years who was trying to start Alcoholics Anonymous and Narcotics Anonymous to help their drug addicts. I understand that the support he got from most of the people in authority he met was scant to say the least.'

'You said the British government. Don't you mean the American?'

'No. British intelligence shared it with ours immediately after the murders in the London Mosque. They were convinced there'd be a revenge attack and wanted to stop it,' Jack replied.

'So, ours might have been that revenge attack. Security in London would have been much tighter than here in the Netherlands. What do you think?' Ilsa suggested.

'I don't know. But the sooner I'm over there the better. If this has to do with karkoubi and Moroccans, as I suspect it does, the world needs to know as soon as possible. Because unless the reasons behind the causes are exposed and dealt with, which they haven't been so far, attacks like this will happen again and again.'

Ilsa digested this. 'Surely if Morocco's influence is as bad as that the world would already know?' she said, slightly defensive of her homeland.

'It's complicated. I will tell you more when I see you. But we have an ace up our sleeve. America gives a lot of money to Morocco, and they will withhold it if they feel so inclined."

'So, what we need know is who committed this horrific act. Then if it was Moroccans and their drugs influenced it, America would be well placed to put pressure on their king to do something about it.' Ilsa summed up the situation, this time deliberately removing any biases.

'That's right'

'If that were to happen, the prospect of a positive outcome should improve,' Ilsa added, 'Although all terrorist attacks are diabolical acts of cowardice, it could mean the Dam Square attack is the catalyst for a shake-up of the world's drug laws and policies that cause many of the problems. Under the circumstances, it would be great if some of that started in Morocco.'

'Another idea the author had is one that Morocco is now in part enacting. Ever since he realised the idiocrasy of the situation, he said it should legalise cannabis and offer its expertise growing it and natural facilities to the firms researching medicinal cannabis.' Jack said.

'What is the other part? Ilsa queried.

'It is one that is well thought out and given Morocco's policies, it is unlikely that without external pressure they would make the necessary U-turn. As the pharmaceutical industry has been doing elsewhere, it admits that what it has done in the past exacerbated Morocco's drug problems, then it makes amends by helping develop an industry there to discover cannabis's medicinal uses.' Jack answered.

'And if that was to take off, Morocco could become one of the richest countries on the planet.'

'Indeed,' Jack said. 'That's why it is known as green gold. Though I would hope if that happened, the pharmaceutical firms involved would demand a fair distribution of the proceeds be distributed to Morocco's huge proletariat. The irony is, before I left Morocco, I had fallen in love with the beauty and nature of the Rif mountains where they grow cannabis and was tempted to buy a plot of land there.'

'Now I suppose you are wishing you had!' Ilsa chuckled.

191

Jack laughed in response. 'Knowing the speed things happen in Morocco, I'm sure I still have plenty of time.'

'Even if the king succumbs to pressure?' Ilsa asked.

'It will still take two or three years, not weeks or months to make the changes that are needed. Though that could change if the letter is made public and the leaders of France, Spain, the Netherlands and America back its contents. They have the most influence in Morocco outside Muslim countries.'

'Do you have a copy of the letter I can read?' Ilsa asked. 'It sounds like it has some, if not all the answers.'

'I can photograph it and send it in a text. But under no circumstances show it to anyone. This is one leak we don't want to happen until the timing is right. I would prefer it if you deleted it immediately after you have read it. The more I know about internet spying, and Morocco's presumed link to Pegasus, the more careful I am.'

'I'm the same. I'd like to talk to you about it after I've read it, though,' she said.

"I'll send it now. We can talk about it next time we speak'

A few moments later they ended their call.

****

Ilsa read the letter twice. She quickly realised she did not know enough about the situation or recovery from drug addiction to make a knowledge-based judgement. However, she could conclude that if what the author said was true, it is amazing the situation in Morocco has got this far without its medical profession or government doing something about it. He clearly has the right experience to analyse the causes and is confident about the solution he proposes. And as he has been saying for over five years that Morocco should back cannabis medicinal research, which until recently it had not, his other views may well be right too.

Reading between the lines, she ascertained that money, pride, a follow the herd mentality and lack of understanding are at the heart of Morocco's past stance. As they are deeply entrenched, they will be big hurdles to overcome. However, the Amsterdam bomb attack may mean the timing is good to make the other changes he says are desperately needed.

After mulling over her thoughts, she sent Jack a text confirming she had read it and deleted it. She did not make a comment, though she had debated adding something personal, *"Ik kijk ernaar uit je te zien en de verloren jaren goed te maken."*

Minutes later she sent him a text saying that as well. Then annoyance at herself set in. She was regretting letting her recent loneliness caused by the pressure of work get to her, *"Looking forward to seeing you and making up for the lost years."*

Chapter 18

The night of the bomb attack, Yashine did not sleep. Every time he closed his eyes his thoughts went back to the bicycle stand incident with the woman. His abiding thought was what was written on her yellow cycling vest, 'Stay calm; Just Do It'. Well, he thought, I did 'just do it', but why did I not 'stay calm'. That is exactly what is backfiring on me.

When the incident actually happened, he'd thought of it as a signal from Allah. He knew he had not faced the camera and thought that by the evening he would be on a plane to Tangier, and from then on safely sleeping there. But now he realised the camera that he had made sure did not see him would almost definitely have seen the Moroccan he'd spoken to whose space he took. And if the police found him, and the female cyclist, they could piece together a description that might well be enough to incriminate him.

Over and over, he fretted over why he had allowed his impatience and fear to let him down. I could have told her I was there before her, he thought, as I think she saw me when she arrived. So she may well have let me take the space without making a fuss. What do I do now? Do I stay here for a night or two and see what happens, or do I take the first plane to Morocco, if I can still catch one without being stopped?

The more he thought, the more confused and frightened he became. He switched his phone off, knowing Hamid and Nadia would contact him, and possibly the others as well. He knew from movies that his phone could be tracked if the police suspected he was involved.

Since three in the morning the news had said that Schiphol airport would reopen at nine the next day. He decided to go back there and take a flight, but only if it seemed safe.

Once on the airport bus, he turned his phone on. To his surprise, the messages from his brother, accomplices and Nadia were all good wishes. Nadia had passed on his reason for not seeing them last night and they each responded positively.

By the time he got to the airport, he knew he could no longer leave his friends to face any fallout that might occur, the more so as it was likely to be because of the altercation he had with the female cyclist. As a result, he got off and took a taxi to his home, knowing Nadia would be there with Mariam and Hamid.

If he had been frightened before, by the time he arrived his fear had doubled. All his life his worst fear had been that dying would be incredibly painful; right now, that was equaled by the concern that his friends would see through the lies he'd told them the night before.

As it turned out, these fears were a waste of time, each of them showing their delight in seeing him and congratulating him on having put their interests before his own. Although their praise partly consumed him with shame, in another way it seemed the success of their crime the previous day bonded them even more closely. It was then he knew he had to tell them about the altercation with the cyclist.

But even that went better than he'd expected. Nadia said immediately she would have done the same and none of the others disagreed. They all knew they had taken risks, and they all thought it most likely they would eventually be caught.

After that, the pleasure of being with the others helped him to relax. There was a positive effect to not being on his own, and when Nadia whispered in his ear, 'Let's go to our room, smoke kif, and have sex,' most things in the world seemed all right again.

****

Soon after Ilsa's second text to Jack, her nerves settled. She had contacted a doctor friend, Mila Bakker at Amsterdam's best-known drug treatment centre.

After exchanging hellos, she said, 'I am sure you are busy, so as it is important, I will get to the point. Is that okay?'

'Yes of course'.

'What do you know about the drug cocktail karkoubi? Anything you can tell me will be useful.'

'I don't know much,' her friend said. 'Until a few weeks ago I had never heard of it. Last week we had two patients who had used it and this week we've already had one. At the moment it seems to be only Moroccans, but I understand its benzodiazepine ingredient is made in Spain, so that might change. That's it.'

'What do you know about its effect?'

'All I know is what I have read on the Internet and what I have heard from my colleagues. It is addictive, highly potent and makes people do terrible things. Why do you ask? Is there someone you are dealing with who has used it?'

'There may be. I knew about its use in Morocco, but only just found about it being sold in the Netherlands. The people you mentioned who had taken it, could you let me have their names and addresses? I need to find out who is supplying it.'

'As you know, that is confidential. I cannot do that.'

Ilsa paused. She and Mila had grown up together and had always been close friends. She decided that under the circumstances she had to take a chance.

'I am sorry to ask you this, Mila, but I believe there is a connection with karkoubi and the bombs in Dam Square.

The problem we have is time. If we don't find out who the terrorists are quickly, we believe they will try to leave the country. They may already have gone.'

Mila had got the message and interrupted. 'I understand. Let me make a call and get back to you. One of our addiction counsellors is Moroccan and knows much more about karkoubi than I do, and he treated them. If I can get him to talk to you, he may be able to give you the information you need.'

'Thanks, Mila. You are a star. If you can do it now, it would be even better.'

'That's fine. I'm happy to help. I will tell him the situation and give him your number. His name is Nasser Mubarak.'

A few minutes later Nasser rang Ilsa. After introducing himself in Dutch, Ilsa responded in Darija. She wanted him to know they had the same origins and, she hoped, the same objectives.

He told her that not only did he have first-hand experience using it when he lived in Morocco. Once he'd got clean eight years ago and moved to Amsterdam, he had been amazed it had not reached Europe.

Ilsa said, 'I cannot tell you the reasons, but I need to know as much about it is possible. But I can tell you it is extremely serious.'

'It has been here a few months and comes from Spain by road through France and Belgium in fruit lorries. To begin with I assumed it was made in Algeria or Morocco, but I now know it is made by a private pharmaceutical company near Algeciras in Andalucía. The lorries though come from Morocco and the karkoubi is loaded on them once they get to Spain.'

'Do you know the name of the company or anyone involved, such as a dealer?' Ilsa asked.

'No. But I am currently treating two addicts who came here out of their minds on it. That was two weeks ago, so they are now detoxed,' Nasser replied.

'Are they still with you?'

'Yes, and one of them I have got to know quite well. At the beginning he was uncooperative but that has changed. Now he talks to me quite openly. I can tell that when he is clean, he is a good guy.'

'Do you think you can get him to meet me?'

'Whether he will do that is another matter. But as you are Moroccan, he might. They are all terrified of being deported,' Nasser said dubiously.

'What if I can guarantee him immunity from being deported or prosecution?' Ilsa said, thinking quickly.

'That could swing it. But you can also do it through me. This man trusts me. I was there when he came out of a coma and gave him the oxygen he needed. I told him my story, how I got clean, how I've stayed that way, and how I took karkoubi when I lived in Morocco. Identification is one of the best bonds to bind addicts together, so he might open up to me,' Nasser replied.

'For starters, what I need is the name of the dealer. I would prefer to do it face to face, though, as that will give it more credibility.'

'I will see what I can do and get back to you. As I said, I believe he is fundamentally a good man and the certainty of not being deported or prosecuted could persuade him to help, and maybe to meet you as well. Mila said I can trust you and that is good enough for me, but I cannot speak for someone else,' Nasser replied.

'Thanks, Nasser,' Ilsa said. 'Call me as soon as you have something. Any time, day or night. This is important. You have my number.'

What Nasser had not told tell Ilsa about was his earlier discussion on the same subject with his friend, Rick Blaine.

****

As there was an NA meeting at the centre that evening, it was likely he would meet Ilyas, his karkoubi contact, there. To respect Ilyas's anonymity, Nasser wanted to see Ilyas's reaction first. For him to talk about being a drug addict to her was fine, but breaking someone else's anonymity in NA was against its principles, and sacrosanct.

As soon as he'd finished talking to Ilsa he sent Ilyas a text: *'Hi Ilyas, I need to talk to you. Let's meet before the meeting tonight. I suggest 17-30 at the centre. Is that okay?'*

Ilyas replied immediately. *'Sure, bro, that's good for me. See you there.'*

By the time Ilyas arrived, he was convinced Nasser had found out something about his past use of drugs and/or crimes that meant he would be expelled from the centre. But Nasser, knowing Ilyas would, like many guilt-ridden addicts early in their recovery think like this, as soon as they met he did his best to make him feel at ease.

'First, I want to tell you how well you are doing. I'm really impressed and so are the other counsellors. If you keep doing what you are doing, one day at a time, like the millions of others who have done it this way, you will stay clean and have a life better than anything you can imagine.'

'Are you sure you aren't just saying that? I feel fearful a lot of the time. And coming here, I was sure you were going to tell me off or expel me,' Ilyas replied, his expression saying as clearly as words would do, 'What's coming next?'

'That's normal at this stage, Ilyas. Drug addiction is like recovery from any serious illness; much like having had a heart attack or a major operation. The patient needs time to heal. What you are doing now is recuperating, and by continuing to apply the NA programme after you leave here, you will make a full recovery, and go on to live a happy life.'

'I hope so, that's what I want. I will do anything I can to get it.' He paused before asking nervously, 'Was there anything else you wanted to talk about?'

'Yes, I need your help with something. The centre's medical doctor has been contacted by a policewoman friend of hers about the karkoubi that is being sold in Amsterdam. I told her it comes from Spain, but because of its potential to cause people to do serious harm, there are fears it might take off here. We've already had three patients here on it in the past two weeks. What I have been asked to find out is, before there are serious consequences, who is dealing in it, and is it too late to do something about it?'

Nasser waited for Ilyas's reply, hoping he had worded his request in a way that would not frighten him so much he wouldn't help.

'I can't help you with that, bro. I'm not a snitch. I've never seen eye to eye with the fuzz about anything,' Ilyas responded immediately.

'I was the same as you. Now I see things differently. When I was using drugs in Morocco, including karkoubi, I was always in trouble with the police. Then when I quit, for months I was still terrified they were going to get me for crimes I'd committed but had never been caught for. But as time's gone by, I've discovered my fears were part of my disease, and mostly unfounded. In fact, I now believe from working NA's 12 Steps, I always had a guardian angel looking after me. This means I now know you do, too, which is why I can ask you to help with this.' Nasser tried to be as persuasive as possible.

'Some of my friends know I come here. If I give you the name of a dealer, it will be easy to pin it on me,' Ilyas answered.

He was right, of course. Nasser framed his next words carefully.

'If you help, I will make sure you get all the anonymity you need. This policewoman is high ranking and most important, she is Moroccan. She assured me she can get the police to guarantee you will not be deported or prosecuted for anything you have done in the past.' He laid his best cards on the table.

Ilyas paused as this last statement sank in. 'That sounds good, but I know what I'm like with fear, it cripples me. It could easily drive me back to using. You are you, not me. I know what I am like.'

Although this was not going as well as Nasser had hoped, the answers Ilyas was giving encouraged him to continue, even though he knew doing so could have negative consequences.

'I understand everything you are saying and agree with all of it. In my experience, when an addict puts his or her recovery before anything else, they stay clean. What you are doing is exactly that. As your counsellor, I cannot ask you to do something that might jeopardise your situation.'

'Thanks, Nasser, and I'm sorry.'

The topic for that night's meeting was from the NA book, *Just for Today*, and the subject was fear.

Towards the end one of the main speakers said how in early recovery she had always been paralysed by fear, but then she added, 'In NA I heard two acronyms for FEAR: Fuck Everything and Run, or Face Everything and Recover. Before NA I always chose the former; since I got clean I do my best to choose the latter. Even though when I first heard these I was a newcomer, I have had to ask myself each time fear began to take control, which of these do I need to apply?'

At the end of the meeting, Ilyas went over to Nasser. Smiling sheepishly, he said, 'I've changed my mind. I will tell you who it is and anything else you want to know.'

NA meetings end with hugs. The hug Nasser gave Ilyas that night was more emotional than any he had given before. He said, 'You are very brave, Ilyas. I could not have done something so courageous in my early days. No one will ever know it was you. I and my friend will do our utmost to protect you in every possible way.'

Tears welled up in his eyes and he began to cry. Though moments like this are the heartbeat of the fellowship of NA, Nasser knew he had just witnessed one that had the potential to equal the best. As soon as he was on his own, he made two telephone calls. The first was to me.

'I was contacted by the police and because of that I met a former karkoubi user I counsel at the centre where I work. He told me the name of the dealer and that he is Moroccan. I now have to tell this to the policewoman who called me. I thought you would want to know first.'

'Thanks, Nasser. Do you know where he lives?' I answered.

'Yes, in Haarlem.'

'Okay, you must give her the details. That is police work. My agenda is different. Like yours, mine is to do as much as I can to help drug addicts and their families. Why don't you come to my hotel? It's near you and we can catch up. There are some things I would like to ask you about NA and AA in Amsterdam.'

****

At 05-00 the following morning, Ilsa Lund and a team of twenty-five 'marechchussee' from the Dutch Ministry of Defence surrounded the address in Haarlem.

From the outside, everything about the house they were about to enter looked normal, but with snipers in place on the street and on the rooftops covering every square metre of the area surrounding it, what was happening there was far from normal.

All Ilsa and her team knew at that time was that this was a potential drugs bust. If the full facts had been known, Jan Walvis would have been there and four times as many police officers, marksmen and helicopters.

Seconds after they hammered on the door, upstairs lights came on. Immediately spotlights were shone on the house and Ilsa spoke into a megaphone: 'This is the police. You are surrounded. Come out with your hands up.'

She waited a moment for a reaction, but there was none. So she added, 'You have thirty seconds from now. Otherwise we are coming in and we are heavily armed. Look outside if you don't believe me.'

Inside the house no one did anything except look at one another. Yashine, like the others, tried frantically to think, but was lost as to what to do. Nothing as sudden as this had been expected.

Nadia was the first to act and went to a window. Seeing the situation outside, she came up with an idea that seemed to make sense.

'We give ourselves up and see what they know. It could be they are doing several raids and we are just suspects. If all they find is the cannabis we've got stashed in the house, they might leave us alone.'

'I agree,' Yashine said. 'We have little choice; otherwise we can get our heads blown off. So, unless you say something to stop me, I am going to open the door and wave a white flag.'

No one spoke. They were all too dazed and frightened to think of anything else. Moments later Yashine opened the door and stood in the doorway waving a white handkerchief. After a few seconds of him doing this in the glaring spotlights, Ilsa issued a new instruction: 'We want all of you to come into the road keeping your hands in the air. Don't stand too close together. We need to see a two-metre gap between each of you, and walk slowly. Don't make any sudden movements.'

As the others followed Yashine and were made to stand in a line in front of a garden wall, Ilsa spoke into her megaphone again: 'We have a warrant to search your house for drugs. If you want to make it easy on yourselves, tell us where to look. And I am not just talking about cannabis. We have reason to believe someone living here has been dealing in karkoubi. Now, starting from the left, one at a time, put any drugs, mobile phones or weapons on the ground in front of you.'

Yashine knew instantly this was not a normal drugs bust. If the police had reliable information that it was being trafficked by them, this would mean big trouble, especially as it was an indirect link between them and the bomb attacks.

However, the only karkoubi they had was well hidden in a garage at the top of a driveway alongside their house where they kept their bicycles. As each pill was contained in a plastic bubble in foil strips in sealed plastic bags, it would be hard to find, and sniffer dogs would not be able detect it. The bigger problem was that this was also where they had kept the explosives, and even though all of it had been used to make the bombs, there may be enough in the form of dust for the dogs to sense it, then for forensic experts to ascertain what explosives had been stored there. If they could link that to the bombs in Dam Square, they would be in deep trouble.

From now on silence was going to be their best form of defence.

At the same time as Ilsa was ascertaining their names and checking their ID cards, her team were searching for drugs in the house. Once she had their details, including how long each had lived in the Netherlands, she rang these through to the Dutch Criminal Investigation Department, asking them to check with Interpol.

It did not take long for her team leader to report that they had found over two kilograms of cannabis resin, but no karkoubi. This was not the news Ilsa wanted or expected, so she decided to look for herself. Twenty minutes later the result was the same. After discussing it with her team leader, she decided to arrest them all for possession of drugs. At least that way she had the right to question them and one of them might break, especially with a threat of prison and deportation hanging over them.

While they waited for an armoured van to take the offenders away, Ilsa spoke with one of the dog handlers whose dog had discovered the hidden cannabis.

'Are dogs familiarised with all drugs?' she asked. 'The drug we are looking for is new to the Netherlands.'

'My dog is trained to detect substances such as explosives, illegal drugs, currency, blood and contraband electronics such as illicit mobile phones,' he explained.

'You said illegal drugs. So, if the drugs are legal, like valium or anti-depressants, and come in foil strips, would he be able to detect those?' Lisa eyed the lively spaniel hopefully.

'Unless the seals are broken, there would be nothing to smell, so they wouldn't. Was there something special you were looking for?'

'There is a new drug on the streets of Amsterdam that comes from Morocco in the form of a tablet that is packed in the same way as pharmaceutical companies' prescription pills. That was what I'd hoped to find here,' she told him.

'I understand. I can do another tour of the house now it's empty if you like. Although it's rare, with so many people around, dogs can get distracted by human smells, perfumes they wear, that sort of thing.' He replied.

'Please do. I am convinced there is more there than just cannabis. And a good lawyer would get them off with what we've found. It would hardly be worth taking them to court.'

'I am not hopeful, but I will give it a try. Give me ten minutes.'

Just as the armoured van arrived and the last prisoner was getting in, the dog handler returned from the back of the house. When he reached Ilsa he said,

'Nothing inside, ma'am, but I haven't checked the garage. I only just saw it. If you give me five minutes, I'll do that now.'

'Okay, I'll come with you,' she said.

As soon as they were near the door the dog started barking, making Ilsa's spirits rise. 'What does that mean?'

'I don't think its drugs, ma'am. For Popeye to bark like this, it's something highly pungent.'

Once the handler opened the door the dog went wild. He said, 'My guess is it's explosives, ma'am. I've never seen him behave like this except in simulation tests.'

'In that case we stop right here. Keep the dog on the lead and go outside. We need to get forensics to comb this place from top to botJack,' Ilsa ordered. 'You must not breathe a word of this to anyone. At the moment we need everyone to think this was a drugs raid where we found cannabis, nothing else. Okay?'

'Of course, ma'am. These are sensitive times. I was on duty Saturday night in Dam Square. Popeye and I were one of the first dog teams to arrive after the explosions. I have never seen such carnage; it was a horrendous sight.'

Back in the soundproofed van, the prisoners had no idea what had just happened.

The next thing Ilsa did was call Jan Walvis.

'Sir, I'm bringing in six suspects. For now, I have charged them with possession of two kilograms of cannabis, but I am hopeful they have karkoubi somewhere on their premises as well. From the reaction of his dog when we opened their garage door, the handler thinks it contains, or has contained explosives. I therefore request you send a forensics team here as soon as possible to check if this is so.'

If it was as she suspected they may be well on their way to early arrests for what looked like being one of Europe's worst-ever terrorist attacks.

"Excellent, Ilsa. I'll do that right away. In the meantime, keep the scene secure. You go with the prisoners to Centrum Station and make sure they are placed in separate non-adjacent cells. I want to leave them for at least two hours to stew in their fears. Then go back to the scene. By the time you get there, I will be there as well.'

Jan Walvis was aware that if Ilsa's assumptions were right, his reputation as head of counterterrorism would soar, not only in the Netherlands but internationally. He wanted to make sure that he, and he alone, was seen to have led this mission.

****

After I'd finished talking to Nasser Mubarak, I telephoned David Smith on the direct number he had given me. I told him that one of my contacts had found out that karkoubi was in Amsterdam and made in Spain. Then I told him I knew the name of the dealer, and because I believed the Dutch police knew that, too, I suggested he liaise with them. 'I understand that the police and a counterterrorism unit will raid the dealer's address. Depending on what they find there, they will know if there is a link to the Dam Square bomb attack.'
'I am amazed things have moved so quickly,' Smith said. 'What will you do now?'
'I am meeting the counsellor from the treatment centre who gave me the information.'
'That's good. Let me know if you hear anything else.'
After this call I spent the time before Nasser arrived reflecting. It seemed as if I may have made some progress in my objective to expose the drug situation in Morocco and its influence elsewhere; but was it enough to be sure of changing anything? The only thing to do in such a situation was to pray for direction and put trust in the result. So that's what I did.

When Nasser arrived, we first talked about the Dam Square bomb attack before moving on to the overall drug situation in the Netherlands and NA and AA's growth there. I asked about the number of Moroccans attending the meetings.

'At least twenty,' he answered, surprising me. 'Most of them go to NA, but there are a few who go to both AA and NA. I can take you to one tomorrow night where there are always at least five. Would you like to do that?'

'Definitely,' I answered enthusiastically.

'The meeting I will take you to is in Sint Jansstraat which is near Dam Square. It starts at four o'clock, so if I meet you near there at three you can see in daylight some of the damage, though most may be cordoned off.'

'Perfect. I look forward to it.'

'There is another meeting at eight, not far away. We can go to that as well if you want,' he said.

'That could be good, but let's see how the first one goes before we decide.' I had hopes more would be revealed by then and I might want to pursue other channels.

****

Once he was in a taxi heading for his Amsterdam hotel, Jack Llewellyn telephoned Ilsa. They had exchanged texts before he left Washington and as soon as he arrived in the Netherlands. In her last one to him, she had written, *'So far, it's all good news. I will give you a heads-up when I see you.'*

Ilsa's text and the prospect of seeing her excited him. Although he wanted to tell her precisely that, he decided it was best to wait until they met. Under the circumstances, the timing to tell her he was a recovered drug addict might be important.

'I got your message,' he said. 'What does good news mean?'

'I can't talk now. I aim to meet you at your hotel at about one for an hour and will tell you then,' she answered.

'Okay. But try to keep the evening free. We have a lot of catching up to do.'

'I'll do my best. It's crazy here at the moment. We charged six Moroccans this morning. The media and our politicians are going nuts. But not a word of that to anyone, including your people in the US.'

'That's incredible. I can't wait to hear what's happened and help if I can.'

"Your timing is perfect. With your American diplomatic hat on, I'll find you lots to do. Now I must fly.'

As Jack turned off his mobile phone, he realised his heart was racing. Ilsa's news had caused a little of that, but mostly it was the memories of his time with her when he had never been happier with a woman in his life.

Once his nerves were more settled, realising he would have several hours free in the afternoon and early evening, he checked for NA and AA meetings near his hotel. But a degree of nervousness returned when he remembered he had not told Ilsa the real reason he had thought about buying a plot of land in Morocco's Rif mountains.

Although he had often smoked cannabis recreationally in New York where he grew up, when he moved to Rabat he had been introduced to some of the best hashish he had ever known. That happened because after just a month of being there, he'd found the perfect girlfriend to introduce him to the best kif in Morocco, possibly even the best in the world.

Her name was Chadia. She had grown up in Chefchaouen, next door to the Rif mountains. From the time they met, one weekend each month they went there for one or two nights and bought enough for the next few weeks. Chadia had smoked it since she was sixteen. She knew exactly who to buy it from and what to buy; she also paid the best price. And although there were at least three police road checks on their drive back to Rabat, they were only ever stopped, never searched. Jack often wondered why. Was it because they knew Chadia, or was it because he was American and had diplomatic plates?

So it was to feed his addiction to cannabis that Jack nearly bought a plot of land in the Rif mountains. In the next few years, including the time he was in Amsterdam and dating Ilsa, his consumption of other drugs increased. After breaking a leg skiing in Colorado the year after he returned to America, he was prescribed strong opiates, and within six weeks was hooked on them. A year later he nearly died from an overdose, ending up in a rehab centre where he had first gone to NA That was nine years ago; he has not taken a mood-altering chemical of any sort, including alcohol, since.

Just before 1 o'clock Jack received a text from Ilsa to say she was running twenty minutes late and that she could only stay half an hour. In that time his anxiety level rose markedly. He was not normally nervous ahead of dates, but this one had so many other aspects to it that his fears flowed like a speeded-up incoming tide.

By the time she walked through the revolving doors, he had said several serenity prayers to calm himself down and called his NA sponsor back in Washington, though for security reasons he could not tell him all the causes of his anxiety.

As soon as he saw her, his worries evaporated. She looked almost the same as the day they had parted at Schiphol airport ten years ago.

211

After an embrace, he knew that if Ilsa felt the same as him, and his stay went as well as he hoped, he could not leave her again. When they let go of each other, all he could say was, 'It is so good to see you. You look great.'

'Thank you; but you haven't looked at me properly yet,' she responded, smiling at his obvious pleasure in meeting her.

'Trust me, you do.' He moved back a little, then added, 'But it's a shame we are meeting because of such awful circumstances, and it's so brief.'

'I am sure we will have time to catch up. So much has happened in the past two days, right now it is almost all I can think about. How long are you staying?'

'It's flexible. I don't have an agenda. My boss has told me to do all I can to help the Dutch police.'

'Well, the way things are moving, I am hopeful it is an open-and-shut case. We have confessions, and all the video camera and forensic evidence we need to prosecute and, I hope, get convictions. Although it was well-planned, they were amateurs when it came to cover-up.'

'So it's not ISIS then?' Jack asked.

'Correct, though it nearly was. The leader decided at the last minute to have his gang of terrorists do it their own way, even though ISIS offered to support them.'

'Is there a connection to Amsterdam's drug mafia? Its reputation is as bad or worse than Italy's these days.'

'None so far that we know of. The group's leader lives on fear. That's why it was easy to break him. Though he had little choice under the circumstances.'

'Let's talk about it over coffee. There's a bar down the hall. I'm still getting over my flight. American Air Force planes' levels of comfort are not exactly like Air Force One's.'

Ilsa laughed.

'I'm sorry I can't stay long,' she said. 'But I hope to make supper, if that's still all right.'

'Definitely. Where would you like to eat?'

'Just around the corner from the hotel is fine. There's a nice quiet place I know that's organic, very healthy and cosy.'

During the next twenty minutes, Ilsa summarised what had happened so far. She started with the help she had been given by her Mila and went on to the property search which led to the discovery of explosives, then the arrests and confessions. Then she explained how these had led to the forensic search of the garage where the karkoubi was found.

'That's amazing. And this all came about because you knew a doctor who specialises in helping drug addicts?'

It occurred to Jack that this could lead to something which for him would be even bigger.

'Yes. It reminds me, I haven't thanked her yet. We have been friends for years. Her name's Mila Bakker. She's a lovely woman.'

Jack decided that this was the perfect opportunity to tell Ilsa about his past drug abuse and recovery.

'I have something important to tell you,' he began.

'I'm sorry, Jack, but it will have to wait until tonight. I've a driver outside and have to go back to the station to continue interviewing our suspects. I also need to write a report with the information Nasser, my contact, gave me which led to the arrests.'

'I understand,' he said, 'It can wait. It's already been good to see you. It will be even better when we have less time pressure.'

'I will aim for 7.30, but may be a bit late. I will let you know if I'm held up.'

Moments later they embraced again and parted.

213

****

After a much-needed and longer-than-expected siesta, Jack set off for the NA meeting with a feeling of excitement in every stride. It was good to be back in Amsterdam, and the prospect of what lay ahead had him beaming. As he walked through the streets, memories returned, mostly of how many cyclists there were in Amsterdam and of its many shops. It was the perfect place for a bicycle bomb attack on innocent people.

As he entered Sint Jansstraat, he knew where the NA meeting was from the moment he saw the huddle of people standing near a street doorway. In almost every city, in every country where he had been to a meeting, this scene greeted him. Today it immediately made him feel at home. As several people put out their hands and said, 'Hi, welcome' that feeling expanded even more.

Upstairs in the kitchen, a young woman offered him coffee. 'Hi, I'm Anna,' she introduced herself. 'Are you visiting?'

'Yes, I'm Jack. How did you know I spoke English?'

'You look British or American. Am I right?' She smiled at him.

He smiled back. 'You are. I've just arrived from Washington. I live there, but I used to live here.'

Standing next to Anna was a man, whom she now introduced. 'Jack, this is Rick. He's just arrived as well,' she said.

'Hi, Rick. Where are you from?' Jack held out his hand.

'I'm a bit of a nomad. I flew in from London this morning, but I've been living in Europe and Morocco for the past few years,' I replied.

'That's interesting. I worked in Rabat a few years ago. Do you know it?' Jack asked.

'I know it well. I'm an author and the co-author of my last book was from Rabat, so we had our meetings there,' I answered.

'What was your book about? Anything to do with Morocco?' Jack asked casually.

'Yes and no. Mostly it was about drugs. I have been going to Morocco for more than thirty-five years, most of it in recovery. When I went there in 2016, I realised it had the worst drug problems of any country I had been to. So I contacted NA World Services to ask for their support and advise me how to start meetings there in Arabic,' I said.

'That's amazing. Do you speak Arabic?'

'No, I used interpreters. Do you?' I responded. I was always pleased to meet members of NA and AA who had been to Morocco; especially when they had lived there and were familiar with its drug problems, my hope always being that they might be able to help.

'No. I was at the US embassy and we used interpreters too. Why do you say they have such bad drug problems?' Jack asked.

'For several reasons. I didn't realise it straight away, it was only after I'd met lots of addicts, families, doctors, psychiatrists and pharmacists there.'

'What do you think are the reasons? I have a few ideas, but I am sure you know more about them than I do,' Jack asked, giving me the opportunity to tell him what I believed.

'There are many, probably more than in any other country. Morocco is the biggest grower of cannabis in the world, yet it's illegal there. There are thousands of drug-addicted children living on the streets and they have a drug called

215

karkoubi, which is probably the most dangerous in the world. Did you hear of it when you were in Rabat?'

I asked this, knowing my enthusiasm for the subject meant I sometimes talked about it too much.

'I did recently, not when I was there. I was more into cannabis. Were you able to help?'

'A little, and I am still trying. The more I saw, the more I wanted to help. The trouble was, the more I understood situation, the more I came to believe that Morocco can only turn its drug problems around if the king gets behind the changes that are needed,' I told him.

As soon as I said this, Jack's attitude changed. He told me later it was because the first time he had come across such an idea and he had heard of karkoubi was mentioned in a letter he had received from British intelligence. But then it was announced that the meeting was starting, so any further chat would have to wait.

Although the meeting was in Dutch, the secretary said that as there were several English-speaking visitors, and as everyone attending spoke English, people could share in either language. After the usual NA introductory readings, she said, 'At the last minute, I asked Rick, who has arrived from London today, to share his experience, strength and hope. So, now Rick, it's over to you to share for up to fifteen minutes. After that it is open sharing.'

I began as always by saying, 'My name is Rick, and I am an addict...'

Chapter 19

'Of all the NA meetings, in all the towns, in all the world, he walks into mine!'

For most of my share I stuck to the guidelines the secretary had proposed. When I expressed the importance of service in NA, I spoke about my time in Morocco and what I had been trying to achieve for drug addicts there. Because some of the frustrations I described replicated those in the letter to King Mohammed VI, Jack told me later it was then he realised the man he was listening to had written it.

At the end of NA meetings, people give one another hugs. Jack saved his last one for me and thanked me at the same time for my share. Then he said, 'If you are not doing anything, let's go somewhere we can talk. You will find what I have to tell you interesting, probably amazing. Ours is no chance meeting.'

'Sure but I need to talk to Nasser, the Moroccan addict who spoke, before I leave. I'll meet you outside after that,' I replied.

'In that case maybe you can introduce me to him,' Jack said. 'I liked what he shared and would like to meet him.'

As soon as I had finished talking to Nasser, I waved to Jack to join us. After being introduced, he said, It's good to meet you. I worked in Rabat for a year which left me with a good feeling for your country and its people.'

'Thanks, it's nice to meet you and hear that.' Nasser smiled with pleasure. 'Not everyone says kind things about my fellow countrymen these days.' To Rick he said, 'Thanks again for what you are doing in Morocco, Rick. I know how hard it is there, especially when you don't speak Arabic. Next time I go, I'll contact you to see how I can help.'

'That would be great, and if you hear of any Moroccans going there, give them my contact details. We need all the help we can get. You don't have to check with me first,' I replied.

'I will. If you are here a few more days, we can meet again. It would be great to know more about the situation there,' Nasser said.

After exchanging hugs again, we parted. As we walked down the stairs to the street, Jack said, 'Can I ask you why you are in Amsterdam? After listening to you speak, it seems our reasons may partly be the same.'

'Because of the bomb attack. I want to know if Moroccans were involved, and if they were, are drugs involved, especially karkoubi? If this is the case, it may sound awful, but it could help with something I am trying to do in Morocco. And you?'

I said this having learned that being open sometimes creates windows of opportunity. Jack's reply proved me right.

'I am here for a similar reason. If you are not busy tomorrow morning, let's have coffee. We have a lot in common and I think I may be able to help you. I am meeting someone for dinner tonight. If that goes well, you will be pleased with what I tell you. You are not the only one who wants to sort out Morocco's drug problems.'

"That sounds good.' I gave him my card. 'You will see on my blog what I write about. Let me know where you are staying and what time to meet,' I said, intrigued. I was convinced he was holding something back.

'I'm staying at the Aalders Hotel. Come at ten. I will text you my email and phone details. My surname is Llewellyn.

You can check me out on Google, but don't believe all you read. The press tends to exaggerate.' He smiled.

As we left the building there were several people who had been in the meeting outside smoking cigarettes. Two of them, a man and a woman, came up to us and introduced themselves as Moroccans living in Amsterdam. They expressed pleasure with what I had said and wished me well.

Jack left then, and I spent a few minutes explaining the NA situation in Morocco to the couple. When I described the frustrations I'd had with its medical profession, religion and drug laws, they agreed these were part of the problem, adding that they were some of the reasons the stigma of being an addict there was so bad. When they told me they were brother and sister and visited their family there twice a year, I gave them details of the NA and AA meetings, telling them how good it would be if they could attend. I also gave them a visiting card and said to contact me any time.

As I got closer to Dam Square, on the way back to my hotel, I thought that already my first 24 hours back in Amsterdam was paying dividends. I had been especially impressed by Jack and looked forward to hearing what he had to say. I had also liked meeting the Moroccans. If they and others in recovery went to meetings when they visited, it would make the probability of getting NA established more likely, so for the first time in weeks I was optimistic.

****

Ilsa was only a few minutes late for her meeting with Jack. In the time since he'd left the NA meeting, almost all he had thought of was the extraordinary coincidence of his meeting

Rick and what he had shared about Morocco. In the time he had been in recovery things like this had happened, but none more serendipitous than this. As he had heard in NA many times, 'coincidences are God's way of revealing Himself', so he was not at all surprised. It did seem as if it was divine intervention.

In the restaurant, once they had been given a table, sat down and ordered drinks, Jack's excitement to tell her his news took over.

He said, 'I know we've got a lot to tell each other. But I need to tell you something first.'

'Go ahead. I'm all ears.' Ilsa leaned forward, beaming at him.

'It's something that happened to me after the last time I saw you in Amsterdam.' He paused, suddenly becoming serious.

Ilsa waited, her smile fading.

Taking the bull by the horns, Jack continued. 'I became addicted to opiates and nearly died from an overdose.'

Ilsa said, 'I remember you broke your leg. Was it anything to do with that?'

'Only indirectly. To begin with the pain was excruciating, so I was put on an opiate called Fentanyl. Have you heard of it?' he asked.

'Yes, and not just because of my job. It's famous because Prince died after taking it and it's fifty times stronger than heroin,' she answered.

'Well, I became addicted to it, and when my doctor stopped prescribing it, I turned to heroin. After my time in Morocco and Amsterdam, I was already hooked on cannabis, and as a result I had become a weed and heroin junkie.' He studied her face for her reaction.

'And now?' she asked.

'I've been off all drugs for nine years. I go to Narcotics Anonymous; their programme saved my life.'

'That's wonderful. I know of NA through my doctor friend, Mila, the one who guided me to the bomb suspects who are now under arrest.'

Relieved to have got this off his chest, Jack said, 'Thanks, I appreciate your attitude.' Wondering how she might feel when she had time to think about his revelation, he changed the subject. 'That's incredible about the arrests. How convinced are you they are the terrorists?'

'Very. I talked to Mila straight after I spoke to you on Sunday night. It turned out that a counsellor working with her is Moroccan and was helping a Moroccan addict who had been taking karkoubi. Through him we found out who the dealer was, and the five others who we think were his jihadist accomplices,' Ilsa said, unable to conceal her satisfaction at this outcome.

'The speed you have achieved that is incredible!, Jack said. 'Well done! If they are guilty, it will be a real coup for you and your team.' He hesitated briefly, knowing that his next question might be sensitive. 'I hesitate to ask you, but I have learned a few things too. Were any of them Moroccan?'

'I am already telling you more than I should. But you helped me, and I know you won't divulge this to anyone. Right?'

'Right. The great thing about being in recovery from drug addiction is that I have to be honest in all my affairs. If I am not, it might lead me to use again and next time that would be curtains for me.' Just stating this reminded him of the life-and-death nature of his drug addiction when he had reached rock botJack.

'They are all Moroccan. Two of them are established cannabis dealers. We think all the karkoubi in Amsterdam to date has been trafficked by them.'

221

'That's the same as the Barcelona attacks. They were all Moroccan and it's almost certain drugs were involved. The police believe the house where they made the bombs was where drugs trafficked in the area were stored,' Jack said.

'I've done some research on it,' Ilsa told him. 'It was the same in Brussels. During the court case it came out that the Moroccans involved were into drugs.'

'It's the diaspora of their people and the country's involvement in drugs that is a recurring theme,' Jack said. Then he added, 'Now it's my turn to give you some good news. You remember the letter to Morocco's king? Well, the writer is in Amsterdam. In the most amazing way, I met him today and I'm having coffee with him at my hotel tomorrow morning.'

'That is incredible!' she exclaimed. 'How on earth did it happen?'

'We met through mutual friends who live here. Once I realised who he was, I told him I had lived in Rabat and worked at the US embassy. That interested him, so he told me what he had been doing in Morocco. Once he had explained, I told him I thought I could help him with his project. After that he was as keen to meet me again as I am to meet him.'

'That really is amazing. This is all happening so fast and so positively. It seems as though every time I blink something new that is good has happened.' Ilsa said, then added thoughtfully, 'I would like to meet him. It would good to hear about his experiences in Morocco.'

'Okay, that's enough about bombs and drugs,' Jack said, noticing the waiter arriving with the menus. 'Now let's enjoy ourselves. I'd like to hear about you and what you've done in the last nine years.'

'I want to hear about you first. And you needn't worry about your former drug problems. The things you have told me make me realise you are on the right track.'

Ilsa put out her hand and held his.

'Where I come from, women go before men. My grandmother would turn in her grave if she knew I was breaking that rule.' Jack winked at her.

'In that case I don't want to upset your grandmother. Except for that stint in The Hague when I met you, I have been in the police force in Amsterdam, in different divisions all the time. I've been promoted four times, and a year ago I was made a CI in the CID. The reason I am involved in the Dam Square bombings is because Jan Walvis, our head of counterterrorism, was put in charge of it and we worked together on several cases a few years ago,' she said.

Jack grimaced. 'I said no more talk of bombs. I know it's a hot subject for us at the moment, but I really would like to know more about you. Did you marry? Are you married? Let's start there.' He smiled encouragingly.

'No to getting married, though I have been engaged. And no children. I often take care of my brother's twins, and that so far has been enough for me. Now it's your turn to answer the same questions.'

'Much the same, but without the engagement, though I did have a six-year relationship with a Chinese woman living in New York,' he answered.

'Where is she now and when did it end?' Ilsa asked.

'Beijing. She's a dentist and has a son who lives there. When Trump became president, she disliked his attitude to China so much, as soon as she could, she went home.'

'I don't blame her,' she said, then she laughed. 'Did you know he had an illegal drug made in his name right after he became president?'

'No. I don't believe it. You are teasing me,' Jack replied.

'In that case, look at this.' She brought out her phone and showed him a picture.

'That's incredible.' Jack gazed at the image of cookies and what looked like a packet of dog treats in disbelief.

'They are ecstasy tablets made in orange called 'Trumpies'. Some were found at Schiphol airport. 24 hours later they were on sale in Australia,' Ilsa said, enjoying herself.

'This should have been on YouTube when he was president. It would have gone viral,' Jack said.

Going back to your girlfriend,' Ilsa said, 'she did the right thing. Several times he singled out China. What worried Europeans was that so many Americans voted for him. My experience is that Americans are good people, whereas his repulsive moral values were a terrible influence in so many areas.'

'I agree, but let's keep off politics as well tonight. The poor quality of politicians throughout the world means it is not going to be an inspiring topic.' Because of his job, Jack hated the subject and was afraid he would express his equally strong views, not great for a diplomat.

'I agree, I'm sorry I brought it up. Tell me about your travel experiences instead. You used to go on some exciting adventures, to places I had never been,' Ilsa suggested.

'Until recently I still did, but now I want to settle. The last interesting place I went to was Greenland. Ever since I was a child, I was fascinated why a country mostly white would be called Greenland, while Iceland next to it is much greener!'

'I know, it is extraordinary. Did you like it?' Ilsa asked.

"I was there in June and flying low over huge icebergs floating down the coast was one of the most thrilling sights I have seen. Another was two years ago. I went island-hopping in the Caribbean. In between Bequia and Grenada we flew low over the Tobago Cays where they made *Pirates of the Caribbean*. This group of tiny islands surrounded by sand and coral reefs was the most beautiful sight I think I have ever seen.' Jack wanted to add how he would like to do that one day with Ilsa, but he knew this was not the right time to suggest it.

'I saw them once from the air when I went to Aruba. Our pilot made a point of flying over them. They are simply heaven. I have wanted to go back ever since.'

Now Jack had his cue, 'I'm up for that. I cannot think of anything better I would like to do than be there now with you,' he said, with a huge smile.

'Thanks for saying that. Just thinking of it is the perfect distraction to what is going on for me in Amsterdam right now,'

'Did you go diving in Aruba?,' he asked, determined not to go back to the bomb attack just yet. 'The Dutch ABC islands are supposed to have some of the best in the Caribbean.'

'No, but every day I went snorkelling. The best thing was swimming with a green turtle. I followed it for some time and videoed it. Whenever I watch it, I am mesmerised by the tranquillity. I stayed two or three metres behind it and it took no notice of me.'

Jack laughed. 'I wonder if it was the same one I followed in the Tobago Cays. Wouldn't it be incredible if it was? They are known to travel huge distances.'

'I was there with my mother who used to watch me from a dive boat. As I didn't have diving gear to put on, I was always first into the water. On one occasion when I jumped over the side, there was a huge barracuda a few metres away under the hull. The boat was motionless and so was the barracuda. I could not believe it and instinctively tried to get back in the boat. Then I remembered it is rare for them to attack humans, so I stayed and looked at it. I'd never seen teeth like it. I was very relieved when a few minutes later it swam off.'

'I had a similar experience when I stayed on Tobago. There had been a storm and the water was murky. The sea was quite rough, and I was on my own. I had been following a shoal of squid which disappeared into the murk. The next thing I knew there was a barracuda less than a metre away staring back at me; I literally froze.' He grimaced at the memory.

'What happened?'

'Like yours, seconds later it swam off, while I turned around and headed for the clear water behind me. In fact, if I remember rightly, I headed back to the beach and safety.'

'I kicked myself after for not taking a photo of mine. I had plenty of time, but my fear let me down,' Ilsa said, thinking that on two occasions since then she had needed a lot of courage when facing armed humans.

'I know! It would have been great to show your grandchildren. I didn't have time to take one, but I had taken some of the squid earlier,' Jack said.

'This is making me hungry. I think it sets the scene for not having fish,' Ilsa said with a smile. She looked down at her menu, the first time she had looked away from Jack since they had sat down.

'I agree. I'm going veggie,' Jack said, smiling back.

They were more or less back on the wavelength they had been on at the height of their affair. It was as if they had been apart months, not years, Ilsa thought. But however strong this sensation was, she knew she had always to live by the adage, 'no going back'.

For the next hour and half their conversation flowed as if it was their first or second date together. The sparks that had been there before kept flowing. So, when the waiter came to take their dessert order, Ilsa had to say unwillingly, 'I'm sorry, but I have to leave. I have to make report and I need to do it while it is still fresh in my mind. We can try to do the same tomorrow if that's good for you?'

'It is, and don't worry, I have things to do tonight too. This job is too much sometimes,' he answered.

'Mine's the same. I am getting to the point when I've had enough.'

Jack told the waiter that they wouldn't be having dessert and asked to settle the bill.

'If I have some questions for the man who wrote the letter, I will call you in the morning. Is that okay?' Ilsa said.

'Of course. I am excited about meeting him,' Jack answered. 'I don't know what he will tell me, but I am sure it will be interesting. I already know a little about what he thinks and wants to do. I will tell you as much as I can when I see you.'

"Thanks, but I really would like to meet him if that is possible.' Ilsa paused, then she said, 'It will be great to see you again. I've enjoyed tonight and we've still got a lot more catching up to do.' She stood up, preparing to leave.

Outside, as the taxi pulled up, just before he opened the door for her to get in, Jack impulsively pulled her to him, put his arms around her and held her tightly. 'Tonight has been very special. I've enjoyed it so much. I hope you have too. I'm already looking forward to the next time I see you.'

'I feel the same, but a lot of water has passed under the bridge. I don't want to rush into something with so many other things lurking in the background. One day at a time I think is what you say in AA.'

Pushing herself further away from him, she looked into his eyes. Jack knew she was talking sense. Although Ilsa was not offering him an opportunity, less than a week ago he could not in his wildest dreams have imagined he would even be in Amsterdam, let alone meeting her, especially under such extraordinary circumstances. Indeed, he thought, let's see what tomorrow brings.

Chapter 20

Just before she went to bed the day after her flight to Tangier had been delayed, Fatima sent Nadia a text. It read: *'I am sure Yashine told you I met him at Schiphol when our flight was cancelled last night. He was most concerned about a relative he was visiting in Tangier and I think I might have upset him. Please tell him I am sorry, and hope his cousin is well soon. He said you might visit him. If you do, let me know so we can meet. Hugs and kisses, Fatima.'*
The first time Nadia read it, was just before she and the others surrendered their phones to the police. As she was at the end of the line, while each was being searched, she had time to read it again. But this was not enough to understand it, so she replied: *'What was it you said that might have upset him?'*
Fatima responded instantly, *'he told me he feared for his cousin's life, and afraid of flying. When we got on our plane to Tangier and the pilot announced we were not taking off because of an incident in Amsterdam, he got worse. Then when we were told we would not be leaving until today, he almost had a fit and had to go to the bathroom twice. Unfortunately, I was not very sympathetic!'*
Nadia kept her reply brief. *'Thanks, I'll deal with it. Hugs Nad'*
It didn't take long for Nadia to work out what must have happened and why Yashine had stopped communicating with her and the others on Saturday night. Her lover had deceived her in an abominable way. He had already annoyed her by being afraid to sacrifice his life for Islam, now he had shown himself to be even more yellow-bellied by being willing to abandon her, his brother and friends for

selfish, fear-driven reasons. But she also recalled how he had returned when he could have caught a flight to Morocco the following day, and wondered about that.

As she sat in silence in the police van, she pooled her thoughts, concluding there was much more that was bad about Yashine's behaviour than was good. By the time they reached the police station, rage and resentment consumed her. What he had done was unforgiveable. She decided that at the first opportunity she would take revenge. Today, in her first interview for questioning under caution at Centrum Amstel police station, that opportunity had come.

Ilsa was renowned for getting confessions from the most hardened criminals. After several training courses on interview techniques, her natural charm, beauty and intelligence, time and again led her to achieve excellent results.

At her first interrogation session with Nadia Benazzi, Ilsa was surprised that when she offered her the counsel of an advocate she refused. After turning on the recording equipment, she introduced those who were present in the interview room.

'The crimes you may be charged with come under the Terrorism Act,' she began. 'If you are convicted, punishment would be from five years to life imprisonment, depending on your role. So, I ask you again, do you want to have an advocate present?'

Again Nadia refused the offer. 'No, I'm happy to talk to you on my own. I want to get this over with and move on with my life.'

'When we picked you up this morning at your boyfriend Yashine's house, you knew we would find drugs. We have already found enough to convict him, his brother and two friends. Now a forensics team is checking to see if the garage recently contained explosives. If that is the case, and they are the same as those used in the Dam Square bombings, other than in court, you will never see any of these people again. Now, are you still sure you don't want an advocate present?'

Ilsa deliberately painted the bleakest picture possible, fear being one of the most effective tools to use in the art of interrogation.

'I want to ask a question. I've heard of plea bargaining. If I tell you everything I know, how will that affect what happens to me?' Nadia asked.

Ever since Fatima's texts, Nadia's anger had been focused on the best way to deal with Yashine. Now they had been caught, and in the knowledge that the tests for explosives would reveal their presence in the garage, she decided this gave her the right to take revenge, while at the same time, it would be best for her.

'I don't do deals with terrorists,' Ilsa said. 'Unless you can prove you were not involved in this most heinous crime, it is unlikely you will be treated differently to anyone else who was.'

'You said unlikely. What did you mean by that?' Nadia asked.

Ilsa regarded her coldly. "I would need to know all the circumstances and be sure of their accuracy. If at any time I found you were hiding something or lying, it would go the other way for you. The seriousness of this crime is at the extreme end of all police work. That means no one will take whatever you or anyone else did lightly, however cooperative they are. There is nothing more cowardly than the murder of scores of innocent people and what it does to their families.'

'You can forget it then,' Nadia retorted, scowling. 'You are all the same. It's all right when Americans, Israelis or the British murder innocent Muslims in Palestine or wherever, but as soon as it's Muslims, we are targeted with all your military might and blame.'

Ilsa remained calm and spoke in Darija. 'I'm as Moroccan as you are. It's just that I don't go around killing innocent people. If you know something, now is the time to speak. If what you say helps our enquiry, I will try to make sure any prison sentence you have is carried out in the UK. Anything else, at this stage, I cannot offer.'

'Are you really Moroccan? Nadia asked, clearly surprised.

This time Ilsa spoke in English, "Yes. But that makes no difference. I am a policewoman first and last. So, is there anything you want to tell me?'

'I am pregnant,' Nadia said.

Was she lying, Ilsa wondered, playing the sympathy card? She must know that public sympathy always favoured mothers-to-be. She asked, 'When is it due?'

'In seven months. I don't want to be in prison while my baby is growing up. My parents can look after it to begin with, but I want to be a hands-on mother and to bring it up,' Nadia answered.

'Is this why you are prepared to tell us what happened?'

'Yes and no. I don't want Yashine to know he is the father. Now I know what he did, I am appalled,'

'Is he definitely the father?' Ilsa asked.

'Yes,' Nadia replied.

'If you were not directly involved, and can prove it, there is a chance you may get a shorter sentence,' Ilsa said. 'But we don't know yet if Yashine and his friends are the terrorists behind the attack. If you can help us prove they were, I would do my best to help you,' Ilsa said, now believing that

Nadia could well be prepared to give them useful information.

'I can tell you now that they were,' Nadia said. 'I knew they were up to something bad, but I was not involved, and because I knew I was pregnant, I kept out of it. I knew about the cannabis in the house, and the karkoubi, which you will find in the garage behind some bricks near the bike rack. But I did not know what they were planning to do with the explosives. I heard them talking, that was all.'

This was going better than Ilsa could have hoped. As two of the other five suspects were being interviewed simultaneously by other officers, she thought it a good moment to take a break. 'I'm stopping this interview now and will return shortly. I need to check on something,' she told Nadia, turning off the recording equipment. 'Thanks, Nadia, what you have told us so far could be helpful. Now it is important I let the officer in charge of the case know. He may want to be with me when I continue interviewing you.'

'Will that help me?' Nadia asked.

'I don't know, but it won't do you any harm. It depends on what you tell us,' Ilsa said.

'In that case, get him. What I tell you will blow your mind. Now I know what happened, I can hardly believe it. But, whatever you do, don't let on I grassed. They have a lot of nasty friends, including members of ISIS, so my life could be in danger,' Nadia said.

Ilsa got up to leave the interview room, registering that Nadia had not shown any significant signs of fear. As she reached the door, she asked one more question.

'Did you mean by what you just said that ISIS were involved?'

'No, I don't think so. But Yashine did speak to them and they offered to help,' Nadia replied.

'We need to get that on tape when I return. I am sure the head of terrorism will want to talk to you too. The more information you give directly to him, the more it will benefit you.' Ilsa stepped into the corridor and closed the door.

Jan Walvis had watched this interview from the observation room. Knowing it was the biggest criminal atrocity in his time as head of counterterrorism in the Netherlands, and the implications it would have globally, he called Chief Commissioner Martin Kuyt.

Once Martin had all the details, he said, 'Let's hope your suspect is telling the truth. What do you think?'

"I think she is. As well as the baby thing, her whole attitude seems to be to save herself regardless of the others. She comes across as a cold, calculating woman,' Jan answered.

"I want you to be in the next interview, and make sure she has a lawyer there. We don't want this backfiring. I will pass on what you have told me to our government minister,' Kuyt said.

'"Make sure you do everything by the book and keep me posted. I will come to Amsterdam later today.'

At the same time Jan Walvis was speaking to Martyn Kuyt, Ilsa called Jack. As soon as he answered, with time tight, she said, 'I wanted you to know we have a confession from one of the two women we arrested. She says she is pregnant, and because of that she's willing to spill the beans. She's already told us where they kept the karkoubi and explosives, so it looks as though she's telling the truth. I thought this information might be useful at your meeting this morning.'

'It is and that's great news. Your timing is perfect, I'm meeting him in ten minutes. You said you might have a question you want me to ask him. Do you?'

'I do but it's about the contents of the letter which he doesn't know I've seen. Unless anything changes, I'll see you tonight.'

'I'll tell him I've shown it to you. Now I know him, I don't think he will have a problem with that. The more he can spread the word about Morocco's involvement in terrorism to the right people, the better from his point of view. Also, I think you will get on well. You sing from the same hymn sheet. I hope the rest of the interview goes well.'

Chapter 21

The nearer I got to Jack Llewellyn's hotel, the more I sensed something special was happening. The timing of our meeting, what he had said yesterday, and my sharing at the NA meeting made me think it could be part of the same divine plan that first inspired me to go to live in Morocco to start NA and AA there. This thought had not entered my thinking when I left the UK for Europe in my motorhome in 2015. I was going there to do research for my book about the history of AA and its knock-on global effect, and lead a life of freedom.

Before I recovered from the disease of addiction, and in the time since, anything that adventurous would not have appealed to me. I had come to enjoy my four-star lifestyle too much. What was more, before that I had been a coward. But that changed because the direction my recovery went had caused me to develop a courage and faith many times more powerful than the false Dutch courage alcohol and drugs had provided previously.

In hindsight I could see that the timing, my circumstances, and everything else that happened was not always within my control. This helped me come to believe I was on some sort of Moroccan magic carpet ride, and now as I approached his hotel, I wondered if Jack Llewellyn was going to be part of this journey.

As my dream to help the plight of Morocco's drug addicts gradually strengthened over the years, this made a little sense. And as I believed it would only be the awfulness of its drug-fuelled problems that would be the catalyst for Morocco to put in place the policies needed to rectify them, I wondered if it had reached the point when this would happen. Was the terrorist attack in Amsterdam the rub this particular Moroccan magic lamp needed to release the much-needed genie?

As soon as I met Jack, the rapport we'd had the previous night returned. In all my years meeting drug addicts, over and over again there was an instant bond that went beyond words. I put it down to the empathy we have knowing the agony and heartache we have been through in our time using drugs, so that unconditional love permeates every such encounter. And even though we all had different backgrounds and experiences, the past pain, and today's gratitude for being alive, penetrates our beings to the core. It taught me that this is what real love is and this love lasts forever.

We sat down and ordered coffee. Jack said the news he had from Ilsa was so important it was the best place to start.

'I'm in Amsterdam for a similar reason to you. You want to expose Morocco's drug problems in a way that makes them change their laws and improve the treatment they give drug addicts. I'm here because Moroccans are involved in terrorism and their drugs are probably behind some of the world's worst attacks. Am I right?'

'Yes. You have surmised my situation well. But how did you know? I did not go into such detail last night,' I replied.

'It's because of my position in America's Homeland Security and our links with MI5 in the UK. I have been shown a letter I believe you wrote and want to send to Morocco's king.'

Jack paused. He would have known I would be flabbergasted by what he said. What he may also have guessed was that I would be instantly filled with fear. I was, and too dumbstruck to say anything.

'You needn't worry, I am on your side. It is amazing to meet you and out of the top drawer of coincidences. The timing could not be more serendipitous.'

His tone and words calmed me.

'I knew my letter had been shown to the Moroccan ambassador in London, but that was all,' I ventured, still shocked but feeling slightly more at ease.

'Anti-terrorism is top of the agenda in most countries. Anything to do with it that will help is channelled to a handful of friendly agencies all over the world. Britain's links with the US are some of the closest,' Jack replied.

'I thought last night there was something more than just NA going on between us. Now I know what that was. You want to help me, don't you?' A ray of hope entered my mind.

'Yes, and that works both ways. What I am going to tell you is highly confidential. If my understanding is correct, because of your commitment to your project you will respect that as you will see how it can help you achieve your aim,' he said.

'Go on,' I said, realising I really did have Jack's support. His commitment to his own recovery meant he would put helping others to recover from addiction ahead of almost anything.

'I am in contact with the policewoman leading the Dam Square investigation,' he continued. 'She is currently interviewing someone who has offered to expose the bombers. They are already in custody and the signs are that they have the right people.'

'Are any Moroccan?' I asked.

'I believe there are six and they are all Moroccan.'

I did not answer. Instead I nodded my head several times, then, as my thoughts progressed, I slowly shook it several times. I could hardly believe what I was hearing. Why had

Morocco let this happen? It was always likely. Why did so many innocent people have to die when there was a solution?

Watching my reaction, Jack said, 'I believe I know what you are thinking. You are asking yourself, why, why, why? Am I right?'

'Yes, one hundred per cent. For four years I have expected something like this. There must be many in Morocco's medical profession and government who dreaded it happening too.'

'I'm sure you are right. But I know what politicians are like. None are going to admit it, or do anything until they absolutely have to,' Jack said.

'That means unless they are exposed,' I said, then asked him, 'So, where do we go from here? How can you help? That is, if you think you can.'

'We wait. I'm seeing my contact tonight and will know more after that. I'll let you know what I can tomorrow,' he answered.

'Given the tragic consequences, my hope is it will be the right time to get countries to put pressure on Morocco to do what it needs to stop more attacks,' I replied.

'What could help do that,' he said, 'is if I show your letter to my contact. If she agrees, and because of the circumstances I think she will, she will want to show it to her superiors. She would also want to meet you.'

'That could cause a problem,' I said. 'The Dutch authorities would have a difficult decision to make. There are four hundred thousand Moroccans living in the Netherlands. Pointing the finger at their former home country's policies could provoke a backlash. And unless handled carefully, it could tarnish Moroccans everywhere. The global diaspora of more than four million could have negative racial repercussions.'

'That is worrying,' Jack agreed. 'However the policewoman is Moroccan. Her parents came here before she was born, and she has always lived here. I know her well. She is as straight as you or I. Everyone is equal in her books.'

'That might help, she may have some useful contacts.' I replied. 'Hopefully she won't be the only person in the Netherlands with that attitude'

'Do you have any other ideas?' Jack asked.

'I've thought about it many times and don't think there is a solution other than forgiveness and time.'

'Like the Nazi concentration camps and Jews, South African apartheid and black people, and Britain and India,' Jack commented.

'That's right, and it slowly works. The only way to get Morocco to change its policies, I believe, is through the king. You saw what he did with the Arab Spring: he made some minor changes which pacified the people. That is what he could do again if the threat of exposure is not made by the global community. Just the Netherlands doing it may not be enough.'

Jack drew in a breath. 'It's more complicated than I thought. Do you think it is doable?' he asked.

'If sufficient pressure comes from influential world leaders, this king will make the changes. Fundamentally, he is a good man. He changed Morocco's less harmful lèse-majesté law after being put under pressure by the media. It is not his fault his policies concerning drugs have been misguided. For some time, I've thought that if he was told the facts and shown there was a way to correct the causes of Morocco's drug problems, he would make at least some of the changes that are needed. Now there has been this attack, if Moroccans and drugs are involved, if he is approached in the right way, he will do his utmost to put things right,' I answered.

'Unfortunately, the timing means he will have some egg on his face. If he had done it sooner, he wouldn't. I became familiar with his ego-driven personality when I lived there.' He shifted in his chair. 'My contact is an intelligent, sensitive woman. If you let me show her your letter, and I tell her what you just told me, maybe there's a way to take this forward that is best for all concerned, including the king.'

'Bearing in mind the sensitivity of the situation and growing strength of the Dutch Mocro-Maffia, it would be good to hear what she has to say. So, show her the letter and arrange for us to meet,' I replied.

Next I asked him something that had been on my mind ever since I began to work out a solution three years ago.

'Of all the leaders in the world who I would like to read the letter, number one is Antonio Guterres, Secretary General of the United Nations. Is there any way you can help achieve that through your American connections?'

'I'm sure it is possible. My colleagues in Homeland have the highest level of contacts at the UN. Why do you think he is so important?'

'For several reasons. He is highly respected for being prime minister when Portugal decriminalised drugs in 2001. Since then it has one of the best records of any country with regard to drugs and addiction treatment. Also, the success of NA and AA there is excellent. I happen to know one of the people who put on the first NA meeting there in 1984. He was on holiday with a girlfriend, and they held an English language meeting near Lisbon. Today there are meetings all over Portugal, in several languages, as well as two hundred in Portuguese,' I explained, assuming this would be news to Jack.

'I stayed there when I was in Rabat and went to English-speaking meetings in the Algarve,' he said. 'Since then, it has amazed me the rest of the world has not followed Portugal's lead. We have proof their stance has worked, whereas the rest of the world's policies definitely have not.'

'The reasons are the same everywhere, money and politics. But in Morocco it's religion as well,' I said.

'It is how to convey that to the rest of the world which is the problem. You and I know what we know from first-hand experience because we lived there and had our own drug problems before NA and AA put them right.' Jack took a sip of his coffee, which by now had gone cold.

'That's why I believe the past Moroccan terrorist attacks, and now this one, can be the door-opener to putting many of the world's drug problems right, not just Morocco's. It will still need controls and education, but if its government and medical profession support NA and AA, as they have in Iran and other Muslim countries, many of their drug problems will be solved,' I said.

'I agree,' Jack answered, 'But I also know the arrogance and pigheadedness of bureaucrats and power of the pharmaceutical industry. That combination is a formidable force. So unless the media and public get behind it, what should be done won't happen.'

'All the time I've been doing this,' I said, 'I've had the same thoughts. But every time I thought of giving up, something happened to keep me going. I believe that although it may not happen now, in God's time it will; as Muslim's say, "Inshallah". Today, there are forces behind this in the form of psychiatrists and pharmacists who live in Morocco, and others who travel abroad who are hearing of the success of

12-Step programmes. As that grows, it can only go in an upwardly mobile direction.'

Jack nodded. 'Like the origins of AA, NA, and other 12-Step Fellowships. In most parts of the world their message of helping people with addictions and emotional problems was established by word of mouth,' he said.

'That's right,' I answered. 'There are many Muslims around the world who have recovered, so we know it works as well for them as it does for everyone else. So the force behind surely cannot fail to penetrate the minds of the people who need it in Morocco.'

Jack stayed silent, so I continued. 'As you know, we often begin the Serenity Prayer at the end of NA and AA meetings. Someone starts by saying, "Who is in charge?" Then we say, "God, grant me the serenity to accept the things I cannot change, Courage to change the things I can, And wisdom to know the difference."'

We stood up and as we moved together to embrace, the last line from the film *Casablanca* came into my mind. I said, 'You know, Jack, I think this is the beginning of a beautiful friendship.'

But it was to be much more than that. What Jack and I did next helped change the world of drugs forever.

Chapter 22

After I left Jack, I walked along the side of Dam Square. Except for the horror of what had happened there, my reflections were positive. The more I thought, the more a warm glow of optimism developed within me. I became convinced God's providence had taken a hand which would result in hundreds of thousands of Moroccan drug addicts recovering.

Leaving the square, I made the telephone call I had been waiting to make ever since I'd heard of the terrorist attack. As the call ended, my feelings of hope and gratitude turned to fear as I realised that if I got what I was doing wrong, I could be exposed to mortal danger.

The call I had made was to Philippa Marlowe, an investigative journalist. She had adopted the name in honour of one of the most successful fictional private detectives of all time.

The previous day I had called her to ascertain whether she would be able to fulfill what would be an urgent need. After explaining what it was, she said that she could. Now, because of my nervous state, I blurted out what I wanted in more detail.

'I will send you the names of the people whose email addresses I need. If you can let me have them tonight it will be fantastic. I want to write to each of them first thing tomorrow, so they arrive simultaneously. Top of the list is King Mohammed VI of Morocco, followed by the head of the *Washington Post* Investigative unit. The rest I will put in an email. Do you think you can you do it?'

'As I told you, it is not a problem. My team has access to everyone on the planet who matters. Even the pope,' Philippa answered.

'It's about forty people, including the editors of international newspapers and news agencies, TV channels, the heads of the UN and WHO, European police chiefs, board of the Global Commission on Drugs, Big Pharma CEOs, several Moroccan ambassadors and Angelina Joli.'

'That should be doable, though it will take a few hours. But why Angelina Joli? Are you hoping to date her?' she asked jokingly.

'Because of her humanitarian work. I want her to endorse the book I have written about the plight of drug addicts and their families in Morocco. Of course, if she wants to date me, I won't put up a fight,' I replied.

This last exchange eased the tension I felt, though I knew it would return because of the possible repercussions for me or my family if what I was doing went wrong. Anonymity was the key, and Philippa knew that. At the same time, she did not need to know the details. It was better I kept them to myself.

After speaking with her, I became excited. I had reached the point I had dreamed of for several years: to expose the situation in Morocco to its king and rest of the world. But I soon came back down to earth. Even though I knew from everything I had learned over the years about addiction and other subjects the thought it was happening now where millions could benefit was impossible to grasp fully.

Before going to my hotel, I went to Amsterdam's Cool Blue store. There I bought a reconditioned laptop. This I would use to send the anonymous emails to each recipient I believed most likely to endorse and expose the content of my letter to King Mohammed. If only one or two of them did that, I thought, it could set the ball rolling and the knock-on effect would do the rest.

Just after 10 p.m. I had an email from Philippa, then a phone call. She had done her work well and had every address I needed.

After an early breakfast, armed with my newly acquired laptop and addresses, I took a bus to Schiphol airport. There I made straight for the Douwe Egberts coffee bar. At a corner table, I sat with my back to the interior, opened the laptop and set up what I needed to send emails, using the airport's free Wi-Fi network. Although I knew the way I was doing it was secure, I still set up a VPN account to guarantee anonymity; sending them from a café in an international airport should confuse anyone trying to trace the source.

Within an hour I had sent a copy of my letter to King Mohammed, to leading newspapers, and to news agencies and TV networks in America, Netherlands, France, United Kingdom, Spain, Belgium and Morocco. Then I sent it to the Moroccan ambassadors and heads of police forces in each of the same countries, each time copying them. After that I sent it to *Charlie Hebdo*, *The Huffington Post* and Al Jazeera, believing they would find the disclosures especially interesting.

Next I did the same to Antonio Guterres, UN Secretary General, Dr Tedros Adhanom, Director-General of the WHO, the chief executives of pharmaceutical firms which make mood-altering addictive drugs claiming to help drug addicts, the commissioners of the Global Commission on Drugs, Saad-Eddine El Othmani, the Prime Minister and Khalid Ait Taleb, Health Minister of Morocco. Lastly I sent it to Angelina Joli; except for her, I copied all of them. Each email had an introduction explaining Morocco's connections to global terrorism plus a history of my research and endeavours.

After sending the last one, I sprayed the laptop with disinfectant and wiped it all over. I restored it to factory settings and securely taped it under the table where I had drunk my coffee. Then I got up and left. In many ways I hoped it would be found, but not before I was safely back in the centre of Amsterdam. By the time I left, the adrenalin that had been pumping through my veins meant I was a nervous wreck.

The first hint of success came on the Dutch NPO1 news at noon. During a report from their journalist who had been at the police briefing by Jan Walvis, he mentioned the Mocro-Maffia and that links to drugs could be behind the Dam Square attack. The second was more specific. It was on the Al Jazeera Media Network in Qatar. A breaking news headline read: *'Moroccan mafia believed responsible for Amsterdam terrorist attack'*

In the course of the next few minutes, this was repeated many times. Then Al Jazeera added another breaking news item: *'Morocco's Dutch Ambassador condemns the attack.'*

These responses were quicker than I had hoped for. The second meant someone had talked to a spokesperson for Morocco, and the Dutch police presumably believed Moroccans were responsible for the attack.

For the next few hours, I scoured the headlines of the newspapers and news agencies to whom I had sent my email. Each had items in the same vein, but there was nothing new, though several highlighted the fact Moroccans were regularly involved in terrorist attacks.

Then everything changed. The *Washington Post*'s morning edition revived an article from *Le Monde* in 2018. Its author had written about the 'Rambo' effect of karkoubi. This was the catalyst the rest of the world's press needed. Most had never heard of karkoubi, so for several it was a front-page story. Each country made reference to the diaspora of Moroccans, and for maximum effect highlighted how many lived in their country, even though they would know readers would feel threatened once aware of this fact.

At the next day's press briefing, Jan Walvis opened the floodgates of fear even more. He said how karkoubi had recently been brought into the Netherlands by the Mocro-Maffia and was responsible for an increase in crime. When he added that it could be linked to the Dam Square attack, he opened up new concerns. He said the main worry was that drug abusers like drugs that are cheap and give the greatest highs and karkoubi ticked both boxes, and if what was being said about it was true, a new drug market could open up, one that would create as much damage as any that had previously existed.

Towards the end of this scheduled fifteen-minute briefing, a Dutch reporter asked, 'I understand karkoubi is made from solvent, cannabis and a benzodiazepine made by a major pharmaceutical company and taken with alcohol. Is that right?'

'Yes. That is our understanding,' Walvis answered, then quickly added, 'There is only time for one more question.'

The same reporter continued, 'Has the company been contacted about their role in its contents? If so, what did they say? And what are they doing about it?'

Taken by surprise, Walvis paused momentarily, then said, 'They have not been contacted yet. That is something we are doing later today. I now close today's briefing and will see you tomorrow unless there are any new developments.'

But the questioner was not finished. He said, 'Because of its links to karkoubi, the Spanish Health Service issued a warning to Spain's pharmacists two years ago to beware of forged prescriptions for this drug. What can you tell us about that?'

'Until we have spoken to the company, I cannot comment. We are making a lot of enquiries and can assure you we are following every lead.' Jan Walvis turned around and walked into Amsterdam Centrum Police Station, more agitated than when he began the press briefing. He had expected difficult questions, but not to be asked one concerning something about which he knew nothing. Why is it, he wondered angrily, the press always uncover something we have missed?

Once inside, he issued an order to a senior officer to find out if the questioner was correct. The officer he chose was Sophie Bakker, the most respected scientist in the Dutch Police's forensic team. He told her to research karkoubi, and then to contact the head of that company's media relations office.

In less than an hour she had all the required information. In the past any queries it would have received about their product and its link to karkoubi would have been fobbed off with 'Refer to our website. It contains all the information you need.'

Before Sophie rang the company she spoke to Jan to tell him what she planned to say and why. She explained that the pharmaceutical industry was renowned for putting any concerning information in the small print of drug prescriptions, relying on doctors to pass that on to patients. But it was known from recent lawsuits that they did not always tell the truth to doctors, nor that doctors passed it on every time.

Jan nodded, telling her that once she had identified herself, and explained the reason for her call, if she got what seemed like a formulaic answer, to quote what it said on the website, then challenge this if it was appropriate.

'That's easy. I've already had a look. Do you want me to tell you what it says? Some of it is quite technical.'

'Yes. I need to know. I cannot afford to miss anything'

'It says that the medication is a benzodiazepine approved for the treatment of most forms of epilepsy, mainly as an adjunct or in refractory cases, and for the treatment of status epilepticus. In some countries it is approved for the treatment of panic disorder with or without agoraphobia. But it says nothing about its addictive qualities, the potential danger of its use as a recreational drug, or its history with regard to violent crime in Morocco, all of which were well documented in newspaper articles.'

'Therefore, your question is, are the medical professionals who prescribe it made aware of those facts? And make sure you record your conversation and let them know you are doing it,' he told her.

The conversation between Sophie Bakker and the media spokesperson went much as Jan Walvis had anticipated. After some automatic diversionary tactics, the spokesperson answered that the information on the website was specifically for the medical profession.

"After so much adverse publicity about its links to karkoubi, especially in Spain, does it not make sense to publish warnings about the dangers?' Sophie said. 'After all, your website is available to everyone, and drug dealers know benzodiazepines have potentially dangerous side effects. Experimenting is precisely what drug users like to do; and taken with alcohol, you must know that the risks become much greater.'

The answer she got was non-commital. The speaker said that as a media spokesperson he was not qualified to answer such questions, suggesting that for anything technical she should contact the CEO's office.

But Sophie was not finished. Knowing their conversation was being recorded, she had another point to make.

First she reminded the company's representative of the seriousness of the situation, and how the Dutch police would do everything they could to prevent similar attacks to the one in Dam Square. Then she hinted that because of recent lawsuits involving non-disclosure of dangerous side effects of drugs by the pharmaceutical industry to the medical profession in the USA, that would be part of their investigation.

****

The afternoon before Sophie Bakker had this conversation, a much feistier discussion took place in Rabat.

When Morocco's health minister, Mohamed Abbas, first read Rick's letter to King Mohammed, because it was written anonymously, he discarded it, telling his secretary it was a hoax. But when the prime minister, Omar Alami, rang him asking for an explanation about its content, his casual approach changed to fear.

As the sender had the right addresses for them, they took the view that this would be the same for the king, though his personal secretary would see the letter first.

For the next few minutes, they discussed what they would say to him when he inevitably contacted them. After that they wondered whether to pre-empt this or not, before deciding it was better to wait and gather as much information as possible first. As the best way forward, they decided the prime minister should speak to Morocco's Dutch ambassador, and Abbas to the country's leading psychiatrists dealing with addiction to find out how much of what had been claimed in the letter was true.

Alami had not made his call before the king's personal secretary beat him to it. This long-time close ally of the king's had received a call from Morocco's British ambassador, who sent him a copy of Rick's letter to the king. He demanded an explanation as to the accuracy of the letter's content. As the prime minister found no obvious falsehoods in Rick's letter, his politically inclined response was to buy time.

'I have only just received it and read it. I need time to investigate its accuracy and authorship,' Alami answered.

'Don't play politics with me, Omar. I need answers now. I have a meeting with the king in forty-five minutes. I am not prepared to hide this,' the secretary replied.

'I have spoken to our health minister and he will contact our leading psychiatrists who deal with addiction,' Alami answered. 'After that I will be better informed and get back to you.'

Knowing how close the personal secretary was to the king, he hoped his reply indicated his understanding that the matter was urgent. But apparently it did not.

'If the contents of the letter are true,' the secretary said, 'Morocco will be ridiculed and accused of negligence by the international community. We know Moroccans have past links with terrorism, but the suggestion this is because we have the worst drug problem in the world is so damning it would have serious repercussions. You have thirty minutes to get back to me. Is that understood?'

After calls to Drs Reda Oumainian and Mohamed Drissi, Abbas became extremely worried. Although both challenged some of the letter's content, they each said they thought they knew who wrote it. When Oumainian explained how he had supported the author when they met, but his team had not, and Drissi said he had not supported him at all, Abbas knew that from now on both his and Morocco's reputation could suffer. And if, as seemed likely, the attack in Amsterdam had been made by Moroccans, Oumainian and Drissi would know their reputations could be on the line.

When he rang the prime minister, Abbas said, 'I have spoken to two of our leading psychiatrists, who both agree there are issues in Morocco that contribute to our drug problems. However, they said we should focus on the influence American drug policies and capitalism have globally and the pharmaceutical industries' bad record with prescription medication as major contributors to the problems. They also said they think they know who wrote the letter and they had met him.'

This did not go down well with Omar Alami. He responded, 'That makes it worse, but I will deal with that later. For now, it is the other things the author says that concern me: the thousands of child drug addicts on our streets, karkoubi, the rest of the world's success treating drug addicts versus Morocco's total failure to do so. When the king opened our addiction treatment centres, he put much emphasis on the need for rehabilitation. Now we are told by an outsider, who is clearly an expert in that field, the way this was done was wrong and there are better ones. Yet you say that our leading addiction psychiatrists met him and presumably knew this, so why didn't they say or do something about it?'

The prime minister indicated that he was highly dissatisfied. He must suspect the road ahead would be littered with difficulties. He would know from his upbringing in Al Houceima and the inability of Morocco's leading

253

psychiatrists to refute Rick's allegations, that what his letter described was accurate. So when Abbas suggested making more enquiries, saying that he would get back to the prime minister with the results, the answer he got was brusque.

'Don't do that. I must speak to the king's personal secretary first. He rang and demanded I call back now as he is about to brief the king. I need to know what he says first.'

As soon as the secretary answered, he went straight to the point. 'I need to know the truth, because that is what I will tell the king. If there is a better solution that other countries apply, he will want to know what it is and why he was not told. Then he will want to know why it has not been implemented here. The last thing he will want are excuses that further undermine Morocco's reputation.'

The prime minister was cornered. On the one hand he represented Morocco's government, lawyers and medical profession, where he had numerous friends who benefitted from the current regimes, on the other he represented the people and the king. For Abbas, the time for diplomacy was over.

'It is not what I want to tell you, but the nature of the letter and authority with which it is written makes me believe it is an accurate account of our situation. If you agree, what do you want me to do?' Alami asked.

'I want to know who wrote it. Find out all you can about him. The more I know the better. If he is right, he may be the best person to sort out the mess Morocco is in. Finding him and getting him, or someone like him, to work as an adviser for us is what I may suggest to the king. That may be the best way forward for us and humanity.'

Soon after his conversation with the prime minister, the personal secretary had his meeting with King Mohammed.

After going through the main points in Rick's letter, he offered his advice.

'Your Majesty, I believe Morocco's situation with regard to drugs is untenable. It has always got worse, never better. Already this attack by Moroccans in Amsterdam has caused more bad publicity than all the other attacks in Europe combined. We have to make changes. I propose we find out who the author is and invite him to become an adviser to your government and our medical profession. As his only agenda is to help our drug addicts, we would not need to worry about his loyalty or commitment. And as he would have no political or financial interest either, we could be sure he would do the best job possible.'

'Find him and arrange for us to meet. I am as committed to resolving our drug problems as he is,' the king answered.

Aware that the king would have his own reputation in mind, the secretary said, 'I have given it much thought and believe that is the right thing to do, Your Majesty. If the result is that the plight of Morocco's drug addicts and their families is better than at any time in the past, the world would say a huge thank you to you and Morocco. Then, if other countries follow suit, and get similar results, you might well be recommended for the Nobel Peace Prize.'

The king did not need to think twice about it. Even the thought of this was the icing on the cake of what he had already done for Morocco.

Chapter 23

I had never met anyone representing a royal family before. So when King Mohammed's personal secretary and I had tea a few days later at the George V hotel in Paris, I was surprised that he seemed to be more tense than I was. I soon found out why.

At the outset he was offensive, saying that the king had taken some of my allegations personally. He then implied our meeting was nothing more than an opportunity to address an issue Morocco took as seriously as any country in the world.

He was accompanied by a female whom he introduced as his personal assistant and two men whom he did not introduce. I had persuaded Jack Llewellyn to accompany me, not as a kindred spirit, but as an American, who because of the way I introduced him, could appear to represent Washington.

After thanking him for seeing us, I assured him that in no way did I blame the king. I then summarised my background and described the drug problems I had observed while living there. After that I explained why some were singularly pertinent to Morocco.

A variety of questions and answers later, he asked me what I thought could be done to solve some of the issues I had highlighted. As I now believed he had accepted that Morocco was responsible for some of them, I phrased my answer more directly.

'Morocco has the capacity to implode with the volatility of this self-made situation or explode onto the world free trade market as producer of some of the world's most sought-after medicines and recreational drugs. The evidence suggests there is minimal downside and much upside potential both internally and globally if your country adopts the best treatment for its drug addicts, continues to legalise cannabis for medicinal use, decriminalises it for recreational use, educates its people about drugs and applies realistic drug controls.'

'We cannot do all of those,' the secretary replied. 'Legalising cannabis in the West may make sense, but for us that would be an anathema to our religion. There is no way around it.'

This was the response I'd expected, so I had my answer prepared.

'You are right, there is no way around that, which is why it must be addressed head on. As Commander of the Faithful, His Majesty, King Mohammed, is well known for doing what he believes is best for Morocco's citizens. I heard your country's most revered psychiatrist, Jallal Toufiq, present the pros and cons of legalising cannabis at an AMA Convention in Rabat. You could talk to him about the case for doing it. And as his father, Ahmed Toufiq is Morocco's Minister for Islamic Affairs, and interpretations of the Qur'an with regard to drugs to many people are ambiguous, you may be able to get them to establish a way forward that would be hard to refute and satisfy your populace.'

The personal secretary did not answer; instead, the beginning of a smile formed which remained as he thought about my response. I assumed from this there may be something about it he liked.

'I will do that,' he said. 'I have the highest regard for both of them. Now I have some more questions. The first is about the success you claim NA and AA have had in other Muslim countries.'

After I'd answered these, he asked about the growth of the global medicinal cannabis market. Fortunately, Jack was well versed on this in North America, so I let him answer. After that I added some facts that were relevant regarding Europe, Lebanon, Israel and Australia.

As King Mohammed VI had made a point of befriending America, the next question the secretary asked was directed at Jack.

'I want to ask you something off the record. Is that all right?'

'It is.' Jack answered without hesitation. 'My aim in meeting you is to do all I can to help.' He then looked at me, I assumed seeking the same approval.

'That's okay with me.' I responded.

'Do you have concrete proof there are links with drugs and the Moroccans who were responsible for some of the terrorist acts?'

I realised straightaway that if Jack answered this he could be compromised. I interjected.

'Given what we know from Mahi Binebine's book about the Casablanca bombings, and facts uncovered after the attacks in Brussels and Barcelona, the answer is definitely yes. Plus, there is the Moroccan mafia in Amsterdam which exists mostly from the proceeds it makes from your country's drugs and trafficking. The way I see it is that if Morocco uses its internal resources to investigate at depth the issue we are discussing, there is little doubt it will uncover enough evidence to help your king realise the desperate need to rectify this situation. But if Morocco does not, and there are more Moroccan-influenced terrorist attacks, your country's public image could be shattered beyond repair.'

I knew my assessment was disturbing; however I was pleased I had said all I had wanted to for several years to someone who could make a difference in Morocco. I had done my homework and knew he was one of the king's most trusted advisors. Jack, though, was more used to diplomacy at this level, so I indicated to him to speak.

'Do you agree, Jack?'

'Every country has people on drugs who cause problems, so Morocco in that sense is no different,' he said. 'At this time, the world loves your country, and King Mohamed has done much good for its people. If the right approach is taken now, it could become even more attractive to visit and lead the way to putting right some of what is wrong with the world's worst drug policies.'

There was a brief discussion in Arabic with his colleagues, each of whom seemed in agreement. The secretary then turned back to us.

'Thank you, Mr Blaine and Mr Llewellyn. This has been a great help. You have given us a lot to consider before I speak to the king. I now understand our situation better and why you are convinced the changes you propose are necessary and could work. King Mohammed will review what you have told me and make a decision. You will hear what that is in due course.'

From this response I believed the meeting had gone reasonably well as it had covered all I had hoped for and even a little more. Now it was time to wait and see just how well.

Part 2

Chapter 24

Casablanca Revisited

After our lunch in Paris, Jack and I took an early evening flight back to Amsterdam. He had arranged for us to be met at the airport by Ilsa Lund. This was the second time I had met her. The first was when we met for a drink at my hotel two days before our meeting with the king's PA in Paris. Jack had arranged it but he could not be there due to a Conference call he had with Washington.

On several occasions during my time in Tangier and Casablanca I had met Moroccan women who impressed me. It was not only their looks that did this, there was a caring attitude to families, life and maturity that appealed to me. In the two hours I spent with Ilsa, I realised she had all these qualities and more.

She told me that proceedings against Yashine and his accomplices, including Nadia and Mariam, had moved forward to the point where they had all been charged. Explaining that their breakthrough came when Yashine realised Nadia had exposed him, so he did the same to her.

Our talk from the outset was convivial. She said how impressed she was with my efforts in Morocco and understood when I said how frustrating it was as well. When she asked if I would go back there, I hesitated before saying no.

'Why is that?' She asked.

'I should have gone there with someone. Being on my own in a strange country doing something so difficult meant I was often lonely.'

'I understand. Sometimes my police work has been like that. It can be a lonely life being a Moroccan female in the Dutch police. If I were to mention racism I could be ostracised or even fired. That's what happened to Fatima Aboulouafa after 25 years' service and reaching a high rank here.'

'I abhor racism' I replied. 'I am surprised something like that could happen in the Netherlands. The problem is that what happened in Dam Square and the activities of the Mocro-Maffia is going to make the life of Moroccan's who live here and in other countries worse.'

'That's for sure.' Ilsa answered. 'I am already thinking of going to live in Morocco. I can do things there I cannot do here or anywhere else. I would also fit in better. The Dutch are not going to welcome Moroccans for a long time after this.'

'What would you do?' I asked.

'Something to help sick animals. On each of my visits there I have seen badly nourished and mistreated street dogs.'

'I know a Moroccan woman, Sally Kadaoui who has created a sanctuary outside Tangier to do just that. It's called SFT. Her sister was a great help to me, and runs a foundation for human development. They are a wonderful family. I can let you have Sally's details. There is a website you can look at.'

'I would like that.' She replied, then what she said surprised me, 'But you must not tell Jack. I have not told anyone except you. Now, I want to know more about you. There are pieces missing from the Rick Blaine jigsaw you have not told me about.'

261

From that moment on the tempo kept moving forward until it became more like the questions and answers on a first date; both of us enjoying the chemistry created by finding many things in common. When we parted she made it clear she had enjoyed our rendezvous too.

'I am sure you will be back in Morocco soon. You are not the giving up type, especially now your goal is in sight. I will aim to be there at the same time and do all I can to stop you feeling alone. What you are doing is important and I would like to be part of it.'

****

On and off since my meeting in Paris, I had a thought that worried me. If the king agreed to some, or all the changes I suggested, would exposing the issues cause more harm to Moroccans who lived abroad than good? And how detrimental would the knock-on effect be to Moroccan tourism and trade?

In the short term the answer would be negative, though the Dam Square bomb attack meant the status quo would do the same. But in the long term, the effect could only be good. As Portugal's turnaround had a positive effect in just a few years, such a massive positive U-turn by Morocco would surely have at least a similar result, I reasoned.

Wanting to be sure my thinking was on the right track, I contacted three people I knew to get their views. The first was Chairman of one of Britain's most successful companies who had personal ties to Morocco. The second the CEO of one of the world's foremost drug treatment centres and the last was Ilsa Lund; knowing she would look at it from the point of view of a policewoman and a Moroccan living abroad.

In each instance their answer was the same, though each came at it from a different angle. In a nutshell what they said was that I must go for it, that for years the world has debated whether to decriminalise drugs and put in place education and controls instead. If Morocco does this and it works, we will know the answer and others will follow, making the world a better and safer place.

To get the view of the Chairman and CEO, I spoke to them on the phone, then I followed that with an email and the Preface to this book. With Ilsa I did the same, but after she had read it, she asked that we meet to discuss it instead. She said she was free for supper the following evening, and for privacy's sake, she would prefer it if it was just the two of us and we meet at her home.

I agreed, though it left me feeling skeptical as I suspected she was going to put my idea down in as gentle a way as possible as she knew Jack thought the same as me.

From the moment she opened the door, she made me know I could not have had my thinking more wrong. She greeted me with a smile and hug, at the same time saying, 'I told you I wanted to get to know you better, now I have you all to myself for a few hours.'

To say I was overjoyed would be a gross understatement. Here was a gorgeous woman, years younger than me, seeming to flirt with me in a way I could never have imagined. Instantly I wondered, how on earth do I respond?

As calmly as I could, I said, 'You know Ilsa, that is the most welcome greeting I've had from a woman for years. And because it is you, it is even better.'

'You are very kind but it is you this evening is about, not me. I have thought a lot about you and your ideas for Morocco. I like all of them. If the answer you get back from your meeting in Paris is not 100% positive, I will do everything I can to help.'

From then until mid-way through supper she explained her thinking. It was very much the future of Morocco and Moroccans she had in mind, not the present or the past. After that she focused her attention on me.

Whether it was her police training and interrogation skills I did not know but her ability to listen and ask sensitive questions was of the highest quality: in another way it was also endearing. Every time I told her something negative about myself or my past, there was no hint of criticism, and on most occasions she found a way to identify herself with me.

As I always do when I meet a younger woman I really like, I tell them my age early on. The first time I did this with Ilsa, she did not respond, so I did it again.

'Why do you keep telling me your age? Are you trying to tell me something? Age is just a number. It's who a person is, what they are doing with their lives, wisdom, honesty and kindness that attract me.'

'I am the same. I realised I am beginning to like you, so I wanted to be honest with you, that's all.' I responded, at the same time inwardly kicking myself for laying my cards so blatantly on the table.

'You needn't worry,' she said, 'your secret is safe with me.' She answered.

'Do you know you have just quoted one of the great lines from *Casablanca*: on that occasion it was said by Ingrid Bergman to her husband, the great freedom fighter,

Victor Laslo.' I responded, romantic ideas flooding through my mind in a way I had forgotten were possible.

'I do. Casablanca is my favourite film. I have always wanted to say them. The way our friendship is going, I am beginning to wonder if we are going to play out a different ending.' She said, smiling mischievously.

Just the thought of what she was saying was blowing my mind. If we were to enact either part of it I would be ecstatic, if it was both, I would spend the rest of my life in never-never land.

The rest of our time together until around midnight continued in the same vein. It made me not want to leave but I knew it would be best if I did. She offered to drive me to my hotel, but I said no. I wanted to relive every moment I could remember on my walk back to my hotel. Also, the Chinese proverb, 'patience is a virtue' came into my mind. All my life I had rushed into things, almost always it was destructive.

Ilsa's parting words made it clear this was her thinking too. 'This evening has been very special for me. I want to do it again. Call me as soon as you hear from the king. I want to be the first person to celebrate with you. I believe I know the perfect way to do that.'

Our parting embrace and her last few words stayed with me all the way to my hotel. They were still there the following morning when I woke up and when I received an email from the king's PA at noon saying he wanted to have a Zoom meeting with me at 5pm.

****

The first thing I did was to call Jack. He was not as excited as me; a few minutes later I found out why. He had received an order that he was to return to Washington immediately. He tried to argue but was told that now the Dam Square attackers were in custody, there was no need for him to stay in the Netherlands. When he told Ilsa, she said he should go. She explained that their meeting up again, and the Moroccan involvement in the attack had shed light on what she should do with her life, and that was to move to Morocco.

After telling me this, he said, 'I'm sure the speed of the Moroccan response and their wanting to follow up immediately are positives. If you want me to be on the call with you, I can.'

'It's better I do it alone.' I replied, 'I may need to be direct with what I say and that might be embarrassing from a US diplomacy perspective.'

Jack agreed, then he offered a piece of advice, 'do not compromise your position. Your understanding of what needs to be done is spot on. If they follow that, they will get good results.'

I thanked him and was about to end the conversation, however, there was something else he wanted to say.

'Of all the people I have met in NA, your gifts and what you have done in Morocco are very special. I know Ilsa thinks the same. If as I suspect you are asked to help establish what you have suggested, you may find Ilsa is the perfect ally. You told me that having someone with you in the past would have helped; well, her being Moroccan and speaking Darija could be useful. You also have similar goals that would mesh well.'

Again I thanked him, this time for his kind words and ideas. I did not mention my more recent thoughts about Ilsa!

****

In the time between my call with Jack and the king's PA, I imagined many scenarios: these ranged from those which would give the worst results to those that would give the best. As it turned out, it was the one I had hoped for since I first moved to Morocco; King Mohammed was to tell Morocco's medical profession to back each of the 12-Step Fellowships that would best help the country's drug addicts and their families.

To get this off the ground, they wanted me to help. I was assured I would receive all the assistance I needed if I went to live there for the next two years. The king would finance the opening of several properly run treatment centres; I would be provided with accommodation and all my living needs. They also agreed to provide a car and chauffeur when I complained about the difficulties I had driving in Morocco.

As a result of their positive attitude, I realised that now would be a good time to address my other concerns. These I explained were important for the long-term success of putting right their overall drug problems.

Morocco must re-model its drug laws in line with Portugal's and that of other countries that worked.

It should not just legalise cannabis for medicinal research, it should be legalised for recreational use too. The money made from these to be used to help Morocco's poor and the rehabilitation of drug addicts.

The king's PA said each of these had already been discussed at the highest levels with the appropriate people. It was then agreed each would come into effect as soon as it was feasible. He added that my taking up their offer, meant that process would be speeded up.

As my friends in AA and NA had told me over and over again, 'Be careful what you pray for; they can come true.' I had done that every day for five years; now it seemed it was going to happen.

I ended the call excited about the prospects that lay ahead. But after a very short time I remembered that actions speak louder than words and politicians are the masters of hyperbole.

****

As soon as my call with the king's PA ended, I texted Ilsa, 'Call me when you can.'

To my delight it took her less than a minute. 'Don't tell me.' She said. 'I just know it went well. Some things in life are meant to be. I finish work in half an hour and will come to your hotel. You can tell me everything then.'

There was only one thing I knew to say, 'This is already one of the best days of my life. I now believe it is going to get even better.'

To which Ilsa gave the perfect response, 'You know Rick, it will. I think it could be one of the best ever for me too.'

'I guess we are living proof of what Shakespeare meant when he said the best is yet to come' I replied.

****

Afterword

As well as the many negatives, there were also good things that happened as a consequence of the terrorist attack in Dam Square.

Randy Cyriax was convicted of manufacturing and dealing in illegal drugs. He was sentenced to eleven years in prison in Spain. As a direct consequence, his father donated £25,000,000 towards the creation of a drug treatment charity in Morocco.

As it was exposed that several pharmaceutical firms had benefitted financially from wrongfully persuading Morocco's medical profession to prescribe their drugs, they each of these contributed as well. It meant there was enough money to provide homes, food and medical support for thousands of the country's street children.

Yashine was convicted of masterminding the murder and maiming of everyone who died and suffered in the Dam Square attack. He was sentenced to consecutive terms of life imprisonment with no remission.

Yashine's accomplices were each sentenced to life imprisonment, the judge saying he hoped that for each person life meant life.

Jack returned to Washington. A few months later he wrote to say he was giving up working for Homeland Security. He realised from meeting me there were other countries in the world that needed 12-Step Fellowships. He aimed to find one and do the same.

Ilsa and I moved to Casablanca where we live on a farm on the outskirts. Before we moved there, she made me agree to a proviso. As I would spend most of my time helping street children and drug addicts, she could spend hers establishing a rescue centre at our farm for street dogs and other animals that need a home. Today, our extended family of humans and animals gives us much satisfaction. Our experiences taught us to follow our hearts, that we live in a wonderful world, and we should do all we could to make it even better. It also taught us to be patient, just because it is not happening now, does not mean it never will, and every cloud has a silver lining.

I learned that an alcoholic and drug addict who has lived for years in the pit of despair can recover. Then, thanks to the programmes of the 12-Step Fellowships of AA and NA, they can live a life beyond any they could have imagined. I know this because it is what has happened to me, and millions of others like me.

Within four years, Morocco had opened treatment centres with professionally trained counsellors and state of the art equipment in Al Houceima, Tetouan, Tangier, Rabat, Casablanca, Marrakesh and Agadir, with plans to open more in the pipeline. Each of these cities now has Alcoholics Anonymous, Narcotics Anonymous, Marijuana Anonymous, Family's Anonymous, Al-anon and other 12-Step Fellowship meetings every week in Darija. As the result, there are more than two thousand former addicts and family members in recovery in Morocco and this number is growing.

It took Morocco three years to legalise cannabis for recreational use. When it happened the world took a deep breath, many predicting that as it was Morocco, given its past, the result would be disastrous. But it was not. Its government took advice from countries that had successfully done the same. This meant they put in sensible controls that work and educated their people about the consequences of taking drugs.

There has not been a Moroccan influenced terrorist attack since Dam Square.

Because of the fall-off in drug trafficking, the Mocro-Maffia in the Benelux countries has shrunk considerably.

King Mohamed VIth' s reputation has been enhanced, and Morocco's standing on the world stage has improved several-fold. The country's tourist numbers are at their highest levels ever. Two major pharmaceutical firms opened cannabis research facilities there. The king and Reda Oumainian have been put forward for a Nobel Peace Prize.

Dedication

American Drug Clouds Over Morocco is dedicated to helping Morocco's 1,000,000 or more drug addicts and alcoholics recover from addiction. At present the treatment they receive is out of date and ineffective, made worse by the country's hypocritical drug laws and unhelpful interpretations of the Qur'an. Combined, these have caused more drug problems and stigma than anywhere else in the world, except America.

The book is also dedicated to those families in France, Spain, Belgium, the United Kingdom, America and Morocco who have experienced the death of loved ones caused by terrorist attacks linked to Moroccans and by global drug policies. However, some of the worst aspects of each of them were affected by America's misguided policies with regard to drugs and addiction, the rest of the world following like lambs to the slaughter, and by pharmaceutical companies' deceptions and greed.

Equally important, it is dedicated to the street children of Morocco, of whom there are tens of thousands. Many of them are barely out of infancy and are often addicted to solvents they sniff from dirty plastic bags. Yet extraordinarily little is done to help these blameless waifs born into, and abused by, Morocco's poverty-stricken society.

Summary

Morocco's drug policies cause some of the worst internal drug problems of any country, and acts of terrorism and creation of mafias by its countrymen are horrendous.

America's influence on the world's drug problems caused by deliberate political misinformation and financial greed by the pharmaceutical industry are devastating.

Russia's veto at the UN Special Session on drugs prevented desperately needed law changes being made.

The controlled decriminalisation of drugs, alongside education and rehabilitation of drug addicts, works.

Based on the ever-growing mountain of positive evidence for legalisation and decriminalisation of cannabis, the rest of the world may well follow the example of Canada, Uruguay, the Netherlands, Portugal and most American states. If this continues, and another G7 country – United States, France, Germany, Italy, Japan, or United Kingdom – follow suit, what began as a desperate attempt to stem its drug, HIV and hepatitis C problems in Portugal in 2001 would pick up momentum. After that the building blocks would be in place to become the biggest advancement in the treatment of a killer disease that destroys people, families and societies since Alexander Fleming won the Nobel Prize for penicillin in 1945.

As the existing evidence is compelling, it means this is likely to happen sooner rather than later, because every minute of every day, the devastating and unnecessary cost of the world's discombobulating drug laws, and predominantly ineffective treatment of drug addiction, make the situation worse, especially in the countries whose policies are inhumane.

Given its global importance, the United Nations and World Health Organisation should act together to expose the truths and demand that the world's medical profession and politicians create a unified approach based on the facts: even if that means changing the UN's veto rule of one country being able to block policies when they are in everyone's best interest, as Russia was allowed to do.

Does the UN really want one country whose motives were altogether dubious making decisions that have negative effects for everyone everywhere in the world? After all, 'united' means 'joined together for a common purpose.'

Such disclosures and the right policy changes would open the way to:

Make Alcoholics Anonymous and Narcotics Anonymous programmes available to the world's millions of alcoholics and drug addicts in the world who need them.

Declare that addiction is a disease, which would remove the stigma of drug addicts being tarnished as weak and, in many cases, criminals.

Lessen the issues caused by men, women and children under the influence of drugs.

Bring harmony to families of addicts and reunite them.

Empty thousands of wards in hospitals and more than halve the number of people in prison.

Save millions in monetary terms in every country in the world.

Opponents, who usually have selfish biases or are misinformed, argue that cannabis on the street today has a higher percentage of THC, the psychoactive part of cannabis, and decriminalisation will lead to more usage, increased crime and abuse of more dangerous illicit drugs.

By studying the results of countries where cannabis has been legalised for medicinal use and decriminalised for recreational use, with proper controls and education put in place, the results prove these sceptics are wrong.

THERE IS NO DOWNSIDE, ONLY UPSIDE if the right policy changes are made by people who have no motive other than to help sufferers, their families and society.

Thanks

My list is long so I will name only a few of those who helped me. It is the cumulative support of all who did which gave me the confidence and determination to persevere when at times it seemed I was fighting a lost cause; especially the help I got from my friends in Alcoholics Anonymous, Narcotics Anonymous, Al-anon and my family. You know who you are. My thanks and gratitude have no boundaries.

In Morocco I especially thank Dr's Ali Sedraoui and Allal Abadi. Without your initial help what I did would not have been possible. My interpreters, Chadia and Meriam, who helped me start the first AA and NA meeting in Arabic in Tangier. Psychiatrists Nazha Fahem and Zineb Haimeur who believe in the AA and NA 12-Step programmes and started a meeting in the addiction unit at the 20th August 1953 hospital in Casablanca. Karima Kadaoui and her husband Abdeslam who gave me 'TLC' when I needed it.

Belinda Braithwaite, whom I met at just the right time and let me park my motorhome on her horse farm when I moved to Morocco. My editor, Hilary Johnson who turned what was previously a jumble of fact and fiction into a book that is a good read as well as one that carries an important message.

Most of all I thank the drug addicts, alcoholics and families I met all over Morocco who so desperately need help. Every time I met any of you, it gave me the encouragement I needed to continue. Not a day passes when I do not think of you. And even though you may never know this book was written – most were illiterate – I have written *Drug Clouds Over Morocco* because I will always love all of you. I just wish I could wave a magic wand and pass on to each of you that which is freely available in the rest of the world which has helped millions of sons, daughters, mothers, fathers, husbands and wives recover from the effects of the disease of drug addiction and alcoholism. But, sadly at this time, the programmes that do this are only sparsely available in Morocco in English and French, not in Darija, which is essential, although they are translated into Arabic and thriving in the rest of the Muslim world.

God bless all of you. Insha'Allah we will succeed.

Drug Policies, Country by Country

An analysis of the evidence from countries that have lifted restrictions on cannabis for medicinal purposes and those that have decriminalised it shows that the results to date are encouraging; whereas those that have not range from poor to bad.

The Netherlands

Drug policy in the Netherlands aims 'to reduce the demand for drugs, the supply of drugs and the risks to drug users, their immediate surroundings and society.'

The Dutch recognise that it is impossible to prevent people from using addictive drugs completely because that would include alcohol and many prescription medications. Coffee shops are therefore allowed to sell small amounts of 'soft' drugs such as cannabis. Applying this approach means that the authorities can focus on criminals who profit from so-called 'hard' drugs.

The result is that rates of cannabis use are equivalent to, or lower than, those of nearby countries (which do not have such coffee shops), and are substantially lower than those of the USA.

Annually, the coffee shops generate an estimated 400 million euros in tax – money that would otherwise have accrued to criminal profiteers – that is used to help the Dutch community. There are some 170 in Amsterdam, and because they are carefully controlled, they are a major tourist attraction with 23% of tourists visiting them, and their close regulation means they are safe.

AA and NA meetings are held in Dutch, where the openness of the Netherlands' drug policies has meant that in a relatively short time they have successfully treated many alcoholics and drug addicts. This is especially evident because today the Netherlands also has such meetings in English, Farsi, French, German, Polish, Portuguese and Spanish, and in March 2019 started one in Moroccan Arabic for their North African population. So the country with the most sophisticated, intelligent controlled drug policies has become one of the recovery capitals of the world.

Portugal

In 1997, about 45% of its reported AIDS cases were among intravenous drug users. By 1999, nearly 1% of the Portuguese population was addicted to heroin, and their drug-related AIDS deaths were the highest in the European Union.

In the year 2000, decriminalisation of drugs was discussed in Portugal's parliament and a year later the policy changed to that. As a direct consequence, blood-borne, sexually transmitted diseases and drug overdoses dramatically decreased, and targeting drug use became an effective HIV prevention measure.

It was then decided to treat the possession and use of drugs as a public health issue, so instead of a criminal record and/or a prison sentence, addicts would get a fine and/or a referral (that wasn't compulsory) to a treatment programme. As a result, money saved from taking individuals through the criminal justice system started being spent on rehabilitation and get-back-to-work schemes.

In the last eighteen years, drug use has diminished among the fifteen- to twenty-four-year-old age group. There has also been a decline in the percentage of the population who have ever used a drug and then continued to do so. Drug-induced deaths decreased steeply and at present Portugal has three overdoses per million citizens, compared to the EU average of 17.3. HIV infection has steadily reduced and become a more manageable problem. There has been a similar downward trend in cases of hepatitis B and C. This policy was complemented by allocating resources to the drugs field, expanding and improving prevention, treatment, harm reduction and social reintegration.

The treatment programmes of AA and NA are widely available in Portuguese. There are more than 200 meetings a week, with some in English and other European languages to accommodate visitors.

Canada

At the United Nations General Assembly Special Session on Drugs (UNGASS) the Canadian government announced that it would introduce legislation in 2017 to decriminalise and legalise the sale of cannabis, making Canada the first G7 country to permit widespread use of the substance.

AA and NA are available in English and French with hundreds of meetings of both Fellowships each week covering all of Canada.

Uruguay

In December 2013, Uruguay became the first country in the world to completely legalise cannabis on a nation-wide level. It is too soon to know if it has been successful; however, there are no signs that it has not.

AA and NA are available in Spanish.

Switzerland

The Swiss policy on drugs comprises four elements: prevention, therapy, harm reduction and law enforcement. The concept of a fourfold approach to the reduction of drug-related problems was developed in the early 1990s and now forms the principle national drug policy. As mandated by law, the Swiss Federal Office of Public Health (SFOPH) endeavours to reduce drug-related problems by being active in the following areas:

Coordination of cooperation between federal, regional and local authorities

Primary and secondary prevention

Treatment (abstinence, substitution, prescription)

Harm reduction and documentation

Training of professional staff

Research

Quality assurance

Although these are their federal policies, America's former president, Ruth Dreifuss, who is a member of the Global Commission on Drug Policy, has made clear her view that regulation by countries and states would take away the possibility for making big money from drug trafficking, therefore legal regulation is the way forward.

Today this view is shared by many of the world's political, business, religious and philosophical leaders and continues to gather pace.

AA and NA are available in German, French, Italian and English.

Iran

In 1990, two brothers from California started the first meeting of NA in Iran. Today there are more than 400,000 members there and 23,000 NA meetings a week. In 2012, a local sports centre hosted an NA World Convention which had 24,000 former Iranian drug addicts attending. If the NA approach was adopted by the Iranian government as its primary source of recovery from drug addiction, these statistics would have the potential to reach all four million of its drug sufferers. (Think of that happening in Morocco!) *NA is available in Farsi and Arabic.*

USA

Since prohibition began in 1920, drug use has increased in all categories. The Reagan, Nixon, Bush and Trump administrations' 'War on Drugs' policy has been a disaster. Today, US prisons have more inmates than any other country in the world, half of whom are there for drug-related offences.

A recent review of its failed policies is now giving way to more relaxed drug laws. Most states are considering rehabilitation as opposed to incarceration for drug users, and the use of cannabis for medical use is widespread; many states have also legalised it for recreational use and more are following.

Another problem in America is the influence in Congress of the drug testing industry. This is worth $4 billion a year and growing, and given its status, its voice gets heard, a voice that is unlikely to support legalisation.

In 2012, Washington and Colorado became the first two US states to approve ending cannabis prohibition and legally regulating its production, distribution and sales. 'Prohibition has been a costly failure, to individuals, communities and the entire country,' said Tamar Ricks, US Drug Policy Alliance.

Washington DC reported the following results after eighteen months:

Minor cannabis offenses down 98% for adults 21 years and older. All categories of cannabis law violations down 63% and cannabis-related convictions down 81%.

The state saves millions of dollars in law enforcement previously used to enforce cannabis laws.

Violent crime decreased and other crime rates remain stable.

Washington collects over $80m in cannabis tax revenues. These are used to fund substance abuse prevention and treatment programs, drug education, community health care, academic research and evaluate the effects of legalisation in the state.

The number of traffic fatalities remains stable.

Youth cannabis use did not increase.

Washington voters continue to support legalisation. 56% continue to approve the state's cannabis law while only 37% oppose, a decrease of 7 points since the election of 2012. 77% believe the law has had either a positive impact or no effect on their lives.

The US Drug Policy Alliance issued this report on cannabis legalisation in Colorado after one year of retail sales and two years of decriminalisation. 'Since the first retail stores opened on January 1st, 2014, the state has benefitted from a decrease in crime rates, a decrease in traffic fatalities, an increase in tax revenue and an increase in jobs. Cannabis arrests and judicial savings according to data from the Colorado Court System have dropped around 80% since 2010. Given that such arrests cost $300 each to adjudicate, it can be inferred that the state is saving millions in adjudicatory costs for possession cases alone. Over the same period, arrests for cultivating and distributing cannabis dropped by more than 90%. Add to this decreases in violent crime rates released by the city of Denver; plus, burglaries fell by 9.5% and overall property crime by 8.9%.'

Along with legalisation, Colorado voters approved a 15% excise tax on wholesale cannabis sales that is only to be used for school construction. In total this brought in $135 million in new revenue in 2015, so $20.25 million goes to schools. There was also a decrease in traffic fatalities in 2014 according to data released by the Colorado Department of Transportation, challenging claims that the legalisation of cannabis would lead to an increase.

If the figures for Washington and Colorado were replicated in all fifty American states, the positive effects would be massive.

The USA has an estimated 20 million drug addicts. Currently there are 23,000 NA meetings a week spread across the country serving less than one million. If its government promoted NA's programme as its primary treatment for recovery from drug addiction the results would all be positive.

The US National Council on Alcoholism and Drug Dependence, (NCADD) says alcohol is the most commonly used addictive substance in the United States. 17.6 million people, one in every 12 adults, suffer from alcohol abuse or dependence, along with millions more who engage in risky and binge drinking patterns that could lead to alcohol problems. More than half of all adults have a family history of alcoholism or problem drinking, and more than 7 million children live in a household where at least one parent is dependent on or has abused alcohol. 88,000 deaths are annually attributed to alcohol use in the US and a large percentage of hospitals and prisons are inundated with alcohol abusers.

Yet alcohol, acknowledged as one of the most lethal drugs, is legal. If AA's programme of recovery was implemented by the US medical profession in every instance of alcoholism, the horrendous results caused by its abuse would be reduced.

AA and NA are available in English and other languages spoken in America.

France

The French, well-known for the people's love of anti-depressants, sleeping pills and prescription narcotics, drug addiction have reached new heights. A study by France's National Drug Safety Agency (ANSM) found that 32% – almost 1 in 3 people – used some form of psychotic medication in 2013, either on a regular or an occasional basis. This is in addition to having one of Europe's highest rates of alcoholism (wine is not alcohol!) and substantial problems with illegal drug addiction.

AA and NA are available in French.

Estonia

Estonia is famous for three reasons: it has the highest number of per capita drug deaths in Europe, the highest for alcohol in the world, and it has one of Europe's healthiest economies!

The reason for the former is fentanyl, a high potency, synthetic opioid with a rapid onset and short active life. It is nicknamed 'China white', 'Persian white' or 'Afghan', but these pseudonyms for this killer drug hide the dangers of taking this innocent-looking powder. It is produced in clandestine labs across the border in Russia, where mafia-influenced pharmacists began making it during a heroin shortage in 2002. Today, it is the drug of choice for Estonia's many addicts, with its scientists saying it is more than 100 times stronger than the heroin it replaced.

It may seem astonishing therefore that it was Russia's veto at the United Nations General Assembly Special Session on Drugs (UNGASS) in April 2016 that prevented the desperately needed changes to the world's drug laws being made. Astonishing, that is, unless Russia's mafia have direct financial links to the highest levels of its government and the KGB!

So, while Estonian addicts die like lemmings (murdered?) Russia's mafia continues to make billions of rubles from illegal drugs.

AA and NA are available in Estonian.

Russia

Alcohol-related deaths per capita in Russia make it the fourth highest in the world, and for drugs overall Russia is ranked sixth.

According to *The Lancet*, Russia has the largest population of injecting drug users (IDUs) in the world – an estimated 1·8 million people. More than a third have HIV, and in some regions, the proportion is about three-quarters of the population. An estimated 90% of their IDUs have hepatitis C, and most are drug-dependent. It is estimated their drug addicts spend 4.5 billion rubles ($70 million) on drugs every day; 1.5 trillion ($23.5 billion) a year. Ironically, that is comparable to its defense budget!

Approximately 30% of all deaths in Russia are attributable to alcohol, says the WHO: this is from alcohol poisoning, cirrhosis, accidents, murder and suicide. The result is that

Russians live some of the shortest lives of any of the big economies. Life expectancy for a Russian man is roughly 65 years, compared to 76 years in the US and 74 for Europe.

Why would Russia veto changes to the world's drug laws that are known to work when their statistics are so awful? The answer one assumes can only be money and internal corruption.

AA and NA are available in Russian and other dialects.

Mexico

Over the course of their domestic drug wars, the number of deaths in Mexico has been at least 100,000 since 2001, with 30,000 people missing. This is influenced by its proximity to the USA, the primary market for illegal drugs trafficked from South America, estimated to make drug cartels US$20 billion annually.

In April 2009, the Mexican Congress approved changes in the General Health Law that decriminalised the possession of illegal drugs for immediate consumption and personal use, allowing a person to possess up to 5g of cannabis or 500mg of cocaine. The only restriction is that people in possession of drugs should not be within a 300 metre radius of schools, police departments, or correctional facilities. Opium, heroin, LSD and other synthetic drugs were also decriminalised, meaning possession will not be considered as a crime as long as the dose does not exceed the limit established in the General Health Law. The law establishes very low amount thresholds and strictly defines personal dosage. For those arrested with more than the threshold allowed by the law this can result in heavy prison sentences, as they will be assumed to be traffickers even if there are no other indications that the amount was meant for selling.

AA and NA meetings are available in Spanish.
Philippines
Rodrigo Duterte was elected president of the Philippines in May 2016 on promises to eradicate drugs, crime and corruption in the country. Duterte, also known as 't The Punisher', even urged Filipino citizens to shoot and kill drug dealers themselves.

'Please feel free to call us, the police, or do it yourself if you have a gun. You have my support,' he said, referring to drug dealers who show violent resistance. 'You can kill him. Shoot him and I'll give you a medal.'

Since his inauguration, more than 10,000 thousand suspected dealers and users have been arrested and killed for illegal drugs activity. In 2018, the International Criminal Court in The Hague announced a 'preliminary examination' into killings linked to the Philippine drug war since it began in July 2016.

AA and NA meetings are available in local languages and English.

Directory of 12-Step Recovery Programs

Alcoholics Anonymous has done far more than achieve success with alcoholism. Today it is recognised as having been a great venture in social pioneering which forged a new instrument for social action, a new therapy based on the kinship of common suffering, one having vast potential for the myriad other ills of mankind.

As a result, many addiction and other recovery programmes have been born from AA's 12 Steps. Each adapted to address a specific problem from a wide range of substance, dependency abuse and emotional issues. Every one of these self-help Fellowships employs the same 12-step principles to recover. These include:

For Drug Addiction.

Alcoholics Anonymous and Narcotics Anonymous programmes of recovery and worldwide success are described in detail in previous chapters. To make contact with **AA** in one of the 175 countries where it is established go to the local AA website. Alternatively go to: **http://www.aa.org/**

NA is also established worldwide. For information, contacts or meetings go to: **http:// www.na.org/**

Cocaine Anonymous (CA), dealing with cocaine and crack addiction. **https://www.ca.org/**

Crystal Meth Anonymous (CMA) is a relatively new 12-Step programme for people addicted to crystal meth. Links provide support for family and friends as well. **http://www.crystalmeth.org/**

Marijuana Anonymous (MA) is a fellowship of people who share their experience, strength and hope with each other that they may solve their common problem and help others to recover from marijuana addiction. Go to their website for more information: **https://www.marijuana-anonymous.org/**

Nicotine Anonymous is a fellowship of men and women who help each other live nicotine-free lives. They welcome all those seeking freedom from nicotine addiction, including those using cessation programmes and nicotine withdrawal aids. The primary purpose of Nicotine Anonymous is to help all those who would like to cease using tobacco and nicotine products in any form. The fellowship offers group support and recovery using the 12 Steps to achieve abstinence from nicotine. **https://www.nicotine-anonymous.org/**

Pills Anonymous (PA) is a fellowship of recovering pill addicts throughout the world who share their experience, strength and hope as to how they stopped using pills. **http://pillsanonymous.org/**

Behavioural Addictions

Gambling, crime, food, sex, hoarding, debtors, and work are addressed in Fellowships such as:

Clutterers Anonymous (CLA) is a 12-step recovery programme which offers help to people who are overwhelmed by disorder. FAQs, literature, meeting list and CLA background information are available at: **https://www.clutterersanonymous.org/**

Debtors Anonymous (DA) helps people recover from compulsive debting and under-earning. **https://www.debtorsanonymous.org**

Emotions Anonymous is for recovery from mental and emotional illness and based on the 12 steps of AA. **https://www. emotionsanonymous.org/**

Food Addicts in Recovery (FA) is an international fellowship of men and women who have experienced difficulties in life as a result of the way they eat and being obsessed with food. They found they needed a 12-step programme of recovery and fellowship of others who shared their problem in order to stop abusing food and begin living fulfilling lives.
https://www.foodaddicts.org

Gamblers Anonymous (GA) is a fellowship of men and women who share their experience, strength and hope with each other that they may solve their common problem and help others to recover from a gambling problem. The primary purpose is to stop gambling and help other compulsive gamblers do the same. They are convinced that gamblers of their type are in the grip of a progressive illness. Over any considerable period of time they get worse, never better.

The fellowship is the outgrowth of a chance meeting between two men in 1957. Both had a baffling history of trouble and misery due to an obsession to gamble. They began to meet regularly and as the months passed neither had returned to gambling. Since that time, the fellowship has grown and groups are flourishing in at least 58 countries in the world; many in local languages and dialects.

They concluded from their experience that in order to prevent a relapse it was necessary to bring about certain character changes within themselves. In order to accomplish this, they used for a guide certain spiritual principles that are today utilised by millions of people who are recovering from other addictions. The word 'spiritual' can be said to describe those characteristics of the human mind that represent the highest and finest qualities such as kindness, generosity, honesty and humility. Also, in order to maintain their own abstinence, they felt that it was important that they carry the message of hope to other compulsive gamblers. **https://gamblersanonymous.org**

Overeaters Anonymous (OA) No matter what the problem with food, whether it is compulsive over-eating, under-eating, addiction, anorexia, bulimia, binge eating, or over-exercising, OA has a solution. Starting in Los Angeles in 1960, they now have 6,500 groups in more than 75 countries, with a total membership of over 50,000 people. **https://oa.org/**

Sex Addicts Anonymous (SAA) is a 12-step fellowship of recovering addicts that offers a message of hope to anyone who suffers from sex addiction. They are addicts who were powerless over their sexual thoughts and behaviours and preoccupation with sex causing progressively severe adverse consequences for them, their families and friends. Despite many failed promises to themselves and attempts to change, they discovered that they were unable to stop acting out sexually by themselves. **https://saa-recovery.org/**

Sex and Love Addicts Anonymous (SLA) is a 12-step programme for people recovering from sex and love addiction. **www.slaauk.org/**

Sexual Compulsives Anonymous (SCA) is a 12-Step fellowship, inclusive of all sexual orientations, open to

anyone with a desire to recover from sexual compulsion. Our primary purpose is to stay sexually sober and to help others to achieve sexual sobriety. Members are encouraged to develop their own sexual recovery plan, and to define sexual sobriety for themselves.
www.sca-recovery.org/
Workaholics Anonymous (WA) is a fellowship of individuals who share their experience, strength and hope with each other that they may solve their common problems and help others to recover from workaholism. The only requirement for membership is the desire to stop working compulsively. **www.workaholics-anonymous.org/**

<u>Auxiliary groups for friends and families</u> of alcoholics and addicts, are part of a response to treating addiction as a disease that is enabled by family systems.

Al-Anon is a worldwide fellowship that offers a programme of recovery for the families and friends of alcoholics whether or not the alcoholic recognises the existence of a drinking problem or seeks help. **https://al-anon.org**

Alateen is part of the Al-Anon fellowship designed for the younger relatives and friends of alcoholics through the teen years.
Al-Anon and Alateen Family Groups are Fellowships of relatives and friends of alcoholics who share their experience, strength and hope in order to solve their common problems. They believe alcoholism is a family illness and that changed attitudes can aid recovery. They are not allied with any sect, denomination, political entity, organisation, or institution; do not engage in any controversy; neither endorse nor oppose any cause. There

are no dues for membership. They are self-supporting through their own voluntary contributions.

Their groups have but one purpose: to help families of alcoholics. They do this by practising the 12 Steps, by welcoming and giving comfort to families of alcoholics, and by giving understanding and encouragement to the alcoholic. The meetings often begin with the suggested Al-Anon/Alateen welcome: 'We welcome you to this Al-Anon Family Group and hope you will find in this fellowship the help and friendship we have been privileged to enjoy. We who live, or have lived, with the problem of alcoholism understand as perhaps few others can. We, too, were lonely and frustrated, but in Al-Anon and Alateen we discover that no situation is really hopeless, and that it is possible for us to find contentment, and even happiness, whether the alcoholic is still drinking or not.'

Al-Anon was co-founded in 1951, 16 years after the founding of Alcoholics Anonymous by Lois W (wife of AA co-founder Bill W) and Anne B.

Alateen began in California in 1957 when a teenager named Bob joined with five other young people who had been affected by the alcoholism of a family member.

Al-Anon and Alateen meetings are held in 56 countries, in local languages and dialects as well as English. **https://al-anon.org**

Adult Children of Alcoholics/Dysfunctional Families. (ACA) ACA's 12-Step programme was developed to deal with the effects of alcoholism or other family dysfunction found in such homes. The term 'adult child' was originally used to describe adults who grew up in alcoholic homes and who exhibited identifiable traits that reveal past abuse or neglect. Its members have histories of the abuse, shame, co-dependency and abandonment found in such dysfunctional homes. Today their groups include adults raised in homes without the presence of alcohol or drugs. Meetings are established in 50 countries and ACA literature is available in 19 languages. **www.adultchildren.org/**

Co-Dependents Anonymous (CoDA) addresses compulsions related to relationships. They have informal self-help groups made up of men and women with a common interest in working through the problems that co-dependency has caused in their lives. CoDA is based on Alcoholics Anonymous 12 Steps of recovery programme and adapted to meet CoDA's purposes. To attend meetings, all you need is the willingness to work at having healthy relationships. This means that all kinds of people attend. Individual members can and do have differing political, religious, cultural, ethnic and other affiliations, but since these are not relevant to the business of recovery from co-dependency, no comment is made about them. CoDA has approximately 2,000 weekly meetings in 60 countries: there are online and phone meetings as well. **www.coda.org/**

There are more than forty other specialist **12-Step Fellowships** that cover other addictions, emotional and psychological disorders. Details of these can be found on the internet or from medical professionals. There is one for everybody who suffers such problems.

Printed in Great Britain
by Amazon